UNHOLY COMPROMISES

TALES FROM THE CENTRAL IMPERIUM

JAN KOTOUČ

TRANSLATED BY ISABEL STAINSBY

UNHOLY COMPROMISES
TALES FROM THE CENTRAL IMPERIUM
JAN KOTOUČ

TRANSLATED BY ISABEL STAINSBY

This edition published by Nazca Press

A division of Misti Media LLC

https://www.nazcapress.com

Available in both Paperback and eBook Editions

1 2 3 4 5 6 7 8 9 10

ACKNOWLEDGEMENTS

The story, *Interspecies Misunderstandings*, quotes from the novel *Crime and Punishment*, by F.M. Dostoyevsky, in David McDuff's translation.

DOSTOYEVSKY, F.M. *Crime and Punishment*. Translated from the Russian by David McDuff, 1991. London: Penguin Books, 1991. ISBN 0-14-044528-5

CONTENTS

Φ

Φ

I

"Mr. August Varviso, Your Majesties."

Daniel Hankerson had been Emperor of the Central Imperium for long enough now, and he could boast an even longer career as an intelligence analyst in the Imperial Navy before then. Which meant that he was good at wearing the appropriate expression.

Nevertheless, when the Imperial guardsman led today's guest into their private sitting room, he had to acknowledge that he was surprised.

He knew that a journalist had come to interview them. Given the commotion his wife Hila Eban had caused during her recent visit to the Bornholm Sector, that wasn't really going to surprise anyone. He also knew that this wasn't a famous journalist. Given the situation, the protocol expert had deliberately not approached the editor of any news outlet favorable to them, but not anyone hostile to the either. This man called himself a freelancer. That was all Daniel knew. His wife was the journalist, not him.

He wasn't expecting their guest to be so *old*.

When he'd given the nod to the idea of a journalist coming to the palace to write the whole story from Hila's—and his—perspective, he'd been expecting a young journalist radiating energy. Instead, they'd gotten this old greybeard. In the Central Imperium, living to over one hundred thirty years, sometimes longer, was entirely normal, even though it did vary from planet to planet. This man looked over one hundred. He was definitely past ninety.

He came over as thin, fragile. White hair and a sunken face only added to that impression. He was wearing a shirt that didn't really fit him but was undoubtedly comfortable.

However, Daniel was a poker player. He quickly recovered from his initial surprise and noticed something else, and much more important. The sparkle in the man's eyes. They were glowing with intelligence.

This man was clever and used to bringing his point to bear. He knew how to get his own way.

And his expression wasn't too different from the one Hila had worn when they met for the first time.

He looked at his wife. She was studying Varviso with the same keen interest—maybe with even greater interest—with the expression worn by any expert when encountering someone else in the same trade.

She stepped in front of Daniel and held out her hand to their guest. The protocol expert would probably have sighed and shaken his head, but he knew this was how Hila did things.

"Welcome to the palace, Mr. Varviso."

With a slight smile, the man took her hand, then Daniel's.

Smiling, but cautiously.

"Thank you, Your Majesties. I am honored to be here."

"Really?" asked Hila.

"Yes, really. I would say that I am not your enemy, but you're a fellow journalist, you know that I'd say that even if I was trying to dig up dirt."

Daniel nodded to him. "Please sit down."

Varviso waited for the Emperor and Empress to sit, and only then sat down himself. The Emperor's personal robot, Sean, had left refreshments on the table and was now waiting in the corner.

"Do you wish shomething to drink, Your Majeshty?" the robot asked with his typical and for visitors slightly confusing pronunciation.

Daniel looked at Varviso, who shook his head. "No thank you, Your Majesty."

Hila also shook her head.

The robot departed and the guardsman followed. The Imperial couple was alone with the journalist.

He observed them and did not bombard them with questions. He was waiting for them to start.

Daniel was scrutinizing him too. He knew that his wife was perfectly able to take care of herself. She had dealt with elite killers and journalists on many occasions—she used to be both.

But he still felt the automatic urge to protect her.

Finally, it was Hila who was the first to speak.

And she jumped straight into her role as a journalist.

"As I understand, you are the chief editor of the *Horgen Daily*, is that right?"

"Exactly, Your Majesty," said Varviso. "For forty-three years now."

"But the *Horgen Daily* is a local paper."

"Yes, it's the only independent media on the planet. Not including the conspiracy bloggers who call themselves the independent media and write stupid clickbait. If you'll pardon the expression. No, I mean that we aren't owned by the Foster Group, which owns most of the media and industry in the Barrondo Sector."

"Understood," Daniel said. "And Horgen is mostly unspoiled nature?"

"Indeed, though of course you were there on your adventures during the war."

"Yes, I rescued my sister from the Black Alps there."

"Yes, I know. We also have plenty of excellent technical colleges and universities, but it's still a very sparsely populated world. Nevertheless, I have one hundred thirty people in the newsroom to cover everything that happens on the planet. It's hard for some newspapers."

"And if I may ask, how did you end up here? I know that the *Westerland News* hired you as a freelancer for this interview."

Varviso smiled. "Once every few years, I leave Horgen and spend some time as a freelance journalist on other planets. I also recommend that my staff in the newsroom do the same. It gives you perspective."

"That's a very interesting approach. But there's something in it," Hila agreed.

Her caution had relaxed a little. So had Varviso's.

The old journalist now fixed his eyes on her. "However. Forgive me, but we're not here because of me, ma'am."

"No. You're here because of me and because of what I did in the Bornholm Sector."

"Yes, but not just that. I want the background. I don't just want you to enumerate the events as you saw them. I want to learn something about you. I want your story."

"I thought you wanted to know exactly what went on in the Bornholm Sector," Daniel objected.

"We'll get to that of course, but even in a local rag we know that the key to any article isn't *who* or even *what*, but *why*." He looked at Hila. "As I'm sure you know very well yourself. Everything possible is being written and broadcast about you across the Imperium, ma'am. And about you, too, of course, sire. About both of you. And you've given so many interviews, and we know so many things about you, but we also know that there are some topics you avoid."

This last comment was aimed at Hila. Daniel frowned, but his wife raised her hand.

"Undoubtedly. And you probably suspect that I have my reasons."

"I'm sure you do, ma'am," said Varviso. "We know you were a member of the Omegas. We know how… suspicious you were of Enhans. We know you lived on Colbran… but context is the key to the story. Details."

It was clear that he wasn't going to drop this subject. And Daniel and Hila both realized that they were going to have to meet him halfway in at least some things.

He was gazing at her fixedly. "Who are you, Empress Hila?"

THE RECRUITED PATIENT

Erden syndrome.

You've just drawn the short straw.

It's a genetic lottery, that's all.

It affects people completely at random. Rich or poor. There's nothing we can do.

I don't know how long you've got. Patients can live with it for years… but months are more likely.

The St Augustine's Order Hospice specializes in these… They'd be able to help you. They don't charge.

Hila Eban walked through the dirty streets of Port Niven on the planet Colbran as her doctor's words played and replayed in her head.

Not that she was exactly *her* doctor. People like Hila didn't have anything resembling insurance. The doctor worked for a local corporation to keep its workers in a condition more-or-less good enough for work, but nobody wanted to overdo it either. If anyone became disabled, or fell ill with some serious disease, nobody was particularly interested. There were plenty of others where she'd come from. So, they threw them onto the street and hired those others.

Which was what would happen to Hila now too.

Erden syndrome.

She'd never heard of it before, but she also didn't have anything that could be described as a proper education. She'd been in the care of the Colbran Children's Institute from the age of eight. It was financed by a local company, Barani Corp. She'd attended school, of course, a school with a robot teacher, where she'd primarily learned to read, write and count, with some of the basics of history and the geography and astrography of the Central Imperium and the galaxy around her planet. She'd looked up most of what she knew herself on the datanet, because she was interested. She'd still known nothing about this syndrome. Until today.

You've just drawn the short straw.

It's a genetic lottery, that's all.

The doctor loved metaphors of that sort, but Hila was lucky to find her sober, which wasn't entirely normal. The doctor probably enjoyed life in this hole about as much as Hila did, but she couldn't get a job anywhere else because of her frequent issues with drugs and alcohol. Of course, Hila had already drawn plenty of short straws in life, as she might consider, living as she did alone on Colbran's streets, at the age of seventeen, with no way of getting out.

It affects people completely at random. Rich or poor. There's nothing we can do.

That might even be true, but Hila knew that many people, including various privileged Enners in Colbran's capital city, took medication from childhood to prevent genetic disorders. However, nobody was going to hand such drugs out to paupers like Hila. In the same way, those who were already ill got better care. Not to mention the fact that the de facto ruling class of Enners, genetically modified people, were scattered across the whole Imperium. They had been ennobled centuries ago. The situation might have changed since then, but they still had a privileged position, and money, and of course those never get ill. Bastards.

I don't know how long you've got. Patients can live with it for years... but months are more likely.

Here Hila was most fascinated by the tone the doctor had used when she uttered this phrase. Not just that it was empty, and impersonal, she understood that it was more the bored recitation of phrases. When Hila asked a question, the doctor's boredom and frustration deepened. As if she couldn't wait for her to go away. She'd told her the diagnosis. Why should she talk to a corpse?

The St Augustine's Order Hospice specializes in these... They'd be able to help you. They don't charge.

Yes, there were plenty of hospices and asylum hostels on Colbran, where religious organizations helped those in need. Although not one of them realized that the greatest help for those in need would be to leave and shoot the Enner scumbags and their minions who ruled here. And the Central Imperium could only brag about "standards of living rising across the Imperium". Maybe, but how did that help when there were holes in the Central Imperium like Colbran and you live in one of them?

Ultimately, however, Hila would probably go to the hospice, or another like it. There wouldn't be anything else she could do.

Her muscles would slowly weaken, she would struggle to breathe, her body would gradually switch off. The doctor hadn't taken the trouble to tell her the details but had given her an information leaflet.

Her legs would probably fail first, then her arms, and finally it would be a competition between her heart and her lungs as to which could hold out the longest.

Modern medicine could treat all these things individually, but not Erden syndrome. It was a combination of genetics and reactions to certain drugs used by humanity for centuries to help them adapt to life on planets other than Earth.

She continued to walk Port Niven's streets. As if the illness had heard her deliberations and had decided to get in touch, her feet grew heavier, and after a while she started to tremble. She had to stop and lean against a cool wall made of cracked karaconcrete.

As she gradually caught her breath, she noticed that there was someone else on the almost empty street. Someone who had probably wandered into this quarter of town by mistake. A tall, elegant woman in a suit of the type that had come back into fashion among the elite on several of the Imperium's planets. Hila wondered how long it would be before the woman was mugged, or worse. She couldn't guess her age, not at that distance. The woman, who seemed to be looking in Hila's direction, turned around and left.

Φ

She wanted to keep working while she still could, even if only for basic survival and delaying the inevitable. She thought of herself as an ant whose queen had died. If, for some reason, the colony couldn't create a new queen, the drones would simply continue to do their work until they died out.

Of course, Hila's robot teacher hadn't taught her this in school, but she'd watched documentaries on the datanet, to which the television screen in their tiny apartment had been connected. It had been her roommate Enrique's idea. When she'd asked him why he'd bought a TV with his hard-earned money when he didn't even have a bed, he'd shrugged and stated that the datanet and TV helped him to get away, while a bed would only keep him here.

She'd held out exactly three more days at work after her diagnosis, then she had a seizure. Her legs didn't obey her, the pain shot through her chest, she staggered and gasped for breath. They had to turn off the machines as a result.

When the foreman had asked what was going on, she'd had to tell him.

And he wasn't a bastard. In his way, he was both perpetrator and victim. He'd also been born on Colbran and had just worked his way up. He couldn't allow her to keep on working when she wasn't able to work and Colbran didn't have benefits or invalidity support. If he didn't throw Hila out, the company management would throw him out and appoint somebody new who would then throw Hila out. That's just how it was. Maybe not in other places, but in this shithole, yes. It was mostly robots who worked in the local dairy factories on other planets. Here someone had concluded that people who have no choice about being paid a pittance were cheaper than robots. It was enough for the corporation to provide a few robot teachers.

Apparently, Barani Corp. had received some award for supporting employment last year.

So, Hila left, with the money for her last week. She said goodbye to a few colleagues, who looked at her with a mix of apathy and sadness. They went through this quite a lot. There'd be someone new within two days. They'd have forgotten Hila within a month.

She wasn't dejected. She wasn't sorry. It was another blow of fate, that's all. She was used to that—fate had already dealt her plenty of blows.

As she made her way home along the familiar street, she had the impression that she saw that strange woman in the suit again, but maybe she was imagining it.

She wasn't imagining the five men who stood in her path.

She didn't know any of them. That was the first thing. Port Niven's streets were full of various gangs, but they stuck to their territories relatively well and didn't inconvenience the locals too much. When Hila was younger she'd worked for a few of them, she'd brought trinkets, stolen things, to the bosses. Of course, the gangs also robbed the locals, but they chose them carefully.

Only there was always someone new here. And as soon as they headed toward Hila, it was clear that this wasn't a misunderstanding. They were after her.

She'd experienced this a few times before. Some of the gangs had the initiation rite of beating up—or killing—random people. A baptism of fire.

She studied them.

The leader was maybe thirty or thirty-five. The others were younger, only a few years older than her. The boss was the only one who didn't look like an idiot. His eyes were watching his surroundings. He knew what he wanted, and he knew how to get it.

His four companions, by contrast, were significantly less intelligent. They'd come for a punch-up, the boss had told them where and who, they didn't care. Their only nicety was forming a semicircle around Hila as they approached.

"What do you want?" asked Hila aloud. Aloud enough for the entire street to hear her, but she knew nobody would come to her aid. That wasn't how it worked on Colbran.

"You pissed off the wrong people, girl," said the leader.

"I've no money," she lied. She had something from work, but nothing worth the effort of five musclemen.

"We don't want money. Not from you."

From what he said, it seemed as if someone had sent this bunch after her. But that made no sense. Who? The foreman at work? He wouldn't give a shit. She must have pissed off a lot of people in the times when she'd stolen for another gang and some traffickers, but they'd probably get even with her boss. If they'd caught her, they might have beaten her up, raped her or even killed her on the spot, but nobody would wait a few years to take revenge. She'd worked in the dairy factory for nearly a year and a half.

She no longer worked there now.

Already, she was just waiting for death.

Her legs were still weak.

She was slowly dying, and someone on the street wanted to beat her up or kill her. Or rape her? She'd encountered a few like that, in the few years in which she'd started to develop a feminine figure. She'd learned to defend herself. But it didn't always work.

She'd experienced many things.

Her entire life was one rotten experience.

And now it was ending. Here, in this way.

She lost her temper.

From documentaries, and even from school, she knew what adrenaline was, and how it works, and now it drowned out even Erden syndrome. She was still debilitated, but she didn't care.

Everything was against her! Absolutely everything!

And now she had a bunch of bastards coming after her!

The semicircle narrowed. The two goons at the edge were ready to form a notional noose around her if she tried to run away.

That was smart. They were counting on it. She had no chance against five guys. Running away would be sensible. Logical. In the historical documentaries she watched, they called it *strategic withdrawal*.

All her life, Hila had tried to do sensible, logical things and it had done her no good.

No good whatsoever!

Anger bubbled up within her.

Genetic lottery.

You bet!

She broke into a run.

They'd expected her to start running in the direction she'd been coming from when they blocked her path, which was why they were ready to cut her off.

They hadn't expected her to attack.

For a few seconds they were confused. Taken aback.

That was enough for Hila.

The leader was standing in the middle of the group, a little further away. Probably he didn't intend to get his own hands dirty. He came over as the type who is nothing more than a charismatic coward. He forced the others to do what he was too afraid to do himself.

He wasn't expecting Hila to come running at him and before he could react, the point of Hila's shoe connected with his crotch and, a few seconds later, her fist hit his Adam's apple.

Hard, fast, brutal.

He grunted and dropped to his knees. Hila rapidly kicked him one more time in the head and he fell to the ground. She turned around.

Two of the remaining heavies took an instinctive step backward. They were hesitating even more now. She needed that.

She didn't know any martial arts. She'd learned to fight on the streets. She knew from practice why it's important to take out the leader first.

Now she threw herself at the boy on her left. He managed to swing his fist, but his blow didn't connect. She punched him in the belly with all her strength. As he came closer, she raised her elbow and rammed it into his nose.

Her arm began to tingle.

She was still high on adrenaline.

One of them seized her from behind, but she tore herself free and jabbed her elbow backward several times. She must have hit his nose;

he grasped her shoulders but couldn't get his hands round her throat.

"I've got her! I've got her!"

Another one of them came to help him. She couldn't see the fifth.

She thrust both hands behind her and found his face.

There were maybe one hundred ways of preventing this. But he didn't know even one and didn't have the time to attempt anything.

She dug in with her thumb and after a moment felt viscous liquid on it as it pressed into his eye.

The dude shrieked so loud that his fellow-fighter slowed down.

Hila was suddenly free. She tugged and, with her bloodied fist, swiped at the man in front of her.

He rallied and Hila herself took a blow to her cheekbone.

The world began to spin.

"You bitch! You fuckin' bitch!"

This time she dropped to her knees and the man raised his foot to kick her in the chest or the head.

She plunged her hand into his crotch and squeezed.

More shrieking. Which got louder when she tugged.

Suddenly, she was on her feet and he was on the ground. Another kick to his head silenced him.

She looked at the fifth boy, who was staring at her and his four pals in horror. The one who'd lost his eye was screaming the loudest. He knelt on the ground, covering his eye socket with a bloodied hand and screaming insults.

Hila kicked him in the head, not taking her eyes off the fifth.

They stared at each other for several seconds. She gasped for breath as the adrenaline raced around her body.

All the injustice in the universe seethed within her.

He stared.

Then he took to his heels.

Φ

Hila had gone three more blocks before the adrenaline drained away and the Erden syndrome made itself felt again.

She should save her strength. That's what the drunken, stoned doctor had advised her.

It didn't help.

She trembled, vomited; pain shot into her chest.

Her legs gave way. She lay on the street in her own vomit.

Genetic lottery.

She wondered if her attackers would find her here. She wouldn't be able to defend herself now.

She'd used up all her energy on them.

Maybe she'd also used up some of the few weeks of life she had remaining.

She didn't know how it worked, but the doctor had mentioned something of the sort.

The most important thing is to rest.

She didn't know how long she lay there, but finally she managed to get up and headed home with trembling steps.

She fell over twice more on the way.

Genetic lottery.

Φ

"For God's sake, Hila, what happened?"

She looked worse than usual, but she'd managed to stagger to the apartment. A small apartment in the slums that she shared with her roommate Enrique.

She fell onto the artificial flooring. She was trembling and could barely feel her left leg.

Enrique knew about Hila's diagnosis. She'd discussed it with him. Now she quickly told him about what had happened on the street.

His reaction didn't really surprise her.

"Are you sure you didn't provoke them?"

"I don't know. But that wasn't even their turf."

Yeah, someone attacked her, and he wondered if it was somehow her fault. Great.

Enrique had also had it rough. They were both street children who'd met in that robot school. Enrique was a year older. She knew that he'd initially lived here with a girlfriend. When the girl had left him for some padrone who had maintained her and bought her nice things, Enrique had protested, so his rival in love had hired some muscle to beat him up. Since then, Enrique had not been able to move the deformed fingers on his left hand, but she knew that they'd hurt him much more than that.

"And did they do that to you?" he wondered.

"No. Erden syndrome did. It's getting worse and I… I…"

It was a while before she could speak again. Her illness really was getting worse.

She could barely feel her legs anymore.

Enrique was still asking if they had maybe followed her, who they were and where they could have come from. She didn't have a clue.

And that wasn't the point.

"I…" she managed to stammer, "…d-don't think I can g-get up."

He helped her by pulling her to the bed. It wasn't easy. Then he gave her some water.

"Do you want some protein bars?" he asked her. "I've got some left. They're good."

Hila thought that she would quickly upchuck any food she ate right now.

She lay and stared at the ceiling. An hour later, she needed to go to the toilet but couldn't walk there herself. Enrique helped her.

He didn't grouse, but she knew that neither of them could live like this.

"Enrique," she said aloud. "In my coat there's the money they gave me at work, before they kicked me out. Take it."

"You can use it too, though, can't you?" he growled. Dragging your roommate to the toilet and back is not an experience anyone has ever enjoyed, unless they chose it as their career. And probably not even then.

Enrique used to tell her how he'd always wanted to be a stage actor, but life on Colbran wasn't exactly conducive to his ambition. Of course, Hila had had her dreams too. Once upon a time a documentary filmmaker had filmed a news story about "Life on Colbran". Apparently, it had won her some prize or other. It was the sort of program that rich, privileged people watched, said "Oh, how terrible", then went to play golf. Hila thought it would be cool to be a reporter like that and tell the truth.

If only anyone would let her.

At least they could dream. Reality was no help.

"Enrique," she said aloud, when the pain had ebbed away a little. "I need you to do something for me."

"Do you want me to get you some meds?" he asked, as he counted the money he'd found in her coat.

"No… I want you to contact the Hospice of the Order of St Augustine."

Φ

It was great in the hospice. They gave her painkillers. And someone who evidently had experience wheeled her to the toilet.

She was no longer in pain, but her body was gradually failing. She watched the television in the common room. As Enrique had always said, television was a means of escape.

But only a little.

The members of the Order were all nice, kind. Hila had probably never seen so many smiling people at once in her entire life. But everyone knew they were only easing her suffering.

"Are you Hila Eban?" asked one of the Order's brothers, one day. "You have a visitor."

"A visitor?" Hila blinked. Had Enrique come to say goodbye? He sometimes got these fits of sentimentality.

But it wasn't Enrique.

It was an elegant lady in a suit.

The same lady that Hila had seen on the street after seeing the doctor, and then several more times after that.

A woman who obviously didn't belong here.

"Are you Hila Eban?"

The lady had brown-black hair and a slightly crooked nose. Her skin indicated she'd been born under a sun that wasn't Colbran's.

"Who are you?"

The woman smiled at her like a teacher smiling at her favorite pupil. The Brother had left them alone and she sat down beside Hila's bed, on a small stool.

"My name is Diana Palmer. And I have come to make you a certain… offer."

"I saw you. On the street."

"Yes, I'm sure you saw me watching you. I know that you have advanced Erden syndrome. And I know you've been told it's incurable."

"Definitely for a street kid like me."

"For anyone, but I represent people who could help you. I'm offering a certain experimental treatment."

"Experimental treatment. I know something about genetics." *From documentaries.* "How do you want to help me?"

"It's complicated. But what do you know about the Ralgars?"

"They're the big lizards who often wage war on the Central Imperium at the frontiers, right?"

"Yes. Ralgars can regenerate. They can grow back entire body parts. And our scientists have managed to isolate their DNA. We think that this mix could be implanted into a human host using genetic manipulation. It would get rid of the Erden syndrome. You'd be able to start a new life."

"That's hooey."

"No, it's an experiment. I'm going to be completely open with you: you may not survive. We're testing it on a lot of people in the terminal phases of various illnesses, and not all of them survive." A gracious smile. "But what have you got to lose?"

Hila moved her hand with difficulty. This woman was making her a good offer, but everyone from the Colbran slums knew all about good but suspicious offers.

"Who are you? No bull."

Palmer gave her another gracious smile.

"I represent the Omega Initiative. Believe it or not, I work for the government. Let's just say that we are… one of the units of the Armed Forces."

"Armed Forces?"

About six months previously Hila had toyed with the idea of joining the Imperial Army. There were recruitment centers on Colbran, and for many young people it was a way of escaping the slums. But precisely for that reason the Army could take its pick, and they didn't select everyone. Not a seventeen-year-old girl. For that, the consent of a legal guardian would be needed, or some other confirmation, and who would wait for that, when so many other candidates were lining up?

"Yes, the Armed Forces," said Palmer. "Technically we come under the Army, but we are… unofficial."

"What do you mean, unofficial?"

"Unofficial in the sense that, if you tell anyone what I was just telling you, I will deny it and wave it off. The ravings of a delirious teenager."

Hila's face twisted, but now she trusted this woman. She didn't make threats; she stated the facts.

"And why would someone from the Army—even unofficially—want to treat Erden syndrome using Ralgar DNA? That's hooey!"

"I'll ask in a slightly different way, Ms. Eban. Tell me what you think about the Enhans. And as you said yourself: no bull. No polite phrases."

Hila took several deep breaths.

She wasn't in pain, but she was thinking clearly.

The Enhans were the artificially created nobility of the Central Imperium. The Imperium's original rulers had created a caste of people with higher resistance, faster reactions and apparently greater intelligence. Resistant and superior. They'd originally been intended to rule and to lead remote colonies, but over time they'd become a nobility, based on something that could be measured. The Enhans even had their own chamber of parliament, and even if the Emperor—also an Enhans—had limited their powers, many of them still did exactly as they liked and were highly influential. An Enhans house ruled Colbran. It also owned Barani Corp. In the Imperium, nobody worried about this, because those bastards were just influential, and so they were permitted to rule planets like Colbran.

"I hate them," she said aloud. "*Hate* them. I don't trust them… And for fuck's sake it's enough to look around and see what they're doing here!"

"Did you know that they have their own chamber of parliament? They gain a great deal of political influence.

"Of course I frickin' know that. I can't stand them."

"And do you know that the Emperor is also an Enhans, even though the other Enhans houses rather identify themselves in opposition to him?"

"I didn't know that, but of course, those bastards want to rule absolutely everything themselves. Make all planets into places like Colbran."

Palmer smiled. That graciousness again. "You have perspective, Ms. Eban. Great perspective. It's almost unbelievable, given where…"

She stopped short. Entirely planned. Hila snorted. "Given where I'm from? I like finding things out! I take an interest. And I know that a hot chick like you doesn't just go round hospices to talk to rabble like me about politics and offer untested treatments. So, what do you want?"

"Aren't you afraid that I'm an Enhans and I wanted to provoke you?"

"No Enhans would be interested in a nobody like me."

"You're probably right. The Omega Initiative is only accountable to the Imperial Intelligence Service. Unofficially. We want to genetically modify volunteers. Volunteers like you, I hope. And to form our unit from them. You'll be stronger and faster than Enhans, and you'd be our secret weapon. You'll receive military training and be an unofficial member of the Imperial Army. You'll fight Enhans actions, frustrate any of their intrigues for which we cannot deploy the Army, because Enhans have great influence in the Army too. They even have special units formed solely of Enhans, called the Superiori Commandos."

"So why don't you take volunteers from the Army? Why are you crawling round hospices?"

"For the same reason. Every soldier is on some list or register somewhere. It would be suspicious if they just disappeared. While nobody knows that you exist and nobody will miss you. Forgive me."

There's nothing like being honest, is there?

Something still felt wrong to Hila. Finally, she asked the question.

"And why me? There are probably loads of dying people across the Imperium. What makes me so special?"

"We're recruiting people from places like Colbran, where we can expect them not to be too fond of Enhans. But I also know about your medical records, and Erden syndrome apart, you're relatively healthy."

"You bribed my doctor to give you my medical records, didn't you?! They're supposed to be confidential!"

"Surely you're not as naive as all that!"

"Well… no. Not about that doctor. She needs something to buy her dope with."

Palmer kept on talking.

"But principally, I know that you are strong-minded and a good fighter. Not just in terms of physical fitness, but also potential. You're not afraid of conflict and you know how to win."

Hila suddenly twigged.

"You hired those heavies to attack me?!"

Palmer nodded.

"You bitch! They could have killed me!"

"I needed to know whether you had it in you. Training is important, but in a place like this it would be easy to become just another apathetic drone. I needed to see you in action. The street has taught you many things and you know how to use them."

"You bitch!"

"You're here, I'm here. They lost. One of them lost an eye. Life isn't fair and you probably don't expect it to be."

Hila said nothing for a long time, then she shook her head. "No, I don't."

Palmer was also taking a long hard look at Hila. "So, Ms. Eban, you now have two options. You can stay here, lying on your back and looking at the ceiling, and enduring your last few weeks, or at best months. Or you can accept the invitation to join the Omegas. I don't guarantee that you'll survive the genetic manipulation, or that you'll get through training, or that you'll even survive the subsequent service.

After all, I'm asking you to do a hard job. When you've completed your training, you'll be a combat commando, a spy, a provocateur. All at once. And it won't be easy. Even if the genetic manipulation is successful, it's likely that you won't live long. Your modified body will simply switch off in time, but it could be twenty or thirty years. I'm therefore deliberately not saying what will come after your service. You sign up for an indefinite period, but the reality is that you can't keep someone who doesn't *want* to be kept. And they send me on these recruitment missions because I'm able to judge this. Don't focus on any glowing future. I'm offering you work and duty. You will do nasty, disgusting things, but they will be necessary for the good of the Imperium. For the people in the Imperium, because we know that people like you don't care too much about the Enhans. And if that's too idealistic for you, then you'll be able to hurt the people who hurt you. One way or another, that will be your life. It won't be an easy life, but it's the life I'm offering you. It's up to you now."

Hila scrutinized Palmer. She remembered what had gone through her head when the doctor had first diagnosed her.

The greatest help for those in need would be to leave and shoot the Enner scumbags and their minions who ruled here.

Palmer was offering her exactly that.

Hila gazed at the ceiling.

The television had been an escape route. The bed kept her inside.

Palmer was offering her a way out. Any way out. The hospice would keep her alive and the Sisters would hold a bowl underneath her and brush her teeth.

"You said your name was Palmer, right?" she asked finally, even though she already knew the answer. The woman nodded.

"That's right."

Hila stared at her.

"Where do I sign?"

‖

"So, you only have a few years left to live?" said Varviso, making sure. "Is there nothing that can be done?"

"Do you think we haven't tried?" said Hila, feeling calmer than she would have expected. Telling this story, finally, had helped her. Her eyes met Daniel's, and he smiled at her encouragingly. He knew the story. Most other people did not.

"The entirety of medical science in the Central Imperium is at your disposal," said the journalist.

"We're trying everything," Hila assured him. "Slowing down my metabolism, genetic implants. But all this can only slow the process, not stop it. One day my body will simply switch off. It's a hodgepodge of human and Ralgar DNA and a great many other untested genetic mixtures. In the next fourteen years, one day… I have a daughter who I know I will never see grow up and…" She looked away. Her eyes filled with tears.

She hadn't been expecting this to hit her this hard. But because of the events in Barrondo, she was afraid for Elda. Afraid of what sort of world her daughter would live in. And Varviso had now uncovered that wound, that awareness, that Hila knew of but wouldn't admit to herself.

She wouldn't be there for Elda.

Daniel took her hand. Varviso could go on pressuring her now. But he didn't. He looked like a fragile old man. "I apologize, ma'am. I shouldn't have said that."

She blinked. "It's… it's fine. It's a relevant question. In your place I'd have asked it too."

"Do you want something to drink?" Daniel suggested.

She took a glass of water from the table. Maybe her husband wanted something stronger. She didn't.

Varviso studied her for a moment. "Would you like to take a break?"

"No, that's fine," Hila heard herself say. "I'm just… shaken. I won't break down, trust me. I've been living with this reality since I had Elda… Princess Elda. And I wouldn't change a thing."

Varviso was silent for a while, then he also reached for a glass of water. "Maybe I could tell you something."

"You? Didn't you say just now that this wasn't about you?"

"That may be true, but I know I'm some strange coffin-dodger that you're telling your life stories to. Maybe some of my experiences would interest you. I've experienced many things during my career."

"In local newspapers on Horgen?" Daniel wondered.

"Well, yes, even there, sometimes, like the time Emperor Daniel and his girlfriend broke into High Gardena in the Black Alps to rescue his sister. But yes, I've experienced more things while traveling around the galaxy." He smiled. "I'm an old man, and I rely on that fact, so I'm sure you will forgive me for sometimes liking the sound of my own voice, won't you?"

Hila burst out laughing despite herself. Varviso went on.

"Once I observed an interesting event on Barrondo. My article was syndicated across the whole Imperium, although it was very censored… and it didn't appear everywhere. Some of the more prudish worlds didn't want to know."

"What happened?" Daniel wondered.

"A highly unusual tourist arrived in Barrondo…"

THE XENOPHILE

"Name?"

"Darren Horn."

"Reason for your visit?"

"Xenophilia."

The immigration official looked up from the travel documents and raised his eyebrows with interest. The tedious, long-drawn-out routine of his job had just been broken by this very atypical answer.

Darren Horn knew that the immigration officer was interested in whether he was coming to the planet Barrondo for business, or as a tourist, but he was always level with people. He didn't want to hide who and what he was.

"S-s-sorry, what?" stammered the official. The planet Barrondo had the reputation of being the planet of forbidden pleasures, so he was used to tourists arriving for all sorts of things, but this had evidently derailed him.

"Xenophilia," Darren repeated. "The Greek term for love for or attraction to the unknown. Since humanity made contact with alien races, it's also been used for someone who is sexually attracted to aliens."

The official looked more interested than shocked. "Well, I'm glad that you're proud of what you are."

"Of course! That's fundamental! We must first and foremost be honest with ourselves."

A long line of people stood behind Darren, but the mesmerized official continued asking questions. In theory, how long he spent questioning each new arrival at the spaceport on the edge of Foster City was up to him.

"We don't have too many aliens on Barrondo…" he began cautiously, but then quickly added: "Although, of course, Barrondo is the world where everyone's innermost wishes come true,"—citing almost verbatim a sentence from the tourist brochure.

"You have some Ralgars here and that's exactly what I'm looking for," said Darren enthusiastically. "Specifically, Ralgars who are going through their sex-change cycle right now."

"You… well… how exactly do you… that is, I mean… Those are interesting desires."

"I've already been to the Gliesans and spent several wonderful nights with one when he was hibernating. But he had consented before he went to sleep, so it was fine, morally and ethically speaking! And with two Silmani I played their third sex, the one that died out over one hundred fifty years ago and that has been cloned since then."

"I know how it works with the Silmani," said the official.

"And last year I went to a Lasian nest. Lasians are giant ants. I couldn't do anything with them, but they allowed me to masturbate in their spawning puddles in the queen's nest…"

"Excuse me!" exclaimed the elegantly dressed middle-aged woman behind Darren. "There are children here!"

Darren looked around. He couldn't see any children, but the woman's outraged expression indicated that there were children somewhere in the spaceport and that he should therefore stop talking.

He didn't get why she was outraged. He'd sat next to her on the journey from Barrondo's orbital station to Foster City, and the entire time, she'd been browsing on a tablet the selection of local companies that provided young men, who for serious money took hormones so that they looked even younger.

Maybe that's why this woman was fixated on children. She desired them, so she saw them everywhere.

A lot of things were legal on Barrondo.

The immigration officer decided it was better not to ask any more questions and let Darren through with a "Welcome to Barrondo!"

As Darren headed along the corridor to Baggage Reclaim, he heard the woman behind him answering the same question about the purpose of her visit.

"I'm here as a tourist. I'm going shopping… for a friend. Listen, what's the fastest way of getting to the nearest branch of GoldenBoys? I want to… buy something for my friend there, you understand."

"You can obtain all that information from your tablet, ma'am. Or from any tourist information point."

"I know, I just… need to make sure. My friend doesn't like leaving digital traces, you understand?"

Darren didn't hear any more.

Φ

At home, on the planet Arnhem, Darren had a relatively well-paid job, no miracle, but he and his wife and their children managed to get along happily, and he had no problems saving for his hobby occasionally.

Barrondo offered the most expensive and most luxurious experiences, but also a great many hotels and entertainments for reasonable prices. Darren was now sitting on the balcony in one such hotel and looking at the night cityscape.

It was full of gleaming lights, colorful towers and strange buildings. One looked like a giant monkey. Barrondo had originally been a small holiday colony for the workers building the FTL gate in this star system. When it was completed, the colony needed to find another source of income. Unfortunately, the planet itself wasn't ideal for colonizing and didn't have too many mineral or natural resources for any sort of mining to be worthwhile. The company that had originally owned the colony had therefore decided to turn Barrondo into the "planet of sin", with all the possible legal and semi-legal amusements that you could imagine, plus several that nobody could ever possibly imagine. Darren had even heard that it was legal to kill someone here. Barrondo had the death penalty, and anyone interested could pay—a great deal of money, of course—to be the executioner. They also held gladiator fights here, and some were fights to the death. Individual gladiators signed an extremely long legal document in which they gave their informed consent. If they died, their families received large compensation packages.

The gladiator fights were what Darren had to go to first. The two Ralgars he was looking for were fighting there right now.

He put down his glass of juice (some strange local fruit) and picked up his tablet. He had bookmarked the information about the Crixus Arena.

The two Ralgar warriors were currently the only members of their race in the arena. Their names were Partar and Gromo and it seemed they fought under the name of the Brothers of the Bloodscales. The arena officially stated that, very soon both warriors would no longer be available, and spectators should therefore come and watch a fight "while you still can!"

A normal person would probably consider this ordinary marketing; "time-limited offers" always sell well. Darren Horn knew something about Ralgar physiology, and he knew that both would undergo the change in the next few weeks.

Ralgars were lizards, over two and a half meters tall, with gigantic paws, a tail and a mouth resembling that of a gecko. They were belligerent warriors who lived in clans that were on worse terms even than human societies, and they spent most of their time at war with each other. They had already waged at least fourteen proper wars, known as "incursions", against the Central Imperium. Sometimes, some Ralgars settled on one or other of the Central Imperium's planets, but they were mostly outcasts from their own clans. In general, they rapidly found work on Barrondo, but they could also be found elsewhere. For example, in parts of elite society a Ralgar bodyguard conferred prestige.

Ralgars regularly changed sex, and Darren, of course, thought this was the most interesting thing about them. Regardless of birth sex, every Ralgar changed sex approximately every fifty or sixty human years. Only males went to war, or incursion. The females stayed on their home planets, laid eggs and protected them from the other clans. It would be possible to describe the two Ralgar sexes as "attack" and "defense" rather than male or female.

The males and the females behaved differently, although from what Darren had read, it seemed that they both retained a certain aggression. Quite simply, Ralgars fascinated and aroused him. He wanted to have sex with a Ralgar female, to be the first to be with her after her change. This could probably not be called "virginity" under even the most indulgent of definitions, but that wasn't the point. It was the bizarre "first" that excited him more than anything else.

He gazed at the city again. In addition to the excellent minibar, the hotel offered top-quality massages and every sort of protein and vitamin formulation. This evening, he was going to take advantage of both. He needed to recover from his journey and figure out his next move.

He had tried to find out as much as he could about Ralgars, but convincing them both—or at least one of them—to go to bed with him, or to wherever Ralgars go at such moments, would be more complicated.

First of all, he needed to get hold of them. Fortunately, the Crixus Arena had a contact form on its datanet page.

Φ

"You want to bang my Ralgars?"

Darren Horn smiled sweetly at the elegant woman in a suit as she invited him into her office. Her name was Angela Riverani, and she probably came from Yuanda; she had a series of dark blue tattoos on her temples and forehead, which were traditional on that world. On Barrondo, she was one of the corporate VPs of Harlequin Entertainment and the Crixus Arena was her direct responsibility. Darren was experienced in these matters and knew that it was a good idea to begin at the beginning. Moreover, as he had saved for this trip, he had money enough for any necessary bribes.

"You could also put it like that. Of course, formally speaking, I want to have sexual intercourse with a Ralgar as soon as he undergoes the change to female."

Riverani rubbed the bridge of her nose with the expression of someone who really hadn't expected to be dealing with this today.

"But sir, Ralgars are giant, aggressive lizards! They regenerate, so they sometimes tear chunks out of each other for fun. Gromo and Partar have lost limbs several times in the arena, but they always grow back. Their speech very vulgar, too. I believe that their favorite human word is 'asshole.'" She shook her head, stood up from the large oak desk and began to walk around the luxurious office. Patiently, Darren watched her. He understood that his desires often derailed people.

"I know what Ralgars are like, Madam Riverani. I have read all the available papers about them. I think that the most extensive is Dartmund's *Ralgar Psychology* and then Noriega's *Models of Ralgar Behavior.*"

"Yet you still want to screw one?"

"I'm sure I remember reading a brochure about Barrondo that promised that my most secret desires will be fulfilled here."

Riverani raised her hand. He knew this argument would be effective.

"Sir, it is not for me to judge any desires or sexual preferences, but… but… they are gigantic lizards, who sometimes *kill* each other for fun!"

"I understand that, ma'am. Nevertheless, I believe that your Ralgar gladiators—Partar and Gromo—are able to follow instructions. For example, they don't kill their manager, or their trainers."

"Well, they're now on their fourth trainer since they started working in the arena. The last one is still getting used to his new legs."

Darren waved his hand. "Even humans can regrow limbs thanks to modern medicine and regeneration therapy. I'm not afraid of that. We don't know much about Ralgar sexuality even from expert literature, but based on their anatomy, we can of course make an educated guess about where their sex organs are located. I even bought a very good program from Tombara, which uses the anatomic features of both species to create models of Ralgar sex and at the same time extrapolates what would be the most suitable positions for sex between a human and a Ralgar. Male or female. They transform completely, it's not just a question of hormones, even though they do play the most important role, of course…"

"Fine, fine, you have studied Ralgars, Mr. Horn, and I really do not need to know anything more, thank you."

"What are they like in person?"

Riverani shook her head. "I've never met them. The Crixus Arena is of course an amazing entertainment venue and it's great that it welcomes millions of visitors every year, but my personal tastes are different. However, you chose to come see me."

"I like to begin at the beginning. And I think that, given the... donation I have made to Harlequin Entertainment, I deserve a hearing.

"Of course. The company is grateful for your donation," the woman assured him. Whether the donation would appear on the company's balance sheet or go directly to her personal account was now up to her.

"Mr. Horn, your plan... I fear it will be difficult to put it into practice. Do you even know that the Ralgars will be *interested*? What do you have that could attract them?"

"My stamina. Both the cloned Silmani and the Lasian queen appreciated it."

Riverani's gaze wandered to the cupboard on one wall of her office. Something told Darren that she kept alcohol in it and really needed a glass right now.

"Mr. Horn, I'm sure you understand that I cannot *force* my Ralgars to... whatever you want to do with them. They're my employees, not my slaves. Slavery is illegal. However, if you would like to try any of our erotic experience houses, they are of course at your disposal. Dozens of our top employees can play the role of slaves so perfectly that you will never know that they aren't. You will think that you fell asleep and woke up in ancient Rome, or in your own harem in Siam, or..." She stopped short, noticing Darren's evident lack of interest.

"I understand that you can't force them," he said, calmly. "I would never want that. I only want the opportunity to meet them. Maybe invite them to dinner. Present my proposal to them. I will persevere, but of course their consent is necessary."

Riverani was silent for a while. "Fine. But I will want you to sign to say that Harlequin Entertainment is not liable for *any* physical or psychological damage or anything else that happens to you."

"That goes without saying."

"Good. I will contact my people at the Crixus… other gladiators—humans, that is—sometimes meet their fans. I will tell my Ralgars to go to dinner with you, that this is part of public relations. Dinner with a sponsor, maybe. But then it will be up to you, and your charm."

Darren smiled. "Thank you, Madam Riverani. Thank you. That's all I ask of you."

"But I have one more condition," said the vice-president.

"Yes?"

"There's a fight this evening. As their sex-change is approaching, we are trying to make the most of them while we still can. Go watch their fight. I'll give you a complimentary ticket. Maybe you will think again!"

Φ

"Ladies and gentlemen! Welcome to the Crixus Arena! We have a spectacular show for you on this glorious evening!"

Darren was crammed into a small hovercar called a "lodge", along with several dozen other spectators. The hovercar had panoramic windows, and screens on which you could see the battles in detail. The Crixus Arena was not a single physical location; fights took place all over the planet. Most of Barrondo was barely habitable desert, so building a small, unpeopled town, or castle, or maze, purely for the purposes of fights, was not a problem anywhere. The lodges and their spectators then hovered over the battleground.

"Today's fight is sponsored by Gamba ASMR Spas! Long-term stressed and want to relax? Have you longed for that amazing tingling sensation on the back of your neck since childhood? Come to Gamba! We can create the Autonomous Sensory Meridian Response reaction in over eighteen thousand ways! Now with an awesome new product: Gliesan ritual brushes that stroke eight different microphones at once. Come give it a try! Come to Gamba!"

Darren made a mental note to try an ASMR spa one day, when all this was over.

He had already spotted the objects of his interest on the screen—they had crawled out of a bunker in the middle of the desert. Two huge Ralgars. Each of them had a few of the swords they called *karba* on their backs, and they held some sort of Ralgar plasma gun in their hands.

"Put your hands together please for our favorite gladiators! Their minutes of glory will soon be over, but today you can enjoy them here to the full! The Brothers of the Bloodscales! Exiled from their own clans, they live only for revenge, for blood, and for your delight. Partar and Gromo!"

Darren applauded and most of the other people in the lodge joined in. Partar was a little smaller than Gromo. They both happily bared their teeth and waved as if they could hear the ovation from the hovercars above them. Not much was known about Ralgar facial expressions and body language, but Darren knew all of it. Nevertheless, he got the impression that Partar's expression was happy, while Gromo's was rather angry. But he remembered what one of his xenology teachers always used to say: you must not ascribe human emotions, and certainly not human facial expressions, to aliens.

"And which naive head-case would dare go up against them? Here we have a group of toughs who decide to bring back-up against these walking heavyweights! Welcome the Steel Riders and their T-38 replica tanks!"

Four steel colossi appeared on the screen. Many centuries ago, people probably had used them as combat vehicles. The spectators chanted. Four tanks against two armed Ralgars. Darren had no idea whether this was fair play, and if so, to what extent, and for a moment he wondered if those tanks would ruin his complex—and extremely expensive— plans for an interspecies date. He hoped that the organizers weren't planning to let their charges be killed just like that. But it also occurred to him that maybe they wanted to go out in glory, like legendary warriors in a battle. If they're going up against four tanks, that's probably legendary enough.

"So, without further ado! Let the show begin!"

For a few seconds, nothing happened, then the tanks began to move.

Darren understood nothing about tactics or anything of the sort, but he knew that Ralgars deal with things directly and aren't interested in any complicated stratagems. The tank crew were probably counting on that, and before Darren could look round, the tanks had opened fire.

Both Ralgars were running in zigzags, and the explosions around them did not slow them down. Darren got the impression that one of them, Partar, had been hit by shrapnel, but he wasn't sure. He thought he could see yellow Ralgar blood.

They were both returning fire now, and one of the tanks exploded. They had modern plasma cannons, which must have torn through a tank built to a seven-hundred-year-old blueprint like a knife through butter. But a hit from one of that tank's guns would also mean certain death.

The tank crews in the remaining three tanks maneuvered their machines, but so did the Ralgars. Explosions, dodges, it was like a crazy dance. Then another tank exploded. And, a few minutes later, a third.

The spectators around Darren shouted and cheered. They were also supporting the Ralgars. Maybe simply because they seemed like the underdogs, as they were so outnumbered?

Finally, one projectile found a target, and Darren despairingly opened his eyes wide as one of the Ralgars flew through the air, a leg behind him; he couldn't see it too well. There was lots of yellow blood everywhere, and probably some internal organs too. He noticed that it was Gromo.

Partar was running directly toward the tank. He hadn't been hit. He roared something as he ran. The tank shot at him again, but missed. There was a heavy machine gun on the hull, but Partar simply threw one of his swords and decapitated it.

By then the Ralgar was already on the tank.

"I bet that screwball will throw a grenade at them now!" said some spectator behind Darren.

But Partar didn't. Instead, he opened the hatch and reached inside with his giant paw. He dragged out one of the tank crew, quickly stabbed him, then discarded him like a broken toy. Then he dragged out another, and another. They probably had some hand-weapons, because they struck Partar several times. He even dropped his sword on the last occasion, then withdrew the final tank crew member with his other hand before crushing his head with his powerful paws.

He crushed his head.

Darren wondered what such a creature could do during sex as it got fired up.

No wonder that Riverani had set the condition of him seeing a match. She'd hoped it would discourage him.

As the spectators began to applaud and Partar and the mutilated Gromo waved—one of Gromo's arms was missing, so he waved with the other—Darren realized that all this only excited him the more.

Φ

Riverani kept her promise and sent the Ralgars on a date with him.

She even reserved a private parlor in the luxury restaurant *Solar Riviera.*

Darren arrived first. He was wearing the tux he'd packed for this trip, and had applied a scent that should act positively on the Ralgars, or at least so he thought.

Ralgars may think differently from people, but he wanted to maintain some customs. That's why he had a flower for each of them. Zergot tulips, which grew on his native Arnhem; he'd brought them with him in a cryobox.

He'd ordered a bowl of full-fat yogurt for both his guests. He knew that ordinary full-fat yogurt from human planets was the greatest delicacy for Ralgars. There was even speculation that it had aphrodisiac properties for them. Darren didn't understand how they could eat it; Ralgars were lizards and couldn't digest lactose well, but evidently it worked *somehow.*

Music was playing in the restaurant, as it had in the arena with the tanks, and here—as across the entire Central Imperium—retro and the 20th century were all the rage, so some female singer sang from the restaurant's speakers in French with strongly emphasized "r"s.

Darren tried not to be nervous but couldn't help it. The efforts of almost a year were to come to fruition here.

What's more, he'd really taken a fancy to those Ralgars.

He'd probably be attracted to them as females too. Humans barely noticed the physical changes, but he'd heard that Ralgar females smelled different, even to humans, due to pheromones.

Finally, the door opened and the waiter led in the pair of lizards.

One of them—Gromo—was still missing an arm, but his other wounds were obviously beginning to regenerate after the fight. Even the arm would grow back, in time.

"Mr. Gromo and Mr. Partar, Mr. Horn," said the waiter, with absolute confidence, as if he introduced two giant lizards into the parlor every day.

"A pleasure to meet you!" said Darren, glowing. He knew that Ralgars didn't shake hands, and he preferred not to try kissing their hands, so he merely bowed slightly and then gave each of them a tulip.

"That's for you."

"So, you're the asshole who wanted to meet us, amirite?" said Gromo.

Darren didn't take it personally. The Ralgars who spoke human language used the word "asshole" on all possible occasions.

"Yes, indeed I am. It's a pleasure."

Partar ate his tulip.

Darren raised his eyebrows. Gromo chuckled and immediately scarfed down his flower too.

"That green shit is good," Partar commented.

The waiter cleared his throat. "Gentlemen, if you'd like to sit down, we can start to serve dinner."

The table had been modified so that both human chairs and chairs configured for Ralgars could fit under it. They all sat down as best they could and then the serving robots, supervised by the waiter, brought in soup for Darren and the yogurt bowls for the Ralgars. He'd ordered an aperitif as well.

The Ralgars didn't wait to be invited—not that Darren would have wanted them to—but immediately started to eat. Gromo seized a large spoon, while Partar grabbed the bowl in his huge paws and gorged himself.

"I… very much wanted to meet you. I would love to know more about you," began Darren, slowly, drinking his aperitif. "I'm Darren Horn, as I already said. I come from the planet Arnhem, in the Bornholm Sector, on the other side of the Central Imperium. I work as a clerk for Jaxan, general sales and purchase of various goods, nothing interesting, but I enjoy it, and it pays well. I'm thirty-eight." He hesitated about giving them more information, but Ralgars didn't have the same social conventions that humans did. And open relationships were nothing unusual even among humans. You only had to look at the planet Tombara. "I also have a wife and two kids, a boy and a girl. Did you know that humans can change sex, if they decide to do so, but they don't do it regularly or automatically, like Ralgars? You know, that's the reason I invited you here…"

The Ralgars had already almost emptied their bowls.

"Well, before we talk about the other reason why I invited you, I'd like to add that I admire Ralgars. I know that some clans wage war against the Imperium, but that isn't your fault, and it isn't mine either. I'd love to know more about the two of you, which clans you're from, how you got to Barrondo and…"

"We hear you want to fuck us," Gromo interrupted him, and looked him over, frowning.

Darren was taken aback. "Well… I wouldn't put it like that… But…" *Oh, dammit, whatever.* "Yes, I do, yes."

Partar laughed. "I told you so! But humans have to say a load of shit first!"

Gromo was still inspecting the stunned Darren. "The fuckwit boss from that corporation told us."

"Do you… do you mean Ms. Angela Riverani?"

Partar waved a paw. "Yeah. We call her the fuckwit boss from that corporation."

He took the lit candle from the middle of the table and ate it too. "Why do you want to fuck us?"

"I… you know. I'm a xenophile. I'm sexually attracted to aliens."

"That's badass. Is that why you smell like a freshly transformed female? So we find you hot?"

"I didn't know that it was like a freshly transformed female, but… yes."

Partar chuckled. "It's working."

"You asshole!" his brother growled at him.

"What is it? It smells good. But I'm afraid that, if I wanted to screw him, I'd break him to bits."

"I must admit that I am fascinated by you changing into females," said Darren. He wondered whether talking openly about his xenophilia disconcerted others like this. The Ralgars were currently turning the tables on him, as they talked somewhat too openly, even for him. "If… both of you, or just one were… I would like, well…"

"To fuck us?" prompted Partar.

"Yes, but… once you have transformed into females."

"The change takes a ton of days and it's pretty shitty," said Gromo. "In every respect. For a fuckton of days—even these long as fuck Barrondo days—it just sucks. There are changes in… what do you call the shit that your body makes and that changes your body and behavior?"

"Hormones?"

"Yeah, that shit. Well, and then suddenly you're female, you don't want to fight, or at least not as much, you want to take cover somewhere and lay eggs."

"But you also want some male to sperminate you, right?" added Partar.

"Yeah, and it's not worth shit. Because we are the only two Ralgars on this whole planet," growled Gromo. "We are exiled from our clans and we won't get to any males. We'll be just two females who'll sit there like assholes and won't be worth shit!"

"Why were you exiled from your clans?" asked Darren.

Gromo seized a large spoon and hurled it across the room. "Because everything stupid in this universe is happening for the same reason: disagreements and assholes!"

Partar wasn't much more forthcoming.

"And what… ehm… well, can't you join another clan?"

"If we could, do you think we'd be sitting here and beating up assholes with other rich assholes like you watching?"

"I'm not rich… I'd say I'm upper middle-class. I saved up for a long time for this trip."

Partar growled. "I don't know what upper middle-class means."

"Well, they're… actually, they're also a sort of asshole."

It probably made sense to communicate on the same level as the Ralgars did.

"So, you want to fuck us," said Gromo, getting back to the point. "But only when we're female."

"If I understand correctly, this will be quite soon?"

"A week or two," said Partar. "But… we have no clans. We'll need to defend our nests, reproduce, and we can't here!"

"No, we can't!" Gromo snarled, waving his stump. "That's why we were hoping that the morons in tanks would kill us."

Darren was taken aback. "You wanted to… die?"

His eyes flitted from one to the other and back again.

Partar said nothing. He even bent his head and stared at the tabletop. Maybe he'd picked that up from humans.

But Gromo spoke up proudly. "Yeah, it's better to be shot to shit in the arena than live in the middle of nowhere as some female fucked up by hormones with nobody to mate with! What's the point in a nest and laying eggs if you have nobody to sperminate you?"

"Another clan could still help us," said Partar.

"No!" snarled Gromo. "No, we already went through enough shit! Fuck them!"

"Maybe I… could help you with that," Darren suggested. "Not with fertilization, of course, but with the… well, physical release."

"With fucking?"

"Well… yes. With the physical stimulus. With new energy. Maybe it would help you get your heads straight in the female cycle. That is what you call it, isn't it?"

Partar gaped at him. "So, I'll change into a female, and you'll fuck me and then I'll be happier?"

"Well… I don't know. Humans and Ralgars are different."

"I know, you're bigger assholes… but maybe it would work."

"You're talking such fucking bullshit!" roared Gromo. "We agreed about this! I decided! We'd go to the arena together and get shot there. We won't be female again!"

"I still think we could maybe rejoin some clan as females!"

"Fuck other clans. I made a decision!" Gromo roared, jumping to his feet and banging on the table, which buckled. "I'm the clan chief!"

"We don't have a clan, bonehead! There's just the two of us!"

"I'm still the chief!"

"Fuck that shit. I don't know if this human is a screwball or only a moron, but so what, maybe I'll have some future as a female. When the female cycle is over, I'll go fighting again and cut off the heads of human assholes!"

Darren didn't need to be an expert in Ralgar body language to know that Gromo was furious.

"I said that's how it would be!"

"And I say no!" Partar also jumped to his feet.

Darren slowly stood up. "Please stop! Allow me to make peace between you."

Partar turned to him. "So do you want to fuck us or make peace?"

"Usually you have to do the second before you can do the first."

Partar laughed.

Gromo looked as if he wanted to lunge at Darren, but then he turned to Partar. "Do you really want to fuck that asshole?"

"When I get hormonal, I'll need something. He's at least enough of a screwball to approach me. So why not?"

Gromo growled. "I don't want anything of the sort."

"I can't force you," cheeped Darren. The giant lizard turned back to him.

"But Partar wasn't joking when he said he'd squish you!"

"I'm sure we can come to some arrangement."

"Some arrangement! You're good at bullshit. Let's stop bullshitting. Do you want to fuck Partar when he's female? Fine. Okay then. But first you'll have to defeat me!"

"What?"

"Are you out of your mind?" asked Partar.

"I'm the clan chief. This human wants to help us. Great. So he can help our entire clan. Both of us. You want to fuck. Enjoy it. I don't give a shit. I want to die in battle."

"You… you want me to kill you?"

"No, I want you to come to the arena with me and fight me there," laughed Gromo, waving his stump. "If you survive, you can do what the fuck you like with sex-starved Partar here. But first you need to defeat the clan chief. Me!"

"But, but… I'm a clerk, I don't have a chance against you! It wouldn't be a fair fight."

"It's never a fair fight, but if you want an advantage, I'll give you one. The last time it was a bunch of assholes in tanks against us!"

Yes, it was, and Darren remembered only too vividly what had happened to them.

"But i-if you want to d-die, why don't you j-just kill yourself?" he stammered. "Or let someone kill you? Why do you want to fight?"

"You'll never understand. You aren't a Ralgar. As soon as the fighting starts, I can't just stop. No, I'll try to kill you in the arena. I'll cut you to shreds with one hand! But if you survive, Partar is yours."

"I'm not yours," growled Partar. "But we'll do like you said. It could be fun."

Darren only gaped at him. At most, he'd expected only one of the Ralgars to accept his offer. But he hadn't expected it to turn out like this.

Gromo waved his hand. "Or you can say fuck that, go home and consider that you aren't good enough for Ralgars, either to fight with or to mate with. After all, you're only upper middle-class!"

At this moment Darren realized two fundamental things.

One, these two Ralgars were even crazier than he'd expected.

Two, that he was crazier still.

Φ

"You asshole!"

"The Ralgars said that word maybe a thousand times over the course of the evening, so please don't you say it too."

Riverani threw up her hands. This time it was dark outside the windows of her luxurious office. Days and nights on Barrondo were each almost as long as two standard days.

"OK. But it's still an accurate description. For god's sake, you agreed to fight a Ralgar to the death!"

"Yes, I did. It was the only way to achieve my aims."

"But that's lunacy! You'll never get them into bed that way! Give it up! Go home." She pointed at his hand that wore a ring. "I get that your wife… tolerates your thrill-seeking, but enough is enough! Gromo has only one hand and he'll still kill you!"

"I know, but I can still try."

"Christ, don't you want to see your children again?"

"Of course I do. But I don't interfere in their hobbies. Or in my wife's. She prefers BDSM. She sometimes goes somewhere to let her hair down. But it's not at all my thing."

"I'll send her a one-week voucher for the best BDSM salons on Barrondo, but for god's sake, give up on this!"

"I have good life insurance. My family would not be left unprovided for."

"You're absolutely nuts!"

Darren was glad that she didn't say 'asshole'.

"I probably am," he said firmly. "But I've also made up my mind. I understand that volunteers can put their names down for the Crixus Arena. And surely a lot of spectators will come for Gromo's last fight?"

Riverani had already opened her alcohol cabinet, taken out a bottle and one glass, and was starting to open the bottle on the table. "You're nuts. You're absolutely nuts! This won't be Gromo's last fight. He'll tear you to shreds!"

"Gromo himself suggested how I can survive. He gave me a greater chance against him."

"Do you have any military experience?"

"No, I've never been in either the army or the navy. I don't like wars."

Riverani knocked back her shot and immediately poured another. "My grandfather served in the Imperial Army. He fought the Ralgars during the Sixth Incursion… and from what he told me it's clear that you have absolutely no chance. You're in admin! What could Gromo offer to give you a level playing field?"

"It's quite simple. He's going to have his *karba* sword and I'll have a nuclear missile."

"*What*?!!"

Φ

"Ladies and gentlemen! Welcome to the Crixus Arena! We have a spectacular show for you on this glorious evening!"

Darren Horn hadn't expected to see the arena again. He certainly hadn't expected not to be a spectator this time.

He was wearing a combat suit, practically identical to the ones the Imperial Army used in contaminated areas. It was designed to withstand a vacuum. Nevertheless, he could hear the commentator's voice in his earphones.

"Today's fight is sponsored by StellarShock Energy Drinks! Do you need to pull an all-nighter? Do you need to concentrate permanently? Do you feel that sleep is only holding you back on your way to success? Drink StellarShock! The best energy drink on the market. Clinically tested. Regular use guarantees you up to six days straight of no sleep!

Drink StellarShock. Read the packaging leaflet for information about possible side effects."

Darren's mouth was dry, but he felt surprisingly calm. He couldn't back out. All the persuasion and insistence and explanation that he was crazy had finally stopped. Riverani had compelled him to sign another heap of documents, in which he absolved Harlequin Entertainment of any liability for whatever happened.

Gromo's choice of weapon didn't reassure her much. In his hands, Darren weighed the weapon officially called a Merkon L-48 tactical guided missile launcher. Any soldier, however, would call it a "nuke gun". This weapon did exactly what its nickname suggested. It fired small nuclear charges. Very small. Darren had no idea how heavy they were, but it was enough to fry a huge area and everything in it. It was the sort of weapon that you didn't need to be able to aim. The disadvantage was that if you hit a target too close to you, the explosion could easily wipe you out with the enemy.

"One half of the Brothers of the Bloodied Scales is here for his final fight! Gromo! He hasn't yet recovered from his last fight, but he only needs one hand to finish off his adversary. One hand, savagery and the urge to kill. Welcome the Ralgar pariah Gromo!"

Darren was well able to imagine the applause. He couldn't see Gromo anywhere near him. The rules that Gromo had made were based on him being put down in the desert several kilometers from Darren, who would have no idea which direction the furious Ralgar would run from. What's more, it's hard to observe the horizon in the desert. Darren's eyesight was good, but that wouldn't necessarily be enough. He also had to keep looking around him.

"But we can always find some naive idiot with a death wish who dares to challenge the master. And here today we have the bravest and craziest of all naive idiots! Someone so off his head that they gave him a pocket-sized nuclear bomb, which means he has at least a small chance against the swords. He's a clerk from Arnhem, he works in an open-space office, he's never been in the army, he's not a sportsman and he last fought

someone in seventh grade. Welcome the biggest screwball on the planet: Darren Horn!"

The commentator had embellished things a little, but not too much. Darren also vaguely remembered getting into a fight with someone in ninth grade.

"So, without further ado! Let the show begin!"

Darren could fully imagine the huge Ralgar starting to move. His bare lizard shanks were thumping across the desert, his single hand grasping his *karba* sword. He knew where Darren was, and he was running right toward him.

Darren checked his weapon. It was loaded and ready. Should he need to reload, he had two more missiles on his back. The instructor, a former marine, had taught him to handle the weapon, but for obvious reasons they hadn't shot live ammunition with nuclear warheads. There weren't too many shooting ranges where they could have, and most of them were already booked out by tourists who had come in to explode nukes for serious money.

Darren had only been able to fire three times, he realized, as he looked around him. He couldn't see the Ralgar anywhere on the horizon. Which didn't mean that he wouldn't miss him in the glow of the local star in the middle of the day cycle...

The marine had assured him that, if he didn't solve the problem with three nuclear warheads, it wouldn't be worth trying with a fourth.

He had also asked Darren about something else. Had he ever killed anyone in his life before? Darren had had to admit that no, he hadn't, and the marine explained that this may be a problem, if he didn't prepare for it. He'd even cited some statistics, according to which most recruits in many wars deliberately aimed above the enemy's head, because they didn't want to kill, even though the enemy was shooting at them.

Of course, Darren had never thought much about this. But Gromo wanted to die. In the same way, Partar wanted to get laid immediately after changing into a female. Darren had talked to both about this for a long time over dinner. For Gromo, it was a case of assisted suicide. Darren was providing euthanasia, which was entirely normal in Arnhem's culture.

Although euthanasia didn't normally involve nukes.

Hang on…

He'd spotted something. On the horizon. He stopped. He watched some movement, some… yes, it was there. Definitely. He saw it.

He aimed, exactly as the marine had taught him, and fired.

The missile launcher had no recoil. The projectile launched, the missile ignited and flew toward the target.

First there appeared a very bright, white light, which fortunately Darren's helmet filtered. Then a mushroom cloud appeared.

The target had been far away, but sand and the pressure wave created by the explosion reached him and he fell into the dune. His suit protected him from radiation and the pressure wave was weak. He'd shot a sufficient distance.

Was it all over?

As he scrambled to his feet, he tried to marshal his thoughts. He'd seen the mushroom cloud. He'd seen the explosion. Had he killed Gromo?

His legs were shaking. Was that the reaction to killing someone for the first time?

Had he even killed anyone?

He forced himself to look around again. He could see nothing in his immediate surroundings. Had Gromo met his end in that huge cloud of churned sand and radiation?

Was he like a knight in some fairy tale? Had he killed the dragon and won the hand of the beautiful princess? Or at least the hand of another dragon who would soon become a princess?

A dragon princess.

Only the heroes of those fairy tales at least knew that they'd vanquished the dragon! Darren could only see the cloud and…

Again, he looked around, and suddenly stiffened. On the other side, he could see a clear streak approaching him, or he thought it was approaching him, and…

That was Gromo!

He didn't know what he'd fired at before, but this time he could see the gigantic Ralgar. He was sure.

He aimed, pulled the trigger, and nothing happened.

Hell, hell, I need to reload!

He took a missile from his back and began loading, just as the marine had taught him, although rather more slowly. He did everything wrong. His hands wouldn't work properly.

He could already make out Gromo's features, he could see he was waving a *karba* sword in his single hand.

Was he too close already? There was only one way to find out.

The missile clicked into place, Darren pressed several buttons, as instructed. He took aim and fired.

Even though his aim was no good and he'd never shot from anything else before, the shot dropped barely ten meters behind Gromo.

The Ralgar pariah, tourist attraction and Partar's brother vanished in a blinding white flash.

Another mushroom cloud.

Then the blast wave hit Darren.

This time he had been really close.

Partar arrived. He looked different.

No, Darren corrected himself, as he entered the hotel room with cautious steps, *she* looked different.

The transformation to female was complete. Partar was now standing opposite him, grinning happily.

Her scent really was different, he realized. Different pheromones make a big difference to perception.

However, Partar wasn't wearing anything, so Darren was also able to notice other, physiological, changes.

Nine days had already passed since his fight. Partar—then still a male—had thanked him for giving his brother a worthy send-off. The Ralgar had, of course, expressed this in many much more colorful phrases, frequently including the word "asshole", but the meaning was the same.

Partar wasn't the only one who needed to transform and recover. Darren had been badly bruised and had broken both legs, but rapid—and expensive—regeneration therapy had mended his bones. Angela Riverani had visited him and told him again that he was crazy, but otherwise she was pleased. The video of his fight had apparently been watched twenty times more than other fights, which made all the sponsors happy and so she was happy too.

Darren started to undress, but Partar suddenly stood before him and tore his clothes off him.

"You've waited so long. You still don't want to scram?"

Darren grinned but shook his head.

"And do you have any idea what Ralgar sex looks like?"

"I know that it's very clumsy."

Partar burst out laughing. "We're aggressive! Whether we're fighting an asshole or fucking one. It's the same thing."

"I know," said Darren.

He could wait no longer.

Months of preparations and waiting were over.

The last of his inhibitions fell away.

He threw himself on her.

He had his female Ralgar.

Φ

This time, Angela Riverani looked even more frustrated than she had after his fight. More than *before* his fight, and that was saying something.

"The media's having a field day over you. 'The man who tested uncharted waters!' Or 'In the vanguard of human experience: the first man to have sex with a Ralgar'. But when they see your photo, I suspect our stocks will go down."

She was standing by his hospital bed, and he smiled at her.

"It hardly hurt at all. I'd taken xeranin to dull the pain. It also stimulates the pleasure centers."

"Well, yes, but…" Riverani was no longer frustrated, she wasn't even scolding him anymore. She only gaped at what was left of him.

Darren had to admit that there were probably nicer views. Long gashes stretched over the left side of his face, caused by the claws that had taken out his eye and ear, and the torn skin on his cheek revealed the edge of his jawbone and teeth. He had similar gashes on his chest, where she had torn out four ribs and, just like Partar's brother Gromo, he now had only one arm. That had happened right at the end when, during the Ralgar equivalent of an orgasm, Partar had been unable to keep a check on her strength and had simply torn Darren's arm off.

He'd been almost flattered. His sexual skill had caused her to lose control in that amazing way. Otherwise, she had made something of an effort not to hurt him.

"You're crazy," said Riverani. "There's no other way of putting it. You're crazy."

"I know," said Darren.

"I think I'll give you a voucher for one of our luxury sanatoriums. On the house, as a thank-you for the PR."

"Thank you."

"And then, please, I'd like to ask you to go home… I hope we won't meet again."

"I'm happy. I'll leave as soon as the worst of it has healed. And thank you. Without your help this could never have happened! I'll never forget you. You have enriched my life and helped me to fulfill my dreams."

Riverani merely shook her head again before leaving the room.

Darren Horn happily rested his head against the pillow and grinned at the ceiling.

The regeneration therapy and the other miracles of modern medicine would do their thing. He'd grow a new ear, eye and face within a few months. His arm would grow back in a year, maybe two.

But oh, the memories!

The beautiful memories…

He would have them forever.

III

Hila's tears had dried up completely. She simply goggled at Varviso as he finished his story.

"And I thought that my love life was strange," Daniel managed to say. Hila poked him in the ribs. A chuckle escaped her, however.

"I understand that you have also encountered Ralgars," said the journalist slowly. "Particularly Nordel Tull?"

He was focusing on them again. Back to reality.

"Yes," said Daniel. "And a great many other Ralgars. During the war against the New Protectorate, we made some… interesting allies."

"And of course, it's thanks to the Ralgar DNA in my genetic modifications that I can regenerate," Hila added.

"Yes, I knew about Ralgar and Omega regeneration." Varviso helped himself to a cookie from the plate of refreshments. "It was undoubtedly extremely useful on many occasions while you were with the Omegas."

"Yes, I must admit that I don't even remember how many times I lost a limb in a gunfight or suffered an internal injury that would have killed a normal person."

"And, like the rest of the Imperium, I too have seen that video of the fight with the Ralgars on Fairview." He took another cookie. "A lot of people—not just Enhans—see the Omegas as being somewhat… controversial."

Hila chortled. "They're right to do so. We sometimes did some rather abhorrent things. Things that the former Emperor wanted to do surreptitiously, to keep under wraps. Some call us a special unit, others a necessary evil, still others terrorists. I've never apologized for what I did, but I've never been proud of it either. And given how I was recruited, I didn't exactly have much choice."

Daniel intervened. "And before you ask, the Imperium currently has no program similar to the Omegas."

Varviso smiled. "And if you had, Your Majesty, would you tell me?"

"Good point."

"Of course you wouldn't. Why would you? But don't worry, I'm not going to ask you about that. This interview is merely for context. But I did want to ask about one specific Omega mission. On Tarlin."

Daniel was taken aback.

Hila sat up straight.

Varviso understood.

There was a reason why he was asking.

He didn't just want the facts, he wanted emotions.

"I know this is a sensitive subject. This mission concerned your friend Captain Golna. I know he was your… can I say mentor?"

"During those godawful months after I… came to the throne, he and Hila were what kept me sane," Daniel managed to say. "He also helped me to… well, get it straight in my head. My responsibilities as Emperor. He was my adviser. But mainly he was my friend, you're right."

"So why do you want to hear about Tarlin, exactly?" asked Hila.

"It's one of the many examples of what was going on in the Imperium. And indeed, is going on. And you are personally involved, via Captain Golna."

"But I wasn't active on Tarlin," said Hila. "That was another Omega team."

"That doesn't matter, ma'am. Even so, I think I'd like to hear about the situation from you, for the overall context."

"Very well."

UNHOLY COMPROMISES

"All rise!"

Courts-martial were traditionally held aboard warships. Although this tradition had been somewhat ignored in recent years, this time the Imperial Navy had decided to follow it, if only because this significantly restricted journalist access, meaning that the entire trial was—as far as possible—out of the public eye.

Alexander Golna stood up with all the others present in the courtroom in the auditorium aboard the battleship *Wisconsin*.

"Members of the military tribunal, arriving," continued the marine's ringing baritone, and he named the tribunal members as they entered, one after the other, led by the most junior in service and rank. They marched slowly, somberly, as if they planned to skip over the trial and go straight to the execution.

"Captain Elena Tafiq of INS *Trieste*, Captain Lawrence Brandon of INS *Owendo*, Captain Valan Raponda of INS *Wisconsin*, Commodore Oliver Starkan, Deputy Commander of BATRON 6, Rear Admiral Cheryl Krause, Admiralty Department of Operations."

They reached the bench and took their places, where they sat down as one. Krause banged an archaic hammer.

"The trial is hereby commenced," she declared, and chairs scraped as those present also sat down. "This court was convened under the laws and regulations of the Imperial Navy's Military Code as part of the Imperial Armed Forces under the government of Emperor Adrian III. The court's task is to examine the charge against Captain Alexander

Golna regarding the incident on the planet Tarlin on the April twelfth of this year."

Golna watched silently.

"The defendant will rise."

He stood motionlessly beside his attorney. The quintet of judges gazed at him.

Their expressions were even more somber now.

"Captain Alexander Golna, the charge against you is that, on April twelfth of this year, as captain of the ship *Mexico City*, units under your command on Tarlin opened fire on a group of civilians. Thirty-two of the said civilians died as a result. You are accused of neglecting your duty as commanding officer under Article 84 of the Military Code, and of second-degree murder under Article 109, as death happened due to your acts and intentions.

"Captain Golna, do you plead guilty or not guilty?"

"Not guilty, Your Honor."

The robot clerk dutifully recorded the information. Golna felt the eyes of the tribunal members burning through him.

"We will keep this in mind. The tribunal members were selected by computer from officers in the Imperial Navy who met the criteria of seniority and availability," Krause continued. "Captain Golna, you have the right to request the replacement of any tribunal member, if you are concerned that they could be biased against you."

All eyes in the courtroom turned almost instinctively to Captain Brandon. Even Golna could not stop himself from looking in that direction. The stocky captain was studying the table edge. They'd never met, and they weren't enemies, but Brandon was renowned throughout the entire Navy as a man with highly indiscriminate opinions about people with a lifestyle somewhat… different to what he considered normal.

Particularly about people like Golna, from a planet known for its specific sexual mores.

"No, Your Honor, I do not wish to request any changes," Golna declared.

Brandon flinched and looked surprised. Krause was surprised too.

She had probably expected to adjourn the court immediately while the computer selected someone else.

Golna had no opinion on the matter, but given what he was charged with, this seemed trivial to him. However, his lawyer had advised him not to request a replacement under the circumstances.

"Very well. You can sit down, Captain Golna," said Krause, and looked at the JAG commander, who sat across the aisle from Golna and his attorney.

"Would the prosecution please take the floor?"

"Thank you, Your Honor. The prosecution aims to prove that Captain Golna is guilty as charged and that…"

Golna stopped listening. He knew only too well what he was charged with.

Some people might feel that the court was merely a formality. Others might say something about a scapegoat and the need to hush everything up. His attorney had repeatedly assured him that he knew nothing about the plaintiff, but he always said the phrases you'd expect.

Golna hadn't paid attention.

He was only too aware of the blood on his hands.

And not only his hands.

He remembered how often he had pragmatically shrugged his shoulders about things going on in the Imperium. About how the Emperor and government always tried to play off both ends against the middle. As a student of history, he understood this.

But now that pragmatism had corrupted not only him, but a great number of other people.

"…I hereby conclude my opening speech," declared the prosecutor. Krause's eyes slid to Golna's attorney.

"The defense may now take the floor."

"Your Honor, we would like to call Captain Golna as the first witness, so he can describe the whole situation to us in his own words."

"Fine. The court calls Captain Golna."

Golna moved to the witness stand, taking the statements from the ship's log and personal diaries that the court had produced as evidence. On Krause's nod, he began to speak.

Φ

The *Mexico City* had docked at the *Walla* space station near Ferrel Kast on April tenth of this year. The crew were on leave on the station and supplies were being restocked. The ship was supposed to depart on the following day. I was also on leave on the station. I, and several of my Tombaran compatriots, were in the Tombara Recreation Center on the station. I admit that, after many months in deep space, I was grateful for the diversion and that I could again enjoy the culture of my home planet…

Φ

"Captain Golna," Captain Brandon interrupted his narrative. "Please speak fully and call things by their actual names. Do not conceal anything from this court."

Golna blinked, but several members of the tribunal did not look at all surprised.

"I'm sorry?"

"The Tombara Recreation Center is a whorehouse, a brothel, is it not?"

"No, Your Honor, it's a place for Tombaran citizens who want to live their own way."

"Which means a great many licentious… sexual practices, doesn't it?" Brandon blushed, as if simply saying the word denigrated him.

"Yes, if you mean orgies, Your Honor. I attended orgies, as is the custom on Tombara."

"A whorehouse, then, as I said."

"No, I didn't pay anyone. It's more like a leisure activity. Like going to play pool, or cards, when you come off duty."

Brandon went red again. "I think that comparison is absurd. And it's highly inappropriate for an officer in your position and of your age to indulge such low urges instead of taking care of his ship."

"My ship was in the dock and I was on leave, Your Honor," said Golna, trying not to sound sarcastic. In a way, it was a good thing that this had come up so soon. But it annoyed him that Brandon was fixating on his leisure activities that had nothing to do with the case.

No, the case is about the marines under my command who fired at civilians.

And the comment about his age was also apt. Golna was over sixty, a good ten years older than Brandon, though Brandon was senior in terms of length of service as a captain. That was why he could be selected as a tribunal member for this court; however, not only did he have plenty of prudish ideas about sexuality, he was evidently offended by the thought that *so old* an officer had enjoyed himself.

"Officers may do whatever they like within the law in their free time," stated Captain Raponda, who was clearly bored by this discussion.

"Yes, but I think that it is also important to consider the character of the said officer," Brandon insisted.

Raponda was about to say something more, but Krause raised her hand.

"This discussion is not relevant to the case. Please continue, Captain Golna."

Φ

As I was getting ready to leave, I got a call from the ship that an urgent call from Commodore Jacobsen awaited me. He's the commanding officer of Cruiser Squadron 30. At that time, his flagship *Melbourne* was docked at the station, like the *Mexico City*. I was taken aback, but I knew immediately that it was important. The Commodore knew that I was on leave. The squadron commander must be informed when a captain under his command spends a night off the ship, and I had complied with that rule. I suggested they connect him directly to my personal comlink, but our radio operator informed me that the commodore did not wish to talk to me from the station and that I should return aboard and take the call there.

My conviction that this was important only intensified.

I crossed the station rapidly, found the intrastation train and traveled to the airlock where the ship was docked. I went on board and ran to my cabin, where I made the connection.

It seemed that the Commodore wasn't at his computer, and I stared at the *Melbourne*'s crest on my screen for less than a minute, but it seemed much longer. When Jacobsen finally appeared on the monitor, the expression on his face also did not fill me with calm.

"Alex," he addressed me informally. "Are you back on board?"

"Yes, sir."

"I need the *Mexico City* to depart immediately. How long do you need to recall all astronauts and set out?"

I wondered what this was about, but professionalism won the day, so I instantly answered the question: "Most of the crew members are already aboard and loading is almost finished. I can set off within two hours. Some astronauts are on the planet below us. If we waited for them, it would be another…"

The commodore interrupted me.

"No, you can't wait for them. Recall them aboard immediately and anyone who doesn't arrive before the *Mexico City* is ready to depart will simply have to stay there."

Once again, I was taken aback by how resolved he sounded. "Commodore, what is this about?"

"There's a revolution on Tarlin. Or an uprising, an illegal coup, whatever you want to call it. The rebels have had enough of the ruling Renton family. Two days ago, they clashed with the local police on the streets of the capital and now it's a full revolution. They've seized the planet's parliament building and occupied the Renton royal palace… There's been a massacre."

"Good God," I said. I can't say I was surprised. House Renton was one of the least popular in the ruling Enhans caste and their arrogance was not counterbalanced by any political skill. I knew that there was unrest on Tarlin. The *Mexico City* had been active in that sector for almost a year. And everyone knew that the situation was on the verge of exploding; everyone except the planet's ruler Aliser Renton, that is. He did nothing except hold dinner parties. Ten years ago, as a great concession to the malcontents' demands, he'd allowed a planetary parliament to be set up on Tarlin, but he personally approved the election of each member and could veto any law that came before the parliament. In the same way, he personally held the budget, controlled most banks, and business was only allowed with the consent of his ministers. When, a few years ago, Tarlin was in danger of losing a lot of people to mass emigration, Renton had restricted opportunities to travel off-planet. He acted cautiously so as not to breach Imperial laws about free movement. But the Central Imperium was built on thousands of tiny compromises. The Emperor needed the Enhans and their House of Parliament to push through other laws and someone like Renton staying in power on Tarlin was pragmatism, pure and simple.

But it seemed that the citizens of Tarlin had had enough.

Which led me to worry about what Commodore Jacobsen's orders would be.

"I want the *Mexico City* to head for Tarlin immediately and make contact with Renton."

"You want us to suppress the uprising?" I asked, shocked. Half of my crew would refuse to obey such an order. While Enhans had privileged status on worlds like Tarlin or Haveloc, they weren't even allowed to hold public office on others, like Enugu or Rosario. The Imperium functioned as one giant unholy compromise.

"No Alex, I don't. Aliser Renton and his closest advisers and family escaped from the capital to his summer residence in the country and have entrenched themselves there. The rebels destroyed his shuttle on the ramp and have gotten hold of some anti-aircraft weapons. They're threatening to shoot him down if he tries to escape."

"Where did they get those weapons?"

"We don't know. What's important is that we assume they won't dare to attack an Imperial shuttle. The *Mexico City* will arrive, her marines will secure the area and we will evacuate Renton and his family. That is all."

"And then what about the planet?"

"The Emperor will recognize Tarlin's new government and the Rentons will keep their seats in the House of Families."

I wasn't surprised. Another unholy compromise. Playing both ends against the middle.

"Wouldn't the Imperial Army be more suitable for this? There's also a troop carrier in the star system."

"No. We want to do nothing, *nothing* that could cause things to escalate. An Imperial Army regiment, with tanks and combat mechs, would certainly constitute such an escalation, just as my entire squadron appearing there would, or any admiral or general or," he smiled, "commodore. No, one ship and one captain to carry off a few refugees, that's another matter entirely. And you're ideal for the job, Alex."

I must confess that I would have preferred not to be ideal for the job. But yes, the history of the Imperium has always interested me. Maybe I came over as a quiet, level-headed, diplomatic captain.

"How many marines do you have aboard?" Jacobsen asked, after a moment.

"Only thirty-five, currently. And some of them will be on the planet right now. I'll need to check with the Personnel Department, but I think that their commander is there too…"

"No matter. I'll send you forty marines from the *Melbourne*. That will give you a big enough force, but go to the surface with them personally. This is a rather delicate situation, and I don't want to entrust it to some marine first lieutenant."

"Understood."

Jacobsen looked as if he were thinking about what else he could add, but ultimately only shrugged. "It sure looks like you drew the short straw here, Alex. The marines will come aboard within the hour, and I expect the *Mexico City* to depart for Tarlin within two."

"You can rely on me, sir," I said. I was certain that we would set sail within that time and that our combat-readiness would make no difference to this.

Nevertheless, I wasn't very certain about anything else.

"Captain Golna, do you think that your orders were sufficiently well explained to you?"

Golna raised his head. Admiral Krause was asking, her face a mixture of honest interest and the need to emphasize this essential matter for the court and the records.

"Yes, Your Honor, the orders were sufficiently well explained to me."

"Do you feel that there is anything that Commodore Jacobsen should have emphasized in his orders, given how events later developed?"

Golna's eyes flickered toward Jacobsen, who was sitting among the spectators in the courtroom.

"No, Your Honor," he said truthfully. "His orders were comprehensible, and I also received them in writing. Direct from the Admiralty."

"Understood. And the written version of the orders is in the evidence, I think," said Krause, making a note in her datapad. "Could you now come to what exactly happened after you arrived on Tarlin, Captain Golna?"

Φ

Silence reigned on the bridge of the *Mexico City* as we reduced speed to Gertz level one and slowly approached the planet.

Someone tapped their foot nervously, until Commander Hamel, my executive officer, yelled at them to stop.

I was monitoring the planet below us. From orbit, Tarlin looked calm.

"Any warships in the star system?" I asked. Some Enhans houses made full use of the services of private military contractors and some of these groups had purchased old warships from the Imperium. In such a situation, they represented a wild card. An unpredictable element.

"Nothing on the sensors," said the tactical officer, Lieutenant Commander Brannigan. "Very little civilian traffic in the area too. I can see only seven civilian ships. And maybe the same number again docked at the orbital station."

That was not many. Tarlin had never been a huge trade junction, but under normal circumstances there would be at least three times as many vessels in the star system. As it happened, the revolution was harming trade, and many captains of freighters and trade ships had probably judged that it would be better to head elsewhere.

Just as a great many people, having found themselves in the crossfire, had undoubtedly already escaped because they could. Maybe the majority of civilians did not support Renton's government, but they still didn't want to wait for some bomb or projectile to destroy *their* home. Anyone who could get out had gotten out.

The only people who had stayed were those who couldn't leave. Such as Renton and his whole family and government.

"How is the situation on the surface?" I asked, as the significance of my thoughts about destroyed houses struck me.

"No answers to our calls have arrived from the surface so far," said the communications officer, Lieutenant Boq. "But I'm picking up signals from local media."

"Let's hear them!"

We watched the news for the next few minutes. The whole bridge, on the main screen. I didn't want to keep any secrets from anyone. They'd have found out soon enough anyway.

The greatest damage had been done to the capital city, but most of the battles there were now over. Datanet broadcasting was working, the main broadcaster had been shut down, but enough people on the planet had their own robot cameras, drones and equipment, so some independent media had sprung into being. Everything indicated that Renton was trying to suppress it. He was again circumventing Imperial laws on press freedom. I understood that he could not officially ban media he did not control, but he could send mercenaries in his service to "express civic discontent" and destroy television studios or beat up or "disappear" troublesome reporters. In civilian clothing, of course. The local police would "arrest" those mercenaries, who then quietly vanished from their cells, were paid off and were subsequently ready for more work.

That was one of the things that people on Tarlin had had enough of, and that had only escalated the current situation.

The media was now working against Renton. And we, on the bridge, could see the destroyed center of the capital city. I understood that everything had begun a week ago when Renton's regime had "disappeared" the popular opposition commentator Alvin Siwisa. A huge crowd gathered on the main square, where it clashed with the police. And things had escalated further into a bloody revolution, the outcome of which we could see on the screen.

Nobody was surprised that things had gone as far as an uprising. But *everyone* was surprised by how effective that uprising had been. The civilians had many more weapons than anyone had expected. Not just pistols and rifles, but anti-tank weapons, anti-aircraft missiles and combat drones. Some older recordings of battles even showed the Proteus firing system, which is used to destroy flying targets.

The rebels may not have had combat mechs or shuttles, but they had the means to rapidly destroy the few of each that Renton had.

And so, they swept through the city like a wave. The police, with Renton's mercenaries, were practically destroyed and everything seemed to indicate that the police chief and last handful of mercenaries were holding out in the municipal court building, which the rebels had surrounded.

The reports repeatedly stated that Renton's youngest son, Lopak, had not survived the street fighting.

The news also showed footage of civilians looting the royal palace. Some of the servants that Renton had left behind had also been killed. Some vloggers were showing videos from the palace on their datanet channels. They particularly reveled in showing all the expensive items that Renton's family owned, from upholstery made of New Jaipur silk, to flooring inlaid with blue wood from Aryona, to the heated pool on the roof and its live heptadolphins. I made a point of finding out: it was very expensive to export these creatures from their home planet and just one must have cost many times more than the average household on Tarlin would earn in ten years.

Even worse, a cell containing the bodies of murdered prisoners, including Siwisa, was found in the cellars of the royal palace.

The popular journalist had become a martyr.

Torture chambers had been found there, as well as a prison.

"And we're supposed to help these people?" asked Brannigan, while the camera panned across the bodies as they were carried out of the palace cells.

"We don't know the context," said Commander Hamel.

"Context? What context could there possibly be for this?!"

"Our task is not to intervene, but to transport away the remaining members of the ruling family and their people," said Hamel, attempting to smooth things over.

"A typical Imperial action," grimaced someone else.

"That crowd killing everyone on the street in fine clothes is also no catalog of virtues," said another officer.

"Renton drove them to it!"

"That's enough!" I've never had a particularly strong voice, but I could shout when I needed to. The bridge fell silent. I went on. "We have our task. Politics is above everyone's pay grade. Let's focus on our work. Communications, connect with the planetary government, let them know we're here."

Maybe I should have formulated my orders more clearly, because *two* contacts were suddenly in touch, both declaring themselves to be the planet's legitimate government. And in a way, they were both right.

I hesitated for a moment, but then I decided to take the call from the rebel spokesman in the capital city first.

Or, as I quickly discovered, from the rebel spokes*woman*.

The face of a woman of around fifty appeared on the screen, her greasy, almost yellow hair flowing over her shoulders. Her eyes were tired, but a fire was burning in them.

"I'm Ella Tiderman, the spokesperson for the Tarlin Opposition Movement."

"I am Captain Alexander Golna of the ship *Mexico City*. Are you the leader of the uprising on Tarlin?"

"The uprising has no leader. Even our opposition movement is a coalition of several organizations." She bestowed a tired smile on me. "Until very recently I was… maybe we could say our organization's accountant. But our leader was murdered in Renton's prison. So was her deputy. The next in command fell in battle on the first day, in the square. So yes, you could say that I currently have some responsibility, but I'm not the leader. When it's all over here, we'll let the people of Tarlin decide who will rule them. I get that this could be a bit difficult to understand for *Imperial* soldiers serving the *Emperor*, couldn't it?"

"Not at all. I'm sure you know that the Imperium has a parliament and an elected prime minister, who must not be an Enhans. And that every member world sends normal representatives to the Imperial Parliament."

"Yes. Renton's cronies are there for Tarlin. They do exactly what they're told." Another tired smile. "If you live in a cesspit, it doesn't help to know that people elsewhere live in nice houses."

"I understand."

"And so, Captain, have you come to destroy our revolution and force us to accept Renton's rule again? Maybe you think you have the entire Imperium behind you, but I know you have only one cruiser, you don't even have a troop carrier, which means you aren't going to land an Imperial Army regiment here. So, what do you want?"

"Our task is to… evacuate the original government of Tarlin. That is all."

"Aliser Renton should stand trial for his crimes."

"Quite possibly. But that's not up to me, nor is it up to you. I am only following orders."

"Throughout history, a great many apologists for dictatorial regimes have said that."

"You're right. The world is not perfect, and the Central Imperium certainly is not. On the other hand," my expression became more serious, "on the other hand, the Central Imperium is willing to recognize Tarlin's new government. Anyone you elect here. And you can send your own representatives to the Imperial Parliament."

Tiderman was silent for a while. "How can I trust you?"

"You don't have to. Your FTL communicators are still working. Contact Hub and ask the government office directly."

"But is that conditional on us letting Renton go?"

I was tempted to tell her that yes, it was, and if I had, maybe there would have been no further incidents. But I decided not to lie. "No, that's a separate matter. The Imperial Navy is evacuating Aliser Renton's government. Tarlin will then get a new government."

"An unholy compromise," declared Tiderman.

"We could call it that. But there's something else that's important. We are preparing to send down shuttles to pick up Renton. Do your people intend to open fire on Imperial units? Do you want to escalate?"

"As I was saying, they aren't *my* people. I have no authority to order anyone to do anything."

"I'm sure you can… *advise*, let's say. The Imperium currently sees this as a local conflict. We do not wish to escalate it, believe me."

"I would be happy to believe you, Captain, but you must understand the emotions of our people. The bodies that were found in the prison under the palace… they weren't only dissidents and agitators. Renton's son was a sadist. Sometimes he had someone abducted or arrested so he had something to play with. And we're not talking sexual stuff. He simply enjoyed hurting people."

"Is he the one who was killed in the capital's streets?"

"Yes, he received his punishment directly from the angry crowd."

"I understand your situation, but we keep coming back to the fact that we are preparing to collect Renton senior and the rest of his family. Will you try to prevent us?"

Another silence. Tiderman possibly consulted someone off-screen. Maybe she was listening to someone. Maybe she was just playing for time.

Finally, she said: "Renton and the rest of his followers escaped to his summer house on an island in the ocean in the northern hemisphere. It's their personal private island and our groups haven't got that far yet. Yet! But we're holding him in check there. We can shoot down his shuttle if it takes off."

"And do you want to shoot down *our* shuttles?"

She shook her head, looking as if the gesture caused her physical pain. "No, Captain. We won't attack Imperial shuttles. But I really cannot speak for the entire opposition. And it's about the people too. There are several towns on the island and their inhabitants are trying to march on Renton's estate. They might not have good weapons, but there are lots of them and they long for justice, just as we all do. I can make no guarantees regarding what will happen."

"Understood. I will see that everything takes place as peacefully as possible."

"I don't know if I should say thank you, Captain. No. I don't want to."

"You don't have to. And while we're on the subject, where did your opposition get those modern weapons from? They're much better than anything a civilian can get on Tarlin… than any civilian anywhere in the Imperium can get, if we include the anti-aircraft guided missiles."

Tiderman smiled. "Goodbye, Captain."

The link went dead.

Hamel could not contain himself. "That went better than I was expecting."

"Yes. We'll see how things continue. Connect me to Mr. Renton."

His file said that Aliser Renton was seventy-seven, but he looked twenty years younger, full of energy, like the successful manager of a large company who goes for a run after work. There were a few threads of gray in his short blond hair, but he looked energetic and active, and his face was rather angry than anything else.

"Aliser Renton here, First Consul of the planet Tarlin. Am I speaking with the Captain of the Imperial cruiser in the star system?"

"Yes sir. I am Captain Alexander Golna, of the *Mexico City*."

"Captain, I am glad you are finally here, but I confess that I rather expected several troop carriers full of Imperial Army soldiers."

"Mr. Renton, our aim is to get you and your family safely off-planet."

The anger on the man's face was transformed into something worse. He didn't shout or swear. It was an expression of cold fury.

"Do you mean to say that you're going to let that murderous riffraff ravaging my capital city, and the whole planet, seize control of all Tarlin? The riffraff who are committing murders?"

"Those are my orders, sir."

"Then I'll give you some new orders! We have a good idea of where the opposition leaders are headquartered. A few kinetic strikes from orbit would be a great help, even if you don't have the army with you."

"You do not have the authority to give me orders. Not to mention the fact that bombing the planet to the extent you suggest must be approved by the flag officer after consulting with two other officers."

I wondered if this was another reason why they had sent a mere captain with a single cruiser.

Renton was still speaking quietly. "Captain, I apologize, I allowed myself to get carried away. I know that you do not answer to me but… this planet is my home. You cannot expect me to leave just like that. To leave it to the mercy of those animals… don't forget that they killed my son!"

The tone he said this in seemed to indicate that he'd nearly forgotten this himself. And I wasn't surprised. It wasn't that people like Renton saw those around them as mere tools for achieving their aims, it was rather that Renton was no longer able to see them as anything else. His whole family was a matter of status, power and opportunity.

On Tombara, I live as part of a family collective. Between us we are bringing up twenty-one children. There are another five men and eight women as well as me. I love them all. For most planets this type of relationship is incomprehensible, but that's how we work.

The Rentons had an extensive family, but I wasn't surprised not to see traces of anything that could be called love.

"I will not forget that, Mr. Renton," I replied aloud. "The revolution on Tarlin, and the loss of life, are regrettable, but our objective is to evacuate you. If you want the Imperium to intervene, you can put your proposals to parliament."

"My sister has already done so. And the Imperium sent you. To evacuate me. I am to run away with my tail between my legs, while those animals destroy everything I have built."

I doubted that he personally had built much.

"Mr. Renton, the reality is that we have come to take you away, and nothing more. I anticipate that we will be able to land at your seat within an hour. I would be glad if you were ready to depart."

Tarlin's overthrown ruler was silent for a moment. He watched me, and what was going on around me, on the bridge, as the camera recorded an entire section.

"Please could we talk privately, Captain Golna?"

I'd expected that question, that proposal. Threats and appeals to my emotions hadn't worked, so he wanted to try something more pragmatic.

I shook my head. "I'm sorry, Mr. Renton, but right now I can't. I cannot leave the bridge during such a critical situation. You can say whatever you want to say to me in front of the whole crew."

Renton hesitated, then finally shook his head. "That won't be necessary, Captain. I will expect you within the hour. Thank you."

He broke off the connection.

I breathed out long and slow and leaned back in the captain's chair.

"Give the order to First Lieutenant M'Hale. His marines should get ready."

"Yes, sir."

Φ

In the end, I left the bridge. Another message came twenty minutes later. This one was equipped with Imperial Intelligence identifiers: For the Captain's eyes only.

I went into my study and made the connection.

No face appeared on the screen, just a blurred silhouette.

"Hello, Captain Golna."

The voice sounded normal, but it was also terse and blunted, which told me that it was not the voice of whoever was calling me. It was a voice generated by artificial intelligence. Modern robots and computers can flawlessly simulate human voices. This caller had imperfectly masked their real voice intentionally, not out of error. To catch my attention?

"Who are you?"

"That is not important. We are on the same side."

"And can I confirm that in any way?"

"Were the official Imperial codes not enough for you?"

"That's how I'm talking to you from my cabin on a secure line, but that does not mean we are on the same side."

The voice on the other end probably accepted this.

"Let's say that it is important to both of us that the situation on Tarlin is calmed without further bloodshed. The government has been overthrown. The Imperium will recognize a new government, and Renton will become another useless figure who pines for the good old days in exile. But he will want more bloodshed."

"Why do you think that?"

"If he successfully draws the Imperium into military action on the planet, if your marines end up fighting the local rebels, it could result in the government of the Central Imperium taking his side and then it really would send in the military intervention he longs for. You talked to Renton, Captain Golna. Are you really going to declare that you don't agree with me?"

I didn't need long to think that one over, but my opinion wasn't relevant.

"Fine. So why are you calling me then?"

"This really is only a friendly, neighborly warning. As I was saying, we are on the same side. Do not trust Renton. He will try something. He will delay and play for time. A crowd is now approaching his residence from the nearest town. He will claim that his bodyguards aren't enough. He will want your marines to take on the job. He will want to provoke bloodshed. I have tried to hold the crowd back, but unfortunately… we can't do everything."

"You are…" Suddenly it dawned on me. "You gave those weapons to the local opposition, didn't you?! Are you Imperial black ops, or what?"

The thought that some secret armed forces units had helped to provoke the conflict on the surface shocked me but didn't surprise me that much.

"I think that there is no need to go into the details of our mission on the surface," said the unknown caller. "Be careful, Captain."

The link went dead.

Φ

I invited the executive officer into my cabin and briefly summarized the content of the call.

He was more shocked than me—Cliff Hamel had never been as interested in history as I was.

I asked him to sit down in the armchair opposite mine. "Opinions, XO?"

"Whoever the caller might have been, I'd say he was right about something. Renton won't want to surrender just like that, sir. He will delay, he will try to talk us round."

"I know. And we have only sixty-five marines commanded by a first lieutenant."

"Indeed, sir."

I took a breath. "I'll fly to Tarlin with the landing force. I'll lead the rescue mission in person."

"Are you sure, sir?"

"Yes. Even if I wasn't ordered to by the Commodore, I can't hand this responsibility to First Lieutenant M'Hale or anyone else under my command. It's all too sensitive and, if anything happens that requires a decision from me, it will happen on the surface. And Renton will probably try to put some sort of pressure on younger officers."

"Pressure that you will probably be able to resist," smiled Hamel. The first smile in the whole of that strange day.

I returned it. "I hope so, XO. I hope so. You'll take care of everything in orbit."

Φ

"I propose that we strike the part of the testimony about the mysterious caller from the record," declared Commodore Oliver Starkan, when Golna paused his narrative.

The courtroom began to murmur.

"Why, may I ask?" asked Captain Elena Tafiq, another tribunal member.

"It isn't relevant to the case under discussion."

"What do you mean by that?" said Captain Valan Raponda. "Warnings of that type, from *Imperial* sources, are without doubt relevant to the case and to the further behavior of Captain Golna."

"And do we know that it even happened?" asked Captain Brandon doubtfully.

"The whole bridge witnessed reception of the message," said Admiral Krause. "And the Imperial codes are entered in the ship's log. Even though the transmission was encrypted and not saved."

"That's what I'm talking about. We only have Captain Golna's word regarding the content of the call."

"It corresponds to the available facts," said Krause, but she hesitated for a moment. "Nevertheless, I think that this… information should be struck from the records."

"I do not agree, Madam Chair," said Raponda.

"Me neither," added Tafiq. "If any Imperial Army secret units were active on Tarlin, a record of it must be kept."

"It is irrelevant," Krause repeated, in a tone that brooked no objections, or even another interpretation. This was clear.

Raponda fell silent. Tafiq stared at her superior for a moment longer.

Murmurs resonated through the courtroom again.

Golna wondered if Krause and Starkan knew something and had

reason to sweep it under the carpet. It was strange that they weren't worried by the fact that the whole courtroom had heard it.

But they obviously weren't bothered by the spread of gossip. And if any secret unit really were operating on the surface, gossip would only help. People in the Army and Navy gossiped about absolutely everything. Everyone took it in their own way. It was important that it wasn't in the official records.

Captain Brandon spoke up. "In that case, it would perhaps also be apposite to remove Captain Golna's remarks about the sexual… communities on Tombara that bring up children. That seems… inappropriate to me."

"Captain Golna used it as a comparison for his impressions of Mr. Renton," said Krause. "It's relevant."

"But… it shouldn't be. I mean that it wouldn't be… things like that do not belong in the records."

Golna wondered what his attorney had been up to when he advised him not to request that Brandon be replaced. The man could barely curb his prudish view of the world. The differences between Golna and Brandon only showed how different and varied the individual worlds in the Central Imperium were.

He didn't get any more time to think. Krause looked at him.

"Captain Golna, please continue and tell us what happened after you arrived on the surface of Tarlin?"

Φ

As we had anticipated, Aliser Renton and his family were not ready to leave the moment we arrived.

We landed on a platform on the roof of his house. *Port Moresby*-class cruisers, like my *Mexico City*, have six shuttles aboard as standard. We landed with four. Even with sixty-five marines and myself aboard, there was space enough for everyone in the entire palace.

If everything went according to plan.

"Welcome to Tarlin, Captain Golna!" said Renton, as he walked toward our shuttles, accompanied by several bodyguards. And nobody else.

"Why aren't you ready yet?" I shouted over the drone of the engines, while the marines behind me were disembarking and taking up formation.

"My apologies, Captain Golna. It's difficult for my family and staff. We need at least a few hours to pack."

"But you don't have a few hours before the crowd arrives from town," one of the bodyguards shouted into the noise.

"Yes, the crowd is enraged. Someone must have incited them, told them that you're coming. You will see for yourself what sort of people they are, Captain."

"I don't want to see it. I want you to assemble everyone in this residence and we'll load them into the shuttle."

"That can't be done quickly."

I suppressed the urge to grind my teeth. "Once, during a drill, my crew evacuated all decks and assembled in the escape modules in under eight minutes. I think that the people in your house can come out onto the roof!"

"My wife is upset by the loss of my son and refuses to go anywhere. You will have to persuade her."

A careful choice of words. "My wife" and "my son". I knew that Renton's wife was not the mother of the son who had died in town.

I wanted to keep arguing, but there was no point. Not now.

I turned to First Lieutenant M'Hale, the Marine commander. "Lieutenant, deploy your people. If the crowd gets as far as the gate, I want you to form a barrier. But under no circumstances should you fire!"

"Yes, sir!" M'Hale, not surprised by this, immediately started to give the relevant orders.

"Bjorn, go with them, show them what and how," Renton said to his bodyguard. "Captain Golna, can we talk privately?"

Φ

The summer residence was furnished in the Hobart Art Deco style, which was coming back into fashion in some parts of the Imperium. It would have appeared opulent if many people lived here but, as Renton led me down a long corridor, it felt like a burial chamber.

The group of marines set off rapidly, and Renton gave some orders by comlink, then he looked at me.

"Captain Golna, I would like… I would like, again, to appeal to your military honor. I cannot leave my world to the mercy of those… elements who have devastated the capital city. It is part of *my* honor."

"As I have told you several times, Mr. Renton, I have my orders. But if we evacuate you in time, I plan to send shuttles to evacuate the rest of your government's police and the mercen… the military contractors who are surrounded in the capital."

"That isn't… Well, I mean, that is not necessary. It's important to go on the offensive. I understand your orders, Captain, but you are the most senior Imperial officer in the star system. If your marines found themselves under fire, it would be your duty to respond. One thing would lead to another. The Imperium would ultimately have to hurry to Tarlin with proper reinforcements. If someone attacks Imperial soldiers, a response is a must."

"Situations like that are very complex," I said, neutrally. "Even if something like that were to happen, hypothetically speaking, it really is impossible to predict the response of the Emperor or his government."

Renton was silent for a moment as we continued down the corridor. In the meantime, I received several reports, first from First Lieutenant M'Hale, who was deploying his marines, and then from Commander Hamel, who reported that nothing was happening in orbit.

Renton spoke again. "Captain Golna, my family is very rich. I'm not just talking about our property as Enhans. I am influential in a great many corporations. And I know that you have a numerous… family on Tombara. That's what you call them, isn't it? I know that you create your families at orgies. I am sure you have many family members you need to… provide for. I also know that times are not ideal. I could help you."

In a period of advanced hacker attacks and cyberthefts, physical banknotes had been reintroduced wholesale into the Central Imperium in the last eighty years. And now Renton withdrew a bundle of them from his pocket.

He wasn't even trying to be inconspicuous.

"I think that what I have here in my pocket is more than your annual salary. The Imperial Navy massively underpays its captains. Take it, as a gesture of my good will."

I sighed. "Mr. Renton, are you attempting to bribe an officer of the Imperial Navy?"

He didn't even try to pretend. "He wouldn't be the first, or the last."

"Mr. Renton, I am *not* interested." I looked at my watch. "All your family must be ready for evacuation and departure within the hour."

"You can't just take us away from here like that!"

"Well, a firefighter can pull someone out of bed and carry them out of a burning building. But I think that the approaching mob will persuade you to leave."

"You're stupid, Golna! So stupid! And you will regret this! My family is powerful! You will regret this!"

He stomped off.

I went in the opposite direction.

Φ

"For the record, I would like to add that we have no evidence that Aliser Renton attempted to bribe Captain Golna," stated Captain Raponda. "It's his word against Renton's."

"I would also like to add that we have no proof that Captain Golna did not accept the bribe," added Captain Brandon. "His moral integrity could possibly be doubted."

"Captain Brandon, please refrain from personal invective," declared Krause. "And although it is impossible to prove whether anyone attempted to bribe Captain Golna, in the light of the ensuing events it is undoubtedly relevant information." She looked at Golna.

"Captain Golna, in your own words, tell us exactly how the incident that concerns this court came to pass."

Φ

The incident happened quickly.

I shouldn't call it an 'incident'; that's too neutral.

The shooting happened quickly.

The mob finally arrived.

The gates to the estate were more decorative than practical. The crowd didn't have top-quality weapons, unlike the rebels in the capital city, or at least not enough, but they had cudgels, sticks, various tools. Nothing that would normally endanger a marine in combat armor. Only the crowd was large, and we had barely forty marines in front of the building. And everyone had seen the recordings of battles in the capital.

They formed lines, shoulder to shoulder, weapons in their hands, but nobody was aiming. The mob shouted at them, a few stones were thrown, or other small objects. The marines stood firm. Some stepped back, but M'Hale held them and at the same time, he tried to persuade the mob to withdraw.

I arrived at that moment. Renton's family had finally started to enter the shuttles when they called me.

I arrived just in time to hear the shouting and some incomprehensible bellowing.

"Imperial whores!"

"Stand aside. This is our fight!"

"You're protecting murderers!"

"Get back to where you came from!"

The shouting was complemented by more thrown objects.

I decided to stand in front of the line of marines. In a mere BDU field uniform, I felt naked and vulnerable, like at the orgies at home.

I raised my hands above my head. I didn't have a weapon, but I was still hit in the chest by some object or other. I have no idea what it was. I staggered and the marines aimed.

"Do not shoot!" I yelled. "Do not shoot!"

The tension was intensifying again, but the crowd, face to face with pointed rifles, was taken aback for an instant. They stopped throwing things but continued to shout.

"Cowards!"

"Imperial whores!"

A tall man emerged from the crowd. He stared at me, but his hands were also raised to show he was unarmed.

He was just as angry as his fellow-citizens.

"You're protecting Enhans murderers!"

"We are merely providing transportation. Only a court can decide whether Mr. Renton is innocent or guilty."

"The Imperial Court will never do anything! Renton will be tried here! And now!"

I was still holding up my hands. "Please take my advice. Disperse! We are only here to evacuate the people in this house."

Another scream, more threats.

The crowd came closer.

I took several steps backward as a defensive reflex. One of the marines was right behind me. The rifles were still being aimed.

"Do you intend to open fire on us?" the man was asking.

I took several steps in his direction. "Given that I'm standing in front of my marines, don't you think it would be stupid of me to order that?"

The man began to repeat himself.

"Renton is a murderer and a tyrant!"

The crowd joined in.

"You're protecting a murderer!"

"Imperial whores!"

"Enhans ass-lickers!"

In my ear, my hands-free comlink buzzed.

I was still watching the crowd, but I touched my ear.

"Charlie Oscar here," I said, announcing myself with my call sign.

"Skywatch here," I heard Commander Hamel's voice say. "Sir, are you okay? The cameras on all combat armor have just cut out."

"What? All of them?"

Every marine had a camera as part of their combat armor, which could see exactly what they could see. One or two might cut out together, by chance, but all of them…?

"Yes, sir, it must be some virus. A hacker attack. We've lost visual."

Suddenly I realized what had happened.

I opened my mouth, but it was too late.

Someone fired into the crowd.

The projectile went right through a woman in the front row, but it was electromagnetic and had a great deal of kinetic energy, and it flew on, through other people, leaving a bloody trail and dismembered bodies in its wake.

And then more of them fired.

The crowd screamed and began to run.

The marines were terrified. They fired and fired. They were carried away by the situation.

"Hold your fire!" I yelled at the top of my lungs. "Hold your fire! Hold your fire! Stop shooting!"

They heard me, and obeyed, but it was too late.

"Good god!" someone screamed.

"What happened? What the fuck happened?"

"Murderers!" shouted someone from the retreating crowd.

The ground was covered with bodies.

Φ

"Was it ever established who was behind that cyberattack that knocked out the cameras?" asked Admiral Krause.

Golna shook his head. "No, Your Honor."

"Was it established which of your marines was the first to open fire?"

"No, that would be impossible."

"I think it would be possible, Captain Golna."

"I was the commanding officer. The operation was my responsibility. I am thus responsible for the actions of the marines under my command."

Many of them were right there in the courtroom. He watched their expressions, and the expressions of other people. Commodore Jacobsen, Commander Hamel, First Lieutenant M'Hale.

"Captain Golna, is it possible that you want to take the actions of your marines onto yourself?" asked Krause.

"I do not think that Captain Golna would be able to take on himself the actions of his marines from some sort of… honor," declared Captain Brandon, almost unwillingly. "I think that Captain Golna does not know who was the first to shoot."

"Nevertheless, it was undoubtedly foolish of Captain Golna to stand in front of the line of his marines," said Commodore Starkan. "When that object was thrown at him, the marines aimed their weapons as a defensive gesture, which increased tension and allowed the situation to escalate even more."

"The question remains, however," concluded Captain Raponda. "Did Captain Golna commit murder?"

Golna did not react.

The silence was broken by Krause. She made no further comments about her colleague.

"What happened next, Captain Golna?"

Φ

We evacuated Renton and his family aboard the *Mexico City*. I and the marines stayed on the surface and attempted to give first aid to the wounded. Commander Hamel sent both our ship's doctors. We evacuated many of the wounded to the nearest hospitals and some of them also came aboard.

Renton insisted that the opposition had attacked the Central Imperium's armed forces. He even used the ship's FTL receiver, several times, to try to persuade the Admiralty and his relatives in the House of Families. But the Imperium refused to escalate the situation further, so we left the planet.

Leaving behind thirty-two dead.

Several marines suffered a psychological collapse, but the ship's doctors and psychologist did their best with them. Others began to talk about leaving the Marine Corps. I wasn't surprised.

When we arrived back at Ferrel Kast, I submitted a detailed report to the board of inquiry…

Φ

Golna fell silent. There was nothing more to say.

The board of inquiry had suggested a court-martial. Golna was accused of murder. And now that court was in session.

"Captain Golna," Krause asked. "Do you have any idea, any suspicion, that any of the marines accepted the bribe that Renton initially offered to you?"

"Allegedly offered to him," Raponda corrected her.

"Alleged bribe."

Golna shook his head. "No, Your Honor. I have no proof and do not wish to speculate."

"Really, Captain? Your career is hanging in the balance. So is the rest of your life."

He shook his head. "I refuse to point the finger at anyone."

Brandon looked as if he wished to make another poisonous remark but stopped himself.

"Fine, Captain Golna. Thank you for your testimony. You may return to your seat."

Golna sat down beside his attorney.

"The prosecution calls the next witness. Commander Cliff Hamel…"

Φ

The court-martial dragged on for another two days. More witnesses were cross-examined: individual marines, civilians who survived the incident, even Commodore Jacobsen. Mr. Renton was not present. He had sent only a brief, contentless affidavit that indicated that he didn't care either about Golna or about the dead; he was only interested in gaining the Imperium's support.

Which he did not get.

Finally, the court made its decision.

"All rise."

The entire courtroom aboard the *Wisconsin* rose to its feet. The tribunal members once again entered in order of rank. And with their verdict. As soon as they sat down, so did everyone else in the room. But Golna was soon back on his feet.

"The defendant will stand."

He obeyed.

"The court's decision is as follows," said Rear Admiral Krause in a clear voice. "On the charge of second-degree murder under Article 109, this court finds the defendant not guilty by three votes to two. On the charge of neglect of duty of a commanding officer under Article 84, this court finds the defendant not guilty by three votes to two. This trial is hereby concluded."

The hammer's blow sounded like the thunder of the gods.

Some people cheered and slapped Golna on the back.

Captain Alexander Golna didn't even notice.

He only stared ahead of him as the tribunal members departed.

An hour after the acquittal, he learned that one of his marines had taken his own life.

Φ

Sitting alone on the observation deck of the *Wisconsin*, he watched the stars behind the transparent steel and thought of nothing. He had received congratulatory messages from his family and friends. He'd even been invited to a Tombaran celebration on the local space station.

He didn't want to go anywhere.

Commodore Stefan Jacobsen found him here.

"Alex!"

Golna raised his head and looked at him. "Sir?"

"I wanted to tell you that you may be interested in how it ended. Krause, Starkan and Brandon voted for you. Yes, Brandon decided it. His prudishness ultimately decided in your favor. I think that either he was unable to imagine that you'd do anything honorable—you were covering for someone out of loyalty—or he was afraid that his own prejudices were clouding his judgment. In any case, a conservative prude from New Canaan help to acquit you."

"Thank you, sir."

This news did not bring Golna any joy. He was numb.

He thought about the dead marine. Commander Hamel had written to him of the death of Private Keith Sloan shortly after the trial concluded. Sloan shot himself in the head with his own weapon. Golna knew he was one of those who'd suffered psychological collapse. He'd cried, but in recent days he'd gotten quieter, only staring emptily ahead. The psychologist had tried to help Sloan, but he couldn't work miracles.

Sloan had shot at civilians. Whatever the courts or public opinion thought, Sloan was one of those who had shot at civilians.

They had tried Golna. They had acquitted him and everyone else with him.

But someone had still paid for it.

"I heard about Sloan," Jacobsen went on. "I'm sorry."

"I would be happier if I'd been convicted and that boy had stayed alive."

"I know. You are a good captain."

"I am? Present tense?"

Jacobsen half-smiled and sat down beside Golna. "What can I say, Captain? An unholy compromise. Is there any speculation that Sloan was the one who fired first?"

"It's impossible to prove. I think that… well, no matter. It wasn't Sloan. I saw how he looked right after the gunfight… no, it wasn't him."

"You're right. In addition, I have heard rumors that even the investigators have an idea of who fired first."

"That's impossible to prove too."

"It is. But Private Debora Marlen left the Marine Corps immediately after the judgment was handed down. And although nothing has arrived in her account, she seems to have a lot of money in cash and is splashing it around. It seems that Renton found someone else to bribe after he failed to bribe you."

Golna was still staring straight ahead. Marlen had been tight-lipped during the entire journey from Tarlin. She hadn't talked to anyone. Not even the psychologist. Maybe they'd been more worried about her than about Sloan.

"As I was saying, we cannot prove that."

"Of course not," agreed Jacobsen.

"And what would be the point? It won't bring any of the dead back to life."

"Surely you didn't expect that?"

"Of course not," Golna sighed. "What about Renton?"

"He'll go into exile somewhere, maybe to Hub, or somewhere else. His family will stay in the House of Families and the prime minister and Emperor have recognized the new government on Tarlin. Exactly as expected."

"Do we know who was the mysterious group that spoke to me?"

"No, and we probably never will. Commodore Starkan has vehemently urged me to remind you that it would be better not to mention that conversation."

"Not mention? Those people probably instigated the whole revolution. They supplied weapons to the Tarlin opposition."

"That's one of the many mysteries of every conflict. Really, Alex. Drop it."

Golna nodded. "Starkan urged you to say that?"

"He and Krause. I'm meant to tell you these things unofficially, as your former commanding officer. You know what it's like."

"I know. So, you're my *former* commanding officer?"

"Yes, unfortunately."

"So, my career is over?"

Jacobsen burst out laughing. "But Alex, do you not know how the Imperium functions? Why do things one way or the other when we can do both?"

"What does that mean?"

"You have been relieved of the command of the *Mexico City*. You will receive official notification today. By the end of the week, Commander

Hamel will be promoted to captain and will take the ship to the Konstantin Sector. To guard the frontiers of the Imperium, far away from all these controversies."

In a strange way, Golna was cheered by this. Hamel was good and should have been given his own command a long time ago.

"And now for that unholy compromise," Jacobsen went on. "Everything is wiped clean, you've been relieved and your old ship is flying to the frontiers. But somewhere on the other side of the Central Imperium, the Ralgars are active again. They've attacked three of our worlds in the Rosario Sector."

"Really?" The Ralgars were an ancient enemy who returned from time to time.

"Yes, the Imperial Navy is sending reinforcements into the area. Including the cruiser *Luanda*, the *Mexico City*'s sister ship." He smiled wryly. "Do you know who is to command the *Luanda*?"

Before Golna could say anything, Jacobsen had handed him an old-fashioned envelope.

"Here are your orders, Captain. The *Luanda* is docked at *Hub Central*, near Hub. They're expecting you aboard within four days. Within seven, the fleet will embark for the Rosario Sector."

Golna gaped at the envelope in his hands. "And... that's it? The situation has been resolved? Swept under the rug? Everything is done by halves..." He fell silent. "Why does this not surprise me? That's just how it works in the Imperium, isn't it?"

Jacobsen stood up. "You know how it is, my friend. More than anything else, the Emperor and the Central Imperium want to hold civilization together. Civilization must continue. That's the Imperium's watchword. And if the occasional unholy compromise will help..." He shrugged, then held out his hand to Golna. The captain stood up, hesitated briefly, then took it.

"Good luck, Captain."

Golna would need to think about what luck actually was.

IV

"Would you say that the situation on Tarlin was unique?" Varviso asked.

"Unfortunately not. Maybe it was one of the most visible cases, but injustice is ingrained in many ways across the whole Imperium," said Hila. "And I'm saying this as someone who married an Enhans and has an Enhans child. But centuries of hate and friction can't be forgotten just like that. The old Emperor was too open to compromise. And yes, I can admit that he had no choice. Unfortunately, that won't stop many people from feeling angry."

She looked at Daniel, who only nodded assent. "That's how it is, sadly."

Varviso finally asked. "And that now brings us to the situation in the Bornholm Sector."

Again, Daniel nodded agreement. "Yes. What happened in the Bornholm Sector relates to how—in a certain way, unfortunately—the entire Imperium is constructed. And it's got even worse since the war. I'm saying since the war as if it were over, but there are still many ongoing conflicts in the Central Imperium."

"I know. I am only too aware of that."

"Only too aware?" asked Daniel.

"Yes, I used to be a war correspondent. During one of my previous… sabbaticals from *Horgen Daily*."

"Where were you?"

"I covered one of those small conflicts. On Manorom."

"That was a skirmish against the Ralgars, wasn't it?" Hila asked.

"Yes, it was. And most people didn't even notice. Back then I followed the fighting from the area with Division 23. Although the most interesting news report that I wrote was about events aboard the hospital ship *Avicenna*."

Sean the robot brought more refreshments and poured glasses of wine. Wisely, he said nothing.

Varviso helped himself to another cookie. "I know that I came to question you, but I really do not want to give the impression that I have come to judge you. But if you're interested, I can tell you what happened aboard the *Avicenna*."

INTERSPECIES MISUNDERSTANDINGS

Nobody ever called it a war.

It was a cross-border altercation.

A defensive action.

A low-intensity conflict.

Only, as Gus Andam discovered, day after day, when they bring you a stretcher with some poor sod who's been hacked to pieces, it really makes no difference whether the hacking was done in a war, an altercation, a defensive action or a low-intensity conflict. They'll still die in your care in exactly the same way.

And you will try, desperately, to save them in exactly the same way.

This had been the main component of Gus's life for the last one hundred and fifty-seven days. Their ship, the *Avicenna*, was orbiting Manorom, a small frontier world that had been attacked by a Ralgar clan.

It wasn't a big offensive. The Central Imperium called big Ralgar attacks 'incursions' and this wasn't one of them. This was not an incursion; it was one clan attacking one planet. The Imperium had sent an expeditionary force, the Imperial Fleet had destroyed Ralgar spaceships, then the Ralgars had used beam weapons on the surface to destroy one troop carrier and had missed the *Avicenna* by inches. She was a hospital ship, but Ralgars were never interested in such subtleties.

The remaining five large troop carriers had deployed their units and started to force the Ralgars out of the residential zones.

Only there weren't enough Imperial Army soldiers to put an end to the fighting. The Imperium had a great many problems elsewhere and there was no point in awaiting reinforcements. Possibly the Ralgars also could not send new warriors to the planet, but so what, there were already enough of them on the surface.

As a result, neither side had enough forces to defeat the enemy. But both sides were trying.

And people like Gus lived with the consequences.

The Ralgars used all types of firearms and explosives, but at the same time they loved personal combat and, whenever the opportunity presented itself, they reached for their favorite swords, called *karba*. That was why fighting with Ralgars resulted in the greatest number of slash wounds and chopped-off limbs since the time of the First World War on pre-cosmic Earth.

And many of the wounded were civilians. The Ralgars showed as much consideration for them as they did for the medical personnel.

But Gus was managing to cope with this. Mostly. The first few hundred wounded were the worst. The regulations of the Imperial Navy stated that soldiers and combat medics should be rotated from war zones after ninety days. A shame he'd been stuck here for five months now. The Imperium had nobody to replace him.

So here Gus and his colleagues remained. The hospital ship *Avicenna* was orbiting Manorom as part of a small fleet supporting battles on the surface. With a bit of luck, the Ralgars would never aim one of their beam cannons at her. Intelligence was apparently *almost sure* that there weren't any left.

"Gus, are you playing or staring at the fucking ceiling?"

Gus tore himself out of his thoughts and back to the present. He looked over the table at his opponent. Dorte Dahlerup was a doctor, like him, and in many respects she was better than him. Even though this seemed unbelievable right now, because her eyes were maybe as sharp as the edge of the blancmange they'd had for dessert with today's lunch.

Dorte was holding a cup of coffee in her hands, but she deceived nobody. It was an open secret that this woman regularly added something to her cup. Gus envied her, in a way. Alcohol evidently helped her. It was a shame he didn't drink.

He had other displacement activities. He liked to laugh. In every possible way. By any means.

He enjoyed cards, and games, all sorts of witticisms. He loved to watch stupid serials on the datanet.

Mostly to stop himself from going mad.

When he met Dorte for the first time, just before they departed for the warzone, he'd switched her hand cream for wart cream. She hadn't said anything, but a few days later, she had shaved his entire body while he slept.

That was the start of a beautiful friendship.

They'd gradually involved many others in their pranks.

Gus looked around. The officers' mess was almost deserted. Most officers had already eaten, and it was an exceptionally quiet afternoon. The slurry they ate here also did not boost morale. It wasn't the fault of the ship's cook, but all the food was made up of protein doses, tank-grown meat, artificial vegetables and synthetic vitamins. They'd originally had fresh food on board too, but they shouldn't have been stuck here for so many months without replacements.

A group of nurses were enjoying some game on their datapads in the corner. Angela and Cliff, two other doctors from a different group, had slipped away together a moment ago. They found stress relief in each other's arms and in pretending that nothing was going on.

Maybe there was some maintenance technician on one of the lower decks who hadn't yet heard about their romance. Maybe.

He looked back at his cards. The fact remained that he didn't much enjoy gambling against an ever more intoxicated Dorte, and a single glance at his cards convinced him that he wasn't going to beat even her.

"Fold."

Dorte chuckled. "Poker is rubbish when it's just two. Do you want to play strategy on your datapad?"

"I don't have the brain for that."

"And you think I do? I know… only too well when I'm… mellow."

"And I still envy you."

Dorte burst out laughing.

"We need a couple more people to play," Dorte mused. "I assume you're not interested in a fling?" She squinted at him, mildly drunk.

They'd been playing this game together since they first met.

"Of course not. You're drunk."

"I usually am when I'm not actually performing surgery."

"Exactly! That wouldn't work!" He laughed. "Have I told you about Linda Heider?"

"No."

"I knew her at uni… Well, she absolutely loved a drink, but you wouldn't believe…"

"Lieutenant Andam!"

That was not Dorte exclaiming that she didn't want to hear this story. It came from the door.

A hacked-off Leopold Krest was striding toward Gus. He was, to Gus's great misfortune, Gus's cabin-mate.

And the only doctor crazy enough to address his colleagues by their rank.

"What's up, Leo?"

"Lieutenant Andam, you know very well what's up!" He raised his hand and waved it before Gus's eyes. This hand, in a surgical glove, was holding something that was slowly beginning to stink.

Gus began to laugh.

"This is what's up!" Krest repeated. "This. This is… this is…"

Dorte decided that she wasn't that drunk and focused her eyes on the item.

"Leo, it's been a long time since my last anatomy class, but that's a… pancreas?"

"Yes. Yes, it's a pancreas. And your idiot pal put it in my uniform pocket!"

"I'm sorry, Leo, but your expression is just…" Gus began to laugh again.

"It isn't funny!" Krest roared. "And this was the last time. It's revolting. And it's disrespectful to the dead!"

"He wasn't dead! Yesterday we removed his pancreas and replaced it with a synthetic one. That was the patient with several stab wounds in the abdomen, don't you remember? He no longer needed his pancreas and spleen, so I… took them from him. When he came round this morning, I told him what I was planning to do with them, and he enthusiastically agreed. Hey, that reminds me, he wanted a photo." Gus pulled out his comlink and snapped the shocked Leo with the pancreas in his hand.

Dorte was already starting to laugh.

"That's enough. That was the last straw! Lieutenant Andam, I'm going to the captain! You'll pay for this and…" He stopped short. "What were you saying about the spleen? You said pancreas *and* spleen?!"

Gus began to laugh again. "Didn't you check your shoes before you came running to find me?"

Leo went red. His veins stood out on his temples. Gus thought that Leo was going to attack. Still with the pancreas in his hand.

"You… you…!"

Maybe he really would have attacked, or at least continued his tirade. But he was interrupted by the sharp whistle of the alarm siren.

The three doctors, taken aback, immediately pricked up their ears. They knew what the signal meant. They'd heard it a thousand times before.

"Attention all hands. Attention all hands! Incoming wounded. I repeat, incoming wounded. All medical personnel report to the admission ward and operation room. Admissions in hangars one and two. I repeat: admissions in hangars one and two."

Gus and Dorte were instantly on their feet. Leo dropped the pancreas and was the first to run out the door. Dorte put down her cup and reached into her breast pocket for a pill, which she rapidly swallowed.

She'd be sober in a few minutes, and would throw up a few minutes after that, but within a quarter of an hour she'd be able to operate.

Φ

Hospital ships like the *Avicenna* could land on the surface of a planet and admit patients directly, but mostly they stayed in orbit, far away from any fighting. On board they had a squadron of medical shuttles, which collected the injured directly from the battlefield or from first-aid stations. The shuttles then arrived in the *Avicenna*'s hangars, from which the medical staff could immediately transfer the patients to admissions and the operating theater.

Gus and a group of orderlies now ran into the hangar and waited.

He was responsible for triage in hangar one. As soon as the first shuttle arrived in the inner hangar, he was instantly on board.

The wounded were held securely in gravitational straps, which immobilized them, however much the shuttle threw itself around.

"What do we have here?" he stuttered, but immediately looked at the first wounded soldier, without waiting for the orderly's reply. The shuttle had a triage robot, a standard component of hospital ships. Someone in command had thought that a robot would be better at triaging patients, because it would not be affected by emotion. Gus and his colleagues generally ignored the triage robot and triaged the patients themselves. Gus was doing this now and half-listening to what the robot was telling him, as he surveyed the patients himself.

A triage card with information was affixed to each of them. The triage robot had added a red, yellow, green or black label to each card, depending on the patient's condition. Gus examined the patients to make sure this information was correct.

The first had lost three limbs. A Ralgar blade had parted the soldier from his left arm and both legs. He was unconscious and a cursory glance assured Gus that he could wait. Another had been scalped when the blade split through his helmet. Yet another had been hit by a projectile, which had torn off almost everything below his waist.

They could all wait.

But two could not.

"Okay. This chest wound and that abdominal wound first!" he called to the orderlies. "Take them to prep immediately!"

He went on, assigning priorities to patients, and had to admit that his decisions matched those of the triage robot almost exactly.

He reached the end of the shuttle, where he noticed something unexpected.

A body. An enormous, yellowish-green, lizard body, with a huge mouth like a gecko.

A Ralgar.

A Ralgar's body.

It wasn't on a stretcher but still bore a triage card with a black sticker.

"What is the meaning of this?" he stared at the body. Someone must have brought the lizard down with several wounds to the chest. It had almost been torn to pieces. "Why have they sent us a dead Ralgar?"

The triage robot rushed over with an explanation.

"The battalion commander had the Ralgar body loaded on the spot, on the battlefield."

"For God's sake, why?"

Now one of the human orderlies from the shuttle crew joined in the conversation. "Apparently, we're to dissect and analyze it here. To learn more about Ralgar biology."

"Whose fricking stupid idea was that?" Gus managed to splutter. "We've had how many wars with the Ralgars over the last hundred years? Not a fucking clue! There are thousands, tens of thousands, of their bodies on the battlefields and we've analyzed them every which way! Xenobiologists and xenoanthropologists have written entire books about them. What the hell are we supposed to find out from one dead Ralgar?!"

The orderly shrugged, but was already helping to carry another patient on a stretcher. The triage robot couldn't shrug; it looked like a levitating ball with mechanical arms sticking out of it. Nevertheless, it still said: "It's an order. Under Article 17 of the Imperial Armed Forces

Code, we are required to obey an order unless it is revoked by a senior officer or unless the order is illegal. Do you have any reason to assume that this order was illegal?"

"No. I only have reason to assume that it's absolutely stupid." Gus shook his head. They did not have time for this. "Shove that dead Ralgar somewhere. The captain can decide what happens next."

He didn't waste any more time on this. The patients from this shuttle were dealt with and he went on to the next one.

Φ

Standard shifts were simply out of the question aboard the *Avicenna* when there was an emergency and they needed to admit the wounded. Although the ship was a sort of flying hospital, the entire Central Imperium was contending with a shortage of doctors, and it was no different aboard Imperial Navy ships. Doctors worked long shifts in the operating room. Robots assisted them, but just as robots had never proved their worth as soldiers or warriors, they could not replace doctors.

The *Avicenna*'s official statistics stated that ninety-six percent of patients who were still alive when they arrived in the OR also left it alive, but when doctors like Gus, Dorte and even Leo worked their way through this butchery, none of them felt that optimistic.

And when, many hours later, Gus finished and wanted to grab a few hours' sleep, he was not at all pleased to be summoned to see the captain immediately.

When he arrived, he found Leo Krest waiting.

The expression on his face was pure schadenfreude.

They were both now standing at the captain's table, waiting. Gus hesitated for a moment, then concluded that he should attempt something military.

"Lieutenant Andam reporting for your orders, Captain."

Wei Meisong, a captain in the Imperial Navy, was not a doctor, but was for the most part a competent manager. He had undoubtedly wanted to command cruisers and battleships, but had not insinuated himself into that elite, so he commanded a hospital ship. At least, that was more-or-less how Gus imagined it.

He sat in his office, reading something on his monitor while a Korean version of the song *My Blue Heaven* played from the speakers. The captain loved to listen to it on repeat.

Finally, he stopped pretending to read and raised his head.

"Lieutenant Andam, I have here an official complaint against you from Lieutenant Leopold Krest."

Leo smiled.

Gus heaved a long sigh. "Really? *Really?* Because of a practical joke?"

"Krest claims that you regularly bully him. You put a… pancreas into his shoe…"

"A spleen. I put the pancreas into his pocket. He's a doctor, he should know the difference."

Leo exploded. "What you did was absolutely disgusting! Unheard of!"

"Unheard of? A month ago, after you gave a dressing-down to two orderlies for something that was your fault, I put a patient's liver into your soup, remember? I felt that if you wanted to chew out your own people that much, a little cannibalism might help."

"You. Did. What?!"

"Yeah. Didn't you notice?"

Captain Wei kneaded his mustache and looked as if he'd rather be almost anywhere else.

"Lieutenant Andam, your behavior is unacceptable. And this isn't the first time you've been sent to me for matters of this type."

"No. But we've all been here significantly longer than we should have."

"I can't help that. But you and Lieutenant Krest are both doctors, and colleagues. You cannot behave like this!"

Gus had had enough. He was too tired for this shit.

"Captain, if you want to throw me out, then throw me out. If you want to lock me up, then lock me up. I've spent the last eleven hours operating on kids who were chopped up in a war that isn't even being reported in the Imperium's newspapers. Believe me, I'd love to be locked up. I didn't want to come here. The recruitment officer gave me practically no choice. Write an official reprimand. Throw me out of the Navy. Do whatever you want, but for God's sake don't force me to stand her and debate how, after five months of service, I should behave toward an idiot who can't tell the difference between a spleen and a pancreas!"

"What did you just call me?" Leo roared.

"An idiot. But you're not just an idiot, you're an arrogant and self-centered idiot. We'd been here barely a week when you lost a patient and convinced the medic that it was his fault. The poor man had a breakdown."

"You…!"

"That's enough!" roared the captain.

"Captain. Sir. You are a witness that…"

"Shut it, Krest!"

Wei was staring daggers at them both. "I don't have time for this. And frankly, I don't know why you're always coming to me about this, Krest."

"Our chief physician refuses to deal with it."

Of course he does. He knows Leo!

The captain sighed. "It's not worth dealing with. Andam, I'll give you a written reprimand, but I know that you don't care. If you can't work collegially, you could at least help us with some independent work. I have orders from the surface for an autopsy on that dead Ralgar they sent us."

"But… sir, I mean, that's stupid! Medical science has already dissected thousands of Ralgar bodies…"

"That's as maybe, but it's an order from the surface, and you will obey it. Look at it as verifying the facts. The body is now in the ship's morgue. It's yours. I want a thorough autopsy. Keep accurate records and then present them to the Intelligence Officer of the expeditionary force we're expecting. Is that clear?"

Gus was too tired to argue. "I assume that this is a more lenient punishment than a whipping or keelhauling, so yes."

Leo was not happy. "But Captain, that isn't a punishment! He'll get his name on scientific publications!"

"Wanna swap?" Gus asked.

"Well, I would gladly…"

"Andam will do it," the captain decreed. "And now, provided neither of you has anything else, go away!"

My Blue Heaven was still playing as the door banged shut behind them.

Φ

He found the Ralgar body in the ship's morgue. It was too big for a coolbox, but one of the crew had improvised, removed the sides from several boxes, and stuffed the lizard inside.

That's where Gus found him. Two robots helped to tip him onto the dissection table.

A robot assistant hovered beside him, the same type of robot as the triage robot. He could have asked for a OR nurse but, given that the captain had entrusted him with this idiocy, it made no sense to involve anyone else.

"Start recording," he ordered the robot, and placed his tray of instruments beside the body. He began to look it over.

Green, scaly skin, a head like a gecko's, enormous paws, a tail. Yesterday he'd been wearing some equivalent of armor or combat suit. It'd been taken off him before he was stored here. That must be why the gaping hole in the Ralgar's chest seemed smaller to Gus than when he'd seen it the previous day during triage. The body was covered in dried yellow blood.

He picked up the electric scalpel.

"Record: Surgeon Lieutenant Gus Andam, add today's date. I am conducting an autopsy on a killed Ralgar. The body looks like a typical Ralgar. It has no obvious anomalies compared to a standard representative of the species. Height almost three meters, weight…" he checked it on the bed display. "Two hundred eighty kilos. The cause of death is most likely several shots to the chest by one of our infantry rifles… what's it called? Fine, that can be added later. The caliber and muzzle velocity can also be added later. As part of the autopsy I will first open the thoracic cavity. I'm going to make a Y incision along the thorax. Why am I doing this? Because I put a pancreas into a colleague's pocket and the captain punished me by making me dissect a Ralgar, because some fuckwit on the surface thinks this body might in some way be different from the bodies of the thousands of Ralgars we've collected over centuries."

"Am I to edit that out later, Doctor Andam?" asked the robot, obligingly.

"Leave it in. Let the captain censor it. And to continue, I'm now going to make the first incision and…"

Suddenly, he had nothing to say.

As he cut into the Ralgar's skin, he discovered that this gigantic lizard did, in fact, differ in one way from the thousands that other doctors before him had dissected over the centuries.

This one was alive.

A sharp inward breath and then a growl forced Gus to take several steps back. The Ralgar began to thrash around. He was breathing, rasping.

"Fuck!"

"Alarm!" said the robot, icily calm. "Enemy on board! Enemy on board!"

The signal must have been sent, because the sirens began to resound through the ship. Gus finally pulled himself together.

"Sedatives! Quick, sedatives!"

The robot obligingly obeyed.

The Ralgar opened his eyes and stared straight at Gus.

Shortly afterwards, the robot gave him a dose strong enough to knock out several hippos.

And the Ralgar really did fall unconscious. At the same moment, two marines ran into the dissecting room.

Gus barely noticed. He was gazing wide-eyed at the supine Ralgar.

Φ

"How can he possibly be alive?" asked Captain Wei. "Wasn't he pierced with fire?"

The group of doctors in Gus's team had gathered in the captain's boardroom, once the news had traveled through the ship. The captain scrutinized the doctors as if they were keeping something from him.

Gus spoke up.

"Ralgars regenerate, Captain. Just like some earth species of lizard. If you cut off their hand, another one grows back after a while."

"But this one was dead!"

"Yes, there are some things that kill them reliably. Just like people."

"Yes," added Leo Krest, in a rapid attempt to contribute to the discussion. "You can live without a hand, but not without a brain."

You seem to manage quite well, thought Gus, but added aloud: "Our soldiers hit the Ralgar in the chest and he seemed dead. Evidently, he has regenerated."

"How did you not jump out of your skin when he came round?" asked Dorte.

"How do you know I didn't? Believe me, I've never been so terrified in all my life. And I am…."

"Fine," said the captain. "We have a live Ralgar aboard the ship. What do we do with him? We could simply shoot him."

"I think we should interrogate him," said Krest.

Dorte glared at him. "Interrogate him?"

"Yes. After all, he must know stuff that our Intelligence would find useful. Plans. Positions. Operational doctrines. We must get all of that out of him." Krest gazed almost imploringly at the captain. "Captain, this is an intelligence goldmine. The Imperial Army will decorate us for this. Everything we get out of him…"

"He's a big lizard who runs around the battlefield with a machete," snapped Dorte. "What sort of information do you think he'll have?"

Krest would not be discouraged. "Details that may seem worthless to us are a goldmine for intelligence officers. They'll put the pieces together…"

"That's horseshit."

"You're only saying that because you don't understand military matters!"

In fact, Leo Krest didn't understand them either, but he thought that he did, which was much worse. He might be a doctor, but he was convinced that he'd be the second Napoleon if only he'd followed a military career.

Captain Wei spoke. "Even if we wanted to interrogate him… how? Honestly, I think it would be simplest just to kill him. Hundreds like him fall on the battlefields down there."

"No."

All eyes turned to Gus. He sat there, stony-faced, hands clenched into fists, leaning on the tabletop.

"Lieutenant Andam?"

"That Ralgar is a prisoner of war and *my patient*. Nobody's going to kill him."

"But he's an enemy!" exclaimed Krest.

"Yes, that's why I said *prisoner of war* as well as patient, Leo. You should try listening."

The captain frowned. "Lieutenant Andam, I understand your position, but the rules on prisoners of war do not apply to aliens."

"Well then, they should start."

"They're gigantic soulless lizards who'd kill you as soon as look at you! Even our civilians! They're animals!" Krest argued.

"Just a moment ago you wanted to extract information from that soulless lizard, Leo."

"I mean that they're monsters and don't deserve our respect."

"I'm not going to spout clichés about being better than them. I don't want to. I'm just going to say that you're an idiot, Leo."

"Captain, did you hear that?!"

"I did. Now, all of you, be quiet for a moment."

"But…!"

"All of you also includes you, Lieutenant Krest!"

Leo fell silent.

The captain ruminated for a while. "Fine. Lieutenant Andam, I understand your position that he's a prisoner of war and a patient, but what do you want to do with him then? We don't have any prisoner-of-war camps, we don't even have the idea of exchanging prisoners. Not to mention that the Ralgars don't take many prisoners."

"There are places where we live with them in peace. Trading ports, like Valakor."

"Yes, but… what do you want to do, take him there?"

"Honestly, Captain, you've already entrusted him to me, so first of all I should try to treat him."

"So he can kill more of our side?" Leo couldn't stop himself from snorting.

"Lieutenant Krest, I believe I have already told you to remain silent," said Captain Wei.

"May I say something, Captain?" asked Dorte.

"Yes."

"I agree with Lieutenant Andam regarding… let's call it treating prisoners. But I don't know what conditions we have for it here."

"I'm afraid of something else," admitted the captain. "Prisoner or not, I would not be happy if that Ralgar broke free from his chains and began running down the corridors and killing everyone he met. And I don't want him to start with you, Lieutenant Andam."

Gus would have liked to argue, but he knew the captain was right. The Ralgar could kill him. If he hadn't administered the sedative on time, the Ralgar would probably have killed him this morning.

"We could tie him up," Dorte suggested. "We have industrial straps aboard that we use to secure the shuttles. They'd hold a Ralgar."

"Yes, that would work. And one more thing. Keep him away from our patients and the hospital." The captain fell silent for a moment.

"Airlock A-26 is right by the medical wing. We'll check it on the plan of the ship. I'd put him in there. With all the equipment you'll need to treat him."

"You want to put him in an airlock?"

"Yes. If he were to break free from his chains—literally—and threaten you or the ship, we'll simply open the door into space and decompress."

"But Gus would be in there with him!" Dorte objected.

"Well, let's hope he runs away in time," said the captain, half-smiling. "Those are my conditions, Lieutenant Andam. For the safety of the ship."

"I understand, sir. And I agree."

The captain looked at Leo for an instant. "But I will inform the Expeditionary Force commander of the situation. Maybe he really will want to send someone to interrogate him. But provided we can persuade him that we have things well in hand, they probably won't worry about it too much."

"What do you mean?"

"Lieutenant Krest was right. We should try to interrogate him. The Ralgar, that is, not Krest."

"I'd prefer to interrogate Leo…"

"Well, yes. Interrogate that Ralgar, that's all."

"We don't even know what language he speaks."

"We have robot interpreters. Try it."

"May I speak, sir?" asked Leo.

The captain only shrugged, so Leo looked at Gus triumphantly.

"You got what you wanted. You'll interrogate him. But I know that you're a softie. You'll need to be hard on him. Sometimes it's necessary to use pressure."

"Let me remind you again, Leo, this is a three-meter-tall lizard with gigantic claws and a gecko mouth. Am I to blow cigarette smoke into his eyes? Or try waterboarding?"

"Be serious!"

"I'm serious about my work. I can't take your comments seriously."

Ф

The main thing that Gus knew about airlocks was that he shouldn't go into them. They were transition chambers, with the inside of the ship on one side and space on the other.

Now he had a surgery inside an airlock. The feeling that only a piece of wall divided him from the vacuum was not exactly pleasant.

What's more, he'd established that, despite everything he'd said about hundreds of Ralgar dissections over the years, he didn't know that much about their anatomy. He'd now downloaded Caldwell's *Complete Ralgar Anatomy*, sixth edition, onto his datapad. Eight hundred pages. He tried to cram as much of it as he could during the evenings, but he wasn't much the wiser.

Now he entered. The Ralgar was restrained by his hands and feet and the restraints really did look secure.

He was upright. Squinting at the ceiling with one eye. The wound on his chest had shrunk some more. In his book, Caldwell stated that the speed at which Ralgars regenerate depends on a great many factors, from the extent of the injuries and loss of blood to the personal resilience of the given individual.

Even though Caldwell had written eight hundred pages about Ralgars, humanity did not know much about them.

Gus plucked up the courage to move closer by a step or two. At that moment he noticed that the marine guarding the airlock had followed him.

"That's fine. You can wait outside."

"Are you sure, sir?" he asked.

"No, I'm not, but please do it anyway."

The marine went out, not too willingly. Gus looked at the Ralgar, who was finally, slowly turning to look at him.

He was enfeebled and still in pain. And although it was said that the eyes are the windows of the soul, this didn't really apply to alien lizards.

The robot interpreter flew in the air above Gus's head. He turned to it.

"Tell him… that there's nothing to be afraid of."

"Understood," confirmed the robot, and began to interpret.

Ralgar society was divided into clans and overclans and they were more disunited among themselves than any human factions. Although some Ralgar clan or other sometimes attacked the Central Imperium, they mostly fought among themselves. That meant that they had languages galore; Imperial linguists had so far identified ninety-six. Someone had been able to identify the language spoken by those on the surface of Manorom, to a limited extent, but nobody was sure of the quality.

When the robot had finished speaking and the Ralgar hadn't reacted in any way, Gus realized that this was going to be very complex.

"Try to tell him that I'm a doctor—a healer—and that I'll take care of him."

"Understood." More chattered interpreting.

"And tell him that I've pledged to ensure that nobody will hurt him."

Another wave of translation. The Ralgar emitted a sort of deep grunting sound and bared his teeth as he did.

"That's their equivalent of laughter," the robot rapidly explained.

"So, he understands."

More laughter, and then the Ralgar spoke. In English.

"That flying ball of yours talks stupid shit. I once saw a guy who'd had half his head shot off and he still talked better than that."

"You… speak English?"

"Yeah, we learn how you talk before we come at you. It's easy, we learn it fast and your language is moronic."

Gus had heard that Ralgars could learn human languages relatively fast. He'd also heard that those who'd mastered human languages had a relatively specific way of speaking them.

He found his tongue. "Well, as I was saying, I'm a doctor. My name is Gus Andam. Gus…" he pointed at himself. "Gus."

"I know you mean yourself. Don't be an asshole."

"I'm a doctor. A physician. I treat humans and Ralgars."

"Why?"

"Well… I wanted to heal people, and I think that even our enemies should receive treatment. Doctors have this rule…"

"You must be an asshole."

"Other people have already told me that. Leo Krest, mostly."

"Who's that?"

"Well… he's also an asshole. Doesn't matter. I mean to say that I want to treat you. Help you."

"Why?"

"It's my job."

"I'll regrow anyway. I don't need you." The Ralgar looked around. "How did I get here? The last thing I remember is chopping up some fucker like you with my *karba*."

Karba was the word in many Ralgar languages for their swords. Gus remembered that.

"Someone hit you. One of… ours. They loaded you into a shuttle. We thought you were dead. We didn't realize that you'd regenerate."

"Yeah, that's what we do." More grunting laughter. "Hey, so someone shot away half my chest and I still survived. What an asshole."

Gus realized that, for some reason, "asshole" was a very popular word among Ralgars.

"Yes, you survived. And I'd like to know if I can help you in any way. Accelerate your healing process."

"I don't know. Doesn't matter. Then what?"

"Well, we don't know, but nobody will hurt you, I guarantee that."

"Why?"

"Well, it's not allowed. You're a prisoner and a patient and…"

"Isn't that a bit fucked up? And have you tied me up so I can't rip you to shreds?"

"That was the captain's idea, but yes."

"Are you going to torture me or something?"

"No! Absolutely not. We don't torture prisoners."

"Where's the fun in that?"

Gus had no idea whether the Ralgar meant it was fun to torture or to be tortured. Maybe his English wasn't that good.

Or, maybe it *was* and he was just… different.

No, he didn't want to admit that. They had to find common ground.

The Ralgar said nothing. Gus walked around him for a while with his medical scanner.

"It's all nonsense anyway," he couldn't stop himself from saying, suddenly.

"What?"

"That we're fighting there. You and us. Against each other. For so long. And we're sitting here talking to each other."

"What else am I supposed to do?"

"Well… not fight."

"Why?"

"So there's peace."

"What? Sometimes you need to chop up a few assholes. Better than sitting on your own ass."

"That's a strange view of the world."

"And what view do you have?"

"Well… that chopping people up isn't good. We're all the same."

"We are not. I'm a giant lizard, you're a little… what do you call the assholes that drink that white shit from the females?"

"Do you mean mammal?"

"Yeah, you're a little mammal."

"But the differences between us really aren't that great. We all want to… live, somehow."

"Yeah, maybe, yeah."

"That's what I thought. Some of our people want to paint you as merciless killers, crazy murderous monsters, but I know that's not the case. As I'm sitting here and talking to you, that's not how it is. Do you have a name?"

"I am Lebroskro, of Clan Pomro."

"Le-bro…?"

"Lebroskro. It's not that hard. But that doesn't matter. Why are you telling me this bullshit?"

"Well, only so you know that I know you're not a murderous monster. We all have our lives, our dreams…"

"Yeah, I want to kill our clan chief. But that's what we all want. He's an asshole, but a powerful asshole. So, we obey him."

"But do you never think about why you're fighting?"

"Because he told us to."

"And that's enough for you?"

"Sure. And cutting off those stupid heads is good fun."

An idea popped into Gus's head. "So, what if you were the chief, not him? Would you also attack us here?"

"Someone from the overclan ordered that. But that doesn't matter. I'd probably attack somewhere. I don't know. It gets boring if you don't attack."

"But you don't want to do anything else?"

"Of course I do. I'll get my female cycle soon. I'll lay eggs. That'll be good fun. It'll be my third time."

From Caldwell's book, Gus knew that Ralgars change sex every fifty or sixty years. That's why there were only males on the battlefield, while the females, who laid the eggs, defended their home planets. Their two sexes were "offense" and "defense".

But in this Gus saw the Ralgar's longing to give up war and start a family.

"Most of our soldiers also want to go home. And to start a family."

"They should go then."

"But it's not as simple as that."

"Yeah, I know."

"Are you looking forward to having young?"

"Yeah. But mainly because the females have that huge new mega cannon they use to protect the nests. I want to try one out. Apparently, they're super shooters!"

Gus decided to ask directly. "Could we not end that conflict down there? It's not going anywhere. Neither side gains anything from it. Why don't we just finish it?"

"Dunno. If you make mincemeat of us, it'll be over, right?"

"Well, yes, but that's not what I want."

"Yeah, because you're treating me. After that it'll be more difficult cos there'll be one more of us." That grunting laugh again.

Gus tried a different tack.

"Do you like music? Or literature?"

"I don't read books."

"You have books?"

"Yeah, someone wrote something down. The Imats teach reading. And we learn that scribbling of yours. But not all clans do."

The Imats… the symbiotic race who made technology for the Ralgars. The female Ralgars protected them on their home planets. Gus didn't know any more than that.

"And what sort of music do you like?"

"Our clan has… this one thing. It's called…" he made a noise that Gus didn't dare even try to work out.

"Would you like to listen to some music?"

"I don't know. Does it make a difference?"

"It does. Do you like music? If you do, I can play you something."

"But you know I'll still rip your head off when the time comes? Just so you don't think we're great friends."

"I'm not afraid of that." Gus looked at his wound. "But I'll treat you."

"But not from too close. I could also bite your head off."

Φ

"I don't know what I was thinking," Gus admitted, sitting by a small table in his cabin, opposite Dorte.

"I don't think you had time to think of anything," she said, pouring some drink from a small flask into a metal cup. She didn't offer him any. She knew he'd refuse.

"But I should have. I was imagining that I could show him that we're the same. I'd show him that war is unnecessary."

"And what would happen if you did? Do you think he'd go home and tell all his mates to stop fighting?"

"I don't know… I was just expecting… something else."

"He isn't a murderous monster, then?"

"Some Ralgars, mostly exiles from their clans, live here and there in the Imperium and work as bodyguards or bouncers."

"Yeah, but that's also true of humans. The outcasts who've left their communities, for good or ill, are also not entirely typical specimens. And there are huge cultural differences even among humans. There were even before we went into space." She threw up her hands. "My ancestors came from Denmark. What about yours?"

"Ghana."

"You see? I'd say we're *very* different in culture."

"Yeah, but we don't tear each other's heads off now."

"Yeah, but maybe in a few centuries we and the Ralgars won't be doing it either."

"I don't know. I want to do something now. Right now… I just want to try to end the nonsense going on down there. Somehow."

"And you do know that the Ralgars attacked first, don't you?"

"Yeah, but the lizard in the airlock isn't responsible…" Gus threw up his hands. Maybe that was stupid. Utterly stupid. He didn't even know what he was trying to do… he just knew he had to try to do *something*.

Dorte took another swig.

"Gus, there are some things that we just can't change. Not you, not me, not that Ralgar. We can't change the world. We aren't gods."

"Every patient wants us to be gods!"

"That's a cute cliché, but it doesn't make us gods."

"Do you find that wisdom at the bottom of your glass?"

She drank again. "No. At the bottom of the glass I can only come to terms with the things I can't change."

Gus was thinking about what to say to that when Leo Krest burst in.

"Woah, Lieutenant Dahlerup, I didn't know you were here. Please keep doing… whatever you were doing."

"We're not doing anything, Leo."

"I know. I just came for my earphones. I'm going to the mess to do some paperwork and listen to an audiobook."

Gus jumped to his feet. "That's it! Audiobooks! I could play him one!"

In a flash, he was beside Leo and peeking over his shoulder. "Do you have that data chip with your audiobooks? What have you got?"

"What do you want? Who do you want to play it to?"

"The Ralgar!"

"You want to give him books? Gus, you're supposed to be interrogating him!"

At least Leo had stopped calling him 'Lieutenant Andam'.

"There are different methods of interrogation, Leo." He was still looking over Krest's shoulder. "What are you listening to now?"

"*The Imperium Through My Eyes* by Empress Ethelreda!"

Ethelreda had been the paranoid, manipulative monarch who was several sandwiches short of a picnic. Gus wasn't surprised to find Leo was listening to this.

"Well, I'm not going to play him that. Can I have a look at what else you've got?"

With a somewhat disparaging glance, Leo handed over his datapad. "You're really interrogating him like that? Has the Ralgar told you anything at all yet, smartass?"

"Yeah, Leo. He's told me something."

Krest obviously was not expecting this. "Seriously? What did he tell you?"

"That we're all assholes. Ralgars use that word for everything and everyone."

Krest grimaced. "I knew you weren't up to it. You let everyone babble bullshit to you."

"So how would you proceed, Leo?"

"You wouldn't believe it," retorted Krest, with the stupidest wannabe cruel expression. Then he turned to the hook holding his working uniform. And stopped suddenly.

"You haven't put anything into my pocket again, have you?"

Φ

"How are you?" asked Gus, entering the airlock.

Lebroskro half-opened his mouth. "Good. I think."

"I've brought you something!" Gus put the small datapad on the nightstand beside the Ralgar's big bed. "You can learn about human culture."

"I already know everything."

"Well, I don't think you know this. Here are some of our books in audio format."

"What?"

"You were saying that you have books too, so I was wondering if you'd like to listen to one to pass the time."

"I thought you didn't want to torture me."

Gus forced himself to laugh. "Yes, I know what it's like. I asked the entire ship and got all possible audiobooks. These are the classics of Earth literature. There's *A Christmas Carol*, by Charles Dickens. It's about a… erm… a man, who is bad and stingy, and ghosts come to him in the night to bring him back to the right path."

"That's horseshit. What are ghosts?"

"Well, they're… supernatural beings. Do you have any mythology?"

"Do you mean that stupid bullshit that isn't true?"

"Mythology. Stories from ancient times, heroic epics, legends about the creation of the world, that sort of thing…"

"We call that stupid bullshit that isn't true."

Gus concluded that he'd better not use this approach to ask about religion. He slid his finger down over the datapad display.

"What else do I have here? Maybe… *Dune*, by Frank Herbert. *A Song of Steel*, by Michaela Merglová. *The Midnight Line* by Lee Child. *In the Shadow of the Protectors* by Hilda Zahid. Or… ooh, *Maladavi* by Wale Okediran. A story from pre-cosmic Nigeria. It's about a man courted by two different women from enemy camps and he… well, he's delicately injured. Humans can't grow back some body parts."

"That's stupid."

"And then there's, what about… *Crime and Punishment*, by Fyodor Dostoyevsky… It's… well, it's about a man who owes money, so he kills two old women with an ax."

"Yeah, that sounds better. And you listen to this shit regularly?"

"As and when, yes."

"And why do you want to play it to me?"

"I think it will bring us closer together."

"Why?"

Gus was tired. He'd explained this over and over and over again, to Dorte, to the captain, to Leo and to everyone from whom he'd gathered audiobook files. He didn't understand why he had to keep on explaining all this.

Why he had to try.

Why he had to face ridicule for simply wanting to do *something* to end this madness. It was like banging his head against the wall.

"Because! Hell, because it's absurd that we're killing each other down there! I'm trying to save kids who aren't even old enough to buy beer in half the Imperium, but we still send them to be massacred. And you don't even know what you want! You only want to fight, to attack, you just wave it off, it's fantastic, but… No, it isn't! It's unnecessary! And people can talk about irreconcilable cultures until they're blue in the face, but Ralgars live in the Imperium too. There are planets where we trade with them, even if it's unofficial. And I know that you have hundreds of different clans and you all hate each other, but hell, why can't we end this senseless slaughter and just go home? Whenever you meet someone, you tell them they're an asshole. And do you think that by behaving like that you're not assholes yourselves? Yes! You are! We're all assholes! All of us!"

Lebroskro was staring at him, open-mouthed.

Gus rubbed his eyes. He hadn't even noticed that he'd started to cry, he'd gotten so het up.

"I've been here for over one hundred and fifty days already! And I want to go home now!"

Lebroskro was still staring at him. Then he bellowed with laughter. "Yeah, it's crap that you feel like that. But you're probably right. We are all assholes. Do you want me to bite your head off?"

Gus sighed. His explosion had also achieved nothing. "Sometimes I wonder if it would help. But…"

The alarm siren sounded.

"Attention all hands. Attention all hands! Incoming wounded. I repeat, incoming wounded. All medical personnel report to the admission ward and operation room. Admissions in hangars one and two. I repeat: admissions in hangars one and two."

Gus looked up at the gigantic lizard. "Your pals have been busy again."

"Yeah, that's what we do."

"I must go, I… must go."

He headed out of the airlock.

"Hey! Hey!" Lebroskro called after him.

Gus stopped and turned around.

"As you want to torture me, torture me then… Play me the one about the ax and killing old crones."

Gus didn't know if this was the Ralgar's attempt at a joke. Finally, he took two steps backward and launched the relevant file on the datapad.

As he was leaving, he heard the first sentence of the novel:

"At the beginning of July, during a spell of exceptionally hot weather, toward evening a certain young man came down on to the street…"

The Ralgar was chuckling as if this was the funniest thing he'd ever heard.

Φ

"The triage robot gave this one priority!" exclaimed an orderly.

"I'll take him!" shouted Gus. He changed his gloves with the nurse's help as two robots carried his last patient away. A woman of around twenty, who'd had a disagreement with some Ralgar projectile and had lost most of her intestines. Gus had to rapidly stitch a cybernetic digestive system into her body. When she got home, she'd get a proper, permanent synthetic prosthesis in a hospital.

Provided she survived the next twelve hours.

The next patient was set down in front of him. A chest wound, caused by something like a hoof.

Gus began to work.

"How many of them are left?" Dorte asked from the next table.

"Dozens. But no more shuttles are arriving."

"At least something." Leo growled. "And by the way. Gus. Where did you put my datapad?"

Gus was glad that Captain Wei's voice came over the intercom, meaning he didn't have to answer Leo.

His mild joy lasted until the captain finished speaking.

"All hands, this is the captain speaking. I'd love to tell you you're going to have less work, but unfortunately, that's not the case. A large Ralgar offensive has been launched near Port Kalantan. It looks like they're throwing everything they've got at us, and we're calling up all reserves."

Gus clenched his teeth beneath his surgical mask. His conversation with Lebroskro was still reverberating inside him.

Pointless. It was all pointless.

But the captain continued.

"We've received the order to land. We'll start our descent in twenty minutes."

Someone gasped for breath.

"Fuck!" Dorte couldn't help saying.

They'd landed only twice in the entire time they'd been deployed on the *Avicenna*.

The captain continued to speak. "We'll touch down right at the edge of the battlefield, as the wounded will be delivered to us more quickly that way. The 23rd Division are getting a thrashing and we'll get their wounded. I'm calling reserve staff into service too. Hang in there, everyone."

"That's too much!" Dorte complained.

Gus tried not to think of those Ralgar ground beam cannon that had shot down a troop carrier on the first day of battle.

Φ

The beam didn't hit them. Several infantry shells hit the *Avicenna* as she descended, but it was mostly scattered fire; otherwise, the Ralgars were aiming at other targets.

The huge juggernaut sank through the atmosphere, the braking jets slowing it down, the Gertz generator switched off. Sweat ran over the helm's forehead as he smoothly and gently touched down on the landing gear's giant legs and antigravity support.

Thanks to them a ship of over one hundred thousand tons reached the ground.

The hatches and doors to the hangar opened.

The captain gave the order that the ship was from this point on to be designated Port Alpha. This meant that it was on the surface near the combat zone.

And aircars and ambulances immediately began to swarm aboard with the wounded.

Φ

The hours went by. One patient after another. Finally, coffee and the like ceased to be enough for Gus and the other doctors; they had to start giving themselves a boost with stimulants.

They had no choice.

Gus, too, shuffled into the prep area, removed his mask and gloves, dropped onto a bench, and took a stimulant pill. Of course, it wouldn't solve everything. His body was still tired, and the stimulant wouldn't stop spasms.

He did nothing, he said nothing. He just sat, staring ahead of him.

Dorte came right after him. She pecked up her pill and flopped down beside him with a long-drawn-out sigh.

"I don't think I'll ever get used to this."

"You already have."

"Yeah, and that's even worse." She rubbed her eyes. "When I joined the Navy, they told me that the worst place for a doctor to serve is aboard frigates and small ships, because there I'd be the only doctor aboard, while on everything from a cruiser up there's more of you so the work is less stressful." She made a sound that might be a chuckle if she were less tired. "The *Avicenna* has thirty-two doctors aboard, of which twenty are surgeons, and we're still exhausted, overworked and burned out."

"Hey, Gus!" said Leo, taking off his mask.

Immediately, Gus felt still more tired, even before Leo hit him with his question.

"Where is my datapad?"

"Your datapad?"

"Yeah, the one you borrowed… I want to download another audiobook onto my comlink from it. There's a second volume of Empress Ethelreda's memoirs."

"Lebroskro has it."

"Who?"

"The Ralgar. Lebroskro. I lent him the datapad so he could listen to audiobooks."

"You lent my datapad to a *Ralgar*? Are you crazy?"

"He wanted to listen to something. I gave him *Crime and Punishment*."

"You gave my datapad to the Ralgar so he could… actually, you know what? I don't want to know. You've already crossed the line. I'm going to go get it. And I'll tell the captain that you're not up to interrogating that Ralgar. He should have been entrusted to someone else long ago. Someone who's a good doctor and a good soldier! I'm on my way!"

Dorte raised her head. "But Leo…"

Leo, however, had already gone.

Gus stared straight ahead. He was tired. So tired. And the pill hadn't started to work yet. That crap had a slow onset, but then again, it also had fewer unpleasant side effects.

"Let him go. I haven't made any progress with Lebroskro, and if he wants to take him into his care, let him."

Dorte was also staring straight ahead. "Do you really want to leave him to Leo's mercy? You came up with the whole the-Ralgar-is-my-patient thing."

"And maybe I was mistaken. Hell, Dorte, maybe everyone is right. The last few days we've been patching up soldiers who got too close to Lebroskro's pals."

She still wasn't looking at him. "Maybe you're right. And maybe all the others are right… But maybe all the others are mistaken."

"But it is true that I can't change the world."

"You can't. In the same way, you can't decide how other people will behave or what they will do. Whether it's Leo, the captain, that Ralgar or even the Emperor. But you can influence your own behavior. How you approach everything. And ultimately, that's what is important. The only thing that's important."

Gus turned to look at her. She returned his gaze.

"Did you find that piece of wisdom at the bottom of your bottle?"

"One of many."

They laughed.

"What are you going to do?"

He stood up. The pill still hadn't kicked in. But that didn't matter.

"Well, I'm going after Leo before he does something stupid."

Φ

"Give me your weapon!" Leo Krest ordered the marine guarding the airlock in which the Ralgar lay.

The astonished marine looked at the doctor in his white coat.

"Sir…"

"Maybe I don't have epaulets, but I'm still an officer. Obey the order, Corporal."

The marine threw his rifle onto his back—evidently, he didn't want to entrust it to the doctor—but he took his pistol out of its holster and handed it over.

Leo opened the outer door and strode inside. He felt exactly like Empress Ethelreda. She also sometimes faced her enemies with a weapon in her hand.

His tablet was lying on the nightstand beside the huge bed to which the Ralgar was bound. He was lying with his mouth half-open, but immediately looked up.

The narrator's voice could be heard coming from Leo's datapad.

"'I am so much in your debt, sir, and so are my orphans and my dead stepmother," Sonya said, hurriedly, *"that if I haven't yet thanked you properly you… mustn't think…'"*

"And you are…?" asked the Ralgar.

Leo aimed the pistol at him.

His hand was only shaking a little bit.

No, he had to be strong. Self-possessed. Like Empress Ethelreda, like Admiral Vaaro, like General Patton.

"I know that you've tried to make my colleague believe a lot of rubbish. But you won't hoodwink me, lizard. You won't hoodwink me! I'm taking over this interrogation. And you will now immediately tell me what your people are planning. Do you understand? And none of the lies you were telling Andam."

The Ralgar observed him but said nothing.

"'Rodion Romanovich has two roads open to him: either a bullet in the forehead, or Vladimirka.'"

His gecko mouth was half-open. "All I told your mate is that you're all assholes. That's the absolute truth." He bent his enormous head toward the datapad. "Rodion Romanovich is an asshole too. He wants to confess but he doesn't have to!"

"You don't think you're clever, do you?" grimaced Leo. "Humanity has already dealt with much bigger irritations than you. So, once again: What are the other Ralgars on the surface planning?"

"To cut off your heads."

"Don't lie!"

"I'm telling the truth."

"You're clever. I must admit that. Clever. But you're still just an overgrown lizard."

"And you're a stunted mammal. Your pal taught me that word. And he also brought me the thing that spouts this bullshit. But the bit with the ax was good."

Leo growled, approached the nightstand and hit the datapad's off button.

At that moment the Ralgar tore off his shackles.

Though actually, he didn't tear off the shackles, he tore one *hand* off the wrist it was attached to. He just propped himself up and ripped off his own hand.

But Leo didn't notice, because he'd started to shriek.

He was splattered with yellow blood and suddenly the stump hit him in the chest with full force.

He ran right across the airlock. The pistol dropped out of his hand.

Φ

Gus Andam ran up to the airlock just in time to see the Ralgar Lebroskro, now unshackled, run full tilt into the marine and throw him at the wall.

He heard bones crunching.

Leo was lying on the floor, cowering, winded, and a little way from the pistol.

Lebroskro focused on the prostrated, wounded marine. He towered over him, a stump where one hand should be. Gus realized that the Ralgar had torn one hand off, knowing it would grow back, and had then used his stump to free himself somehow.

Gus had a few seconds. The thought of quickly reaching for a weapon, aiming and firing leaped to mind.

But he couldn't do that.

He wasn't capable of it.

He couldn't shoot.

Principally, he couldn't kill.

And so he stood there, rooted to the spot, until Lebroskro finally turned toward him.

He's good at killing, Gus thought, wishing for the cool detachment he didn't have.

He was scared of the enormous lizard towering above him.

He swallowed.

"Are you going to kill me?"

He immediately thought of arguments why Lebroskro should not do that. He was a healer; he only wanted to help him. He wanted to bring their two species closer, to show them that they could do more than just kill each other…

But he hadn't managed to do any of this.

Something flickered in his peripheral vision and Lebroskro also reacted.

Leo was running out of the airlock.

"Your pal?" growled the Ralgar, as if he hadn't just broken half the marine's bones or torn off his own hand.

This was so bizarre that Gus stopped short. "No… I wouldn't call him a pal." He thought of something the Ralgar would appreciate. "I wouldn't put a pancreas into a pal's pocket. A pancreas is…"

"I know, it's some of the crap you have in your bodies that doesn't grow back."

"Well, yes."

The Ralgar laughed. "Fine, but next time you should make him eat it, that would be funnier."

There will be a next time, then?

Gus hardly dared to hope.

Then he discovered that he shouldn't hope.

The airlock's inner doors closed with a hiss behind him.

He turned around.

The Ralgar, snarling, ran round him and charged into the hatch with all his strength.

But it didn't budge.

Gus turned to the large window beside the door. There, on the other side, stood Leo at the control panel.

He looked terrified and, at the same time, determined, as if he was going through lists of his favorite historical military psychopaths in his head and wondering who would say what.

"I'm opening the airlock to space!" he said through the speaker. His voice was shaking, but he was also trying to play the part of a decisive leader. "I'm sorry, Gus, you were my friend. My brother in arms. But we must stop that monster! It's the only solution. I'm launching you into space! Forgive me!"

Gus opened his eyes wide.

The Ralgar began to hammer on the window, but it was made of the finest transparent steel and didn't even buckle.

Despite this, on the other side Leo instinctively stepped back before forcing himself forward and pressing the big button.

Gus was still gaping.

"Leo, you idiot…"

The outer door of the airlock opened with a hiss.

"…we're planetside!"

A refreshing wave of Manorom air wafted in.

He could hear birdsong.

The sounds of battle in the distance.

Leo stared, his expression terrified, at the hole to the outside.

Lebroskro also turned toward it. A few meters away was his path to freedom.

Then he turned back to Gus.

The doctor swallowed again.

"You're assholes," declared Lebroskro. He pointed his stump at the window. "But he's the bigger asshole."

The corners of Gus's mouth turned shakily upward. "I didn't know that we'd agree on precisely that, but I agree with you."

The Ralgar bellowed with laughter. He turned around and took two steps toward the hatch, then stopped.

He turned back to the nightstand and grabbed the datapad.

"Rodion Romanovich Raskolnikov is an asshole too."

Gus nodded jerkily. "The author was going to be executed but the sentence was commuted at the last minute. Just now I understood exactly how he felt."

Lebroskro laughed again, then ran to the external hatch and jumped.

Gus only saw the lizard jump and slide down over the ship's hull.

Finally, he dropped into the mud and ran off in the direction of the battle sounds. To his own people.

The *Avicenna* could not fire at him in any way. She was a hospital ship, so any type of offensive weaponry was banned.

And a hospital ship she continued to be.

Gus tore his gaze away from Manorom's horizon and knelt beside the wounded marine.

The inner door opened, and Leo burst in.

Gus filtered out his stammered apologies as he provided first aid.

Φ

Captain Wei Meison drummed his fingers on the desk in his office.

My Blue Heaven was playing from the speakers.

Gus and Leo stood in front of his desk. Leo looked even more terrified than he had when standing face to face with the Ralgar.

"So, Lieutenant Krest, you took it upon yourself to interrogate a prisoner entrusted to Lieutenant Andam and in doing so you enabled him to escape. By trying to release him into space, along with Lieutenant Andam and Corporal Savit. And the only thing that saved them was the fact that you were too obtuse to realize that the *Avicenna* was planetside?"

"I… sir, that isn't entirely fair. I've always been a loyal member of the Central Imperium's armed forces. My father…"

"This isn't about loyalty and it's not about your father. This is the truth."

Leo's mouth dropped open. For a moment he looked like a Ralgar with a gecko mouth. Then he nodded jerkily. "Yes sir. But I strongly object to… the word 'obtuse'. I… made a human error and I am willing to take the consequences… but please don't include it in my records, sir!"

Wei turned to Gus. "How is Corporal Savit?"

"Seven broken ribs, collarbone also broken, the shoulder bone got the worst of it in two places. But he'll survive and, ultimately, he'll be okay."

"That's very good news." The captain turned back to Leo. "Is there anything else you want to say, Krest?"

"I… no, sir. Only that I'm sorry."

"Lieutenant Andam, is there anything you'd like to add?"

"No, sir."

There wasn't anything to say.

The captain heaved a sigh, looked intently at the edge of the table, then drummed on it again. "I've just received a message. We're flying home."

The two doctors exchanged glances. They couldn't help it.

"Reinforcements arrived in orbit an hour ago. Including the hospital ship *Galen*, which will replace us. In six hours, any wounded able to return to their units will leave the ship. Then we'll take off. We'll be out of the star system within sixteen hours."

Gus stood there in shock. Joy and euphoria hadn't yet made themselves felt. He wasn't expecting this.

He wanted it to be over.

He'd hoped it would be over.

But he hadn't expected it this… soon. This suddenly.

He couldn't react.

But Leo could.

"That's… great news, sir!"

"I'm glad you think that, Krest. Because the last thing I want to deal with now is the paperwork around your disciplinary proceedings. And now get lost and give thanks to all the saints you honor."

"Y…yes, sir."

"And you, Lieutenant Andam."

"Yes, sir?"

"Would you like any personal input into this situation? I may choose to ignore it, but if you decide to take the case to the public prosecutor…"

"I… no, sir, I think it's better to draw a line under this. A very thick line."

"I'm glad you see it that way. Dismissed, gentlemen."

Dorte was waiting for them in the corridor. Any questions she might have had about the Ralgar's escape and Leo's stupidity were drowned by her enthusiastic whoop when Gus told her they were flying home.

She jumped on Gus and hugged him. Then, a little more hesitantly, she also hugged Leo.

But he was still staring at Gus.

"Gus, I… I'd like to thank you. Thank you for… for not wanting to take it to the prosecutor. I'm grateful… and I… I'm sorry about what happened. But… I hope you agree that we don't need to talk about it any longer. Let's forget it. Yeah?"

He held out his hand. Gus took it.

"That smells good."

For the last two days, Leo had been amazingly humble and obliging. Not just to Gus and Dorte, but also to all other crew members, even his subordinates.

The *Avicenna* had taken off from the surface of Manorom and was heading out of the star system; meanwhile, the Imperial Army reinforcements were disembarking onto the planet. The *Galen* had arrived with them. Her doctors would now treat the wounded. New soldiers would replace the old ones. The fighting would continue.

It was possible that the army with its fresh reinforcements would make a breakthrough. Force the Ralgars off the planet.

Gus sometimes wondered what Lebroskro was doing. Whether his

Ralgar patient was still alive or had become one of the thousands of bodies left on the battlefield. He'd have liked some sort of resolution, but knew he couldn't expect one, not here. There was no way he'd ever know.

So, as the *Avicenna* powered away from Manorom, through Gertz space, and the doctors finally had the chance to take a breather, Gus invited Leo and Dorte to the officers' mess for a special meal.

"It really does smell great," Dorte confirmed Leo's words as the robot placed steaming portions in front of them. Gus had let her in on it and to his surprise, she'd agreed.

"So, let's eat," he urged them.

Leo heaped food onto his plate and began to eat enthusiastically.

"That's a strange seasoning. Is it chicken?"

"Yes, sure, it's chicken," Gus confirmed in a serious voice.

Lebroskro may have vanished and nobody would ever know what had happened to him. But Gus could get at least some sort of resolution here.

Lebroskro had left something behind. The enormous Ralgar hand that he'd torn off his arm.

Leo thought it was delicious.

"This chicken really is excellent."

V

"Do you know what happened to Doctor Andam?" asked Hila.

"As far as I know, he left the Navy and now has a private practice somewhere in the Imperium."

"That's good. Maybe I'll do an interview with him myself, one day. I still think like a journalist, yes. And I do know that he'd probably be surprised if the Empress appeared at his door."

"Well, he's definitely experienced worse things," Daniel reasoned. "Stranger things, certainly."

The mood was a little more relaxed again.

"The Imperium has, of course, seen many conflicts like the one on Manorom in recent years. I believe that you and the Imperial government—not to mention the armed forces—must feel that you are putting out thousands of small fires."

Daniel nodded. "You could put it like that, yes."

"I know. And would you agree, sire, that the situation is worst in the Bornholm Sector?"

That subject, again.

"That depends on your perspective, but the New Protectorate fleet withdrew across that sector after we'd defeated them at the Battle of Hub. And it left behind saboteur groups. Ships that remained in the rearguard and attacked our convoys. And that's not all. There's been sabotage, espionage and hacker attacks."

"Are you talking about the famous Henry Corp. expedition?"

"You heard about that?" asked Hila.

"Only in passing. I know that a colonization fleet heading for the planet Palo Alto and financed by Henry Corp. was attacked by hackers."

"Yes, several times over. But that wasn't a matter only for the Bornholm Sector. It first happened in Sol."

Varviso frowned. "In Sol? Near Earth?"

"Yes, that's where the entire colonization fleet assembled." Hila smiled. "The journalist monitoring all that back then was my former colleague. Maybe that too will give you some of the context you wanted."

NEW HORIZONS

The lounge aboard the luxurious space yacht *Gloriana* was furnished tastefully, but not as pretentiously as Nick Gramo expected. Escorted by the ship's robot-steward, he walked over an ordinary crimson carpet and sat down in one of the comfortable upholstered armchairs to wait for the man he was going to interview.

However, he soon stopped paying attention to the interior décor and turned it instead to the gigantic observation port. The lounge was located right in the bows of the ship, and a magnificent panorama of stars was visible through the observation port of the ship as it sailed through the Solar System.

It had been a few years since Nick Gramo was last in space, and he thought he remembered what it was like, but he was used to traveling on overbooked scheduled flights. This was his first time in a private yacht and the first time he'd been able to observe the stars with the naked eye.

There was a hiss as the door opened.

"Mr. Gramo. I apologize for keeping you waiting so long," said Mr. Doug Henry, glancing at the untouched tray of refreshments on the side-table between two armchairs. "I see that you've been taken care of."

"Yes, Mr. Henry, thank you."

The two men shook hands, and Henry invited him to sit down.

Nick Gramo was technically Doug Henry's employee, but only in the sense that one of the regional CEOs of a gigantic corporation could be considered the "boss" of an ordinary employee working at a subsidiary.

Nick was a reporter, and he worked for Horizon News, the news station belonging to the Henry Corp. conglomerate that was also the driving force behind the colony expedition to the Bornholm System.

Nick was on this flight on his own initiative. He had coaxed his boss—that is, his immediate superior—into letting him set out for Saturn's orbit, where preparations for the colony expedition were underway. As a bonus, he'd been offered a ride aboard Henry's personal ship, the *Gloriana*, and an interview with Mr. Henry himself.

"I understand that you have a few questions," said Henry with a smile, as if to indicate that his time was precious, and that Nick should finally take the plunge.

"Yes, Mr. Henry, thank you." He switched on his robot-camera. The small sphere rose into the air and its lenses began to record Henry's face.

The microphones activated.

Behind Henry, the panorama of space was visible.

"It's been said that this colony expedition is a new start for humanity. Can you make a statement about that?"

Nick Gramo asked the question as Henry turned to the tea-table and poured himself a glass of juice from some fruit that the journalist did not recognize.

"I don't know about all of humanity, but it's definitely a new start for the Central Imperium. That's why the Emperor and the government have supported us so generously. The Imperium has come through a nasty war, and this is a step into the future. We're building again, not destroying. What's more, this will also help repair the damage caused by the war. As I'm sure your viewers know," he continued, although they were both sure that the ordinary viewer would not know this, "Henry Corp. financed the colonization of three worlds in the Bornholm Sector. I personally coordinated the entire process from the station *Lonely Star*. Only, before the first colonists could leave, the war started and as you undoubtedly know, *Lonely Star* was destroyed after we attempted to stop the enemy fleet from approaching. Captain Esau Biwott died a hero during the attack. He sacrificed himself so that the rest of us had time to evacuate. That is one of the reasons, but not the only one, why the frigate, the flagship escorting our expedition, bears his name. His son Loran christened it. Loran was only thirteen at the time of the evacuation."

Nick Gramo nodded. At this point, his editor would probably insert some footage from the launch of the *Esau Biwott*, in which the now fourteen-year-old orphaned boy, with tears in his eyes, pressed the button to detonate a bottle of champagne over the hull of the new ship.

"Are you planning to colonize all three planets immediately?" he asked, for the viewers' sake, although of course he already knew the answer.

"No, the economy is still in the postwar phase and so the entire project will start on planet Palo Alto. Of our three candidates, it's the best one for colonization. If everything goes well, we will colonize the other two next year."

"How many vessels are taking part in this expedition?"

"Thirty colony ships are currently in preparation at the stations around Saturn."

"Is it true that the Imperial Navy will provide the fleet with protection?"

"Yes, to a certain extent. The fleet will be accompanied by several Imperial frigates."

Nick judged that the time had come for a few more difficult questions.

"Mr. Henry. There are almost ninety inhabited planets in the Central Imperium. Many of them suffered during the war, the economy isn't even at fifty percent of where it was a few years ago, infrastructure is collapsing. Many of our readers and viewers may, with justice, ask why the Imperium, and why so influential a corporation as Henry Corp., are investing so much money into settling new planets, when those same funds could be used to improve infrastructure on existing worlds. Half the planets in the Wuwei and Rosalio Sectors are still on a rationing system. So why aren't we pushing the economy in that direction?"

Henry did not answer immediately. Nick hadn't expected him to. The magnate must have reckoned with questions like that; he was thinking, he didn't want to answer by smiling, waving his hands and spouting PR-bullshit.

At least, not too much PR-bullshit.

"The Central Imperium has been through, indeed is going through, difficult times. Henry Corp. is helping on at least eight worlds. We're renewing infrastructure, assisting the economic relaunch. But the colony expedition is part of that too. The Imperium must look to the future, and indeed at the symbolism. We wanted to settle those new worlds before the war, and this is evidence for all people in the Central Imperium that civilization is continuing. Indeed, that is the motto of the whole Central Imperium: civilization must continue." He shrugged. "And for your more practically minded readers and viewers, I may add that all the colony ships we are using were already built, and after the war, there were a great many homeless people on Earth, particularly in the Europe region. They form the core of our new colonists. And that is also the reason why the colony expedition is starting from the Solar System, not from another part of the Imperium. Last but not least, I would also like to add that a freshly settled world will rapidly become a market for other worlds in the Imperium, and again, that will help the economy."

Here, Nick could not refrain from a follow-up question: "And what do you think the returns will be? Practically all colonies lose money during their first few years. What then?"

"Palo Alto is rich in raw materials, including special plants for which there will be a market even in the old Imperial worlds. I have no concerns there."

Nick looked at his notes for the next question. "You mentioned the Imperial Navy escort, but what about other security? As far as I know, the Bornholm Sector is still unsafe. The enemy fleet crossed it at the end of the war and some places still have isolated ships supporting themselves by piracy. There is speculation that entire mercenary fleets, paid by our enemies, are operating in the sector. Hacker organizations too."

"The Central Imperium is providing military assistance as well as the escort, and an Imperial Navy fleet is active in the region. And as you rightly point out, we also have concerns about hacker attacks. Unfortunately, there have been several cyber-attacks in the Central Imperium in recent months. Last month, a cyber-attack disabled the manufacturing line in the Hobart shipyards. Of course, Henry Corp. does not want to risk anything, so we intend to hire a cyber-security firm to protect our colony expedition."

"Which one?"

Henry smiled. "That remains to be seen. I am currently traveling to inspect the colony fleet anchored at the Henry Corp. stations *Gar K. Nelson* and *Adamcak*. When I have finished my inspection, I will meet the representatives of three organizations aboard the *Nelson*. I'm going to interview the candidates, in fact."

Nick nodded and glanced at his notes again. "Our viewers would also be interested to know how…"

Φ

"Mr. Gramo, may I ask you a favor?" asked Henry, half an hour later, when the interview was over. The station *Gar K. Nelson*, the *Gloriana*'s first stop, was growing closer in the observation port.

"Certainly, Mr. Henry. Of course," said Nick, as he switched off his robot-camera and put it away in its case.

"You're transferring to *Nelson* now, is that right?"

He already knew the answer.

"Yes, Mr. Henry. I have some appointments there, and tomorrow some of the colony expedition volunteers are giving me interviews."

"You are free today?"

"Well…" Nick paused in surprise, but it made no sense to quibble. He wasn't a good traveler and he wanted to rest. But Mr. Henry, although not his direct boss, was a boss.

"Yes, I am," he finally managed to say. "What do you need?"

"It's a somewhat delicate matter. As you already know, the *Gloriana* will only dock for a short while at *Nelson*, then she will continue to Iapetus and the Sol FTL gate, where I must negotiate with some contractors before returning to the station tomorrow. I would be glad if you would interview the three representatives of our cyber-security companies. The ones I will interview, in a different sense, tomorrow. They aren't managers, they're hackers. They call themselves *white hats*, which means they're on the right side of the law." He chuckled. "In any event, I would be glad if you could talk to them and give me your own observations tomorrow. I have studied the expertise of the three companies, and their histories too," he laughed again, "indeed, I even know which of them is the lowest bidder. But I don't want to entrust the fate of a colony expedition simply to price and some history. I would like to know your observations, your opinion."

"But Mr. Henry, I'm not a cyber-security expert..."

"No, but you're good at external perspectives. You know nothing, you're not biased. And as I discovered over the last half-hour, you're good at asking the right questions."

Finally, Nick Gramo nodded.

"Okay then, Mr. Henry. I will certainly interview them and try to give you some impressions tomorrow."

"That's all I ask. Show me your comlink. I'll send you the details of where to meet them."

Nick pulled his PDA comlink from his pocket. Henry tapped his own a few times, then Nick's device beeped to confirm that everything had been received.

"And to motivate you even more, I understand that you asked the management of Horizon News to allow you to travel with the expedition."

"Yes, Mr. Henry. I wanted to fly with them, but Horizon News already has someone there."

"Don't worry about that. If you help me, I think that more journalists will fit onto the expedition ships. I'll see to it."

Now it was Nick's turn to smile.

Φ

As soon as the *Gloriana* docked, Nick Gramo set off through the bowels of the station *Gar K. Nelson* to the hotel that Henry had indicated. He'd also booked a room for him in the same hotel, which was handy.

Nelson wasn't large, certainly not when compared to *Hub Central* at Hub or *Agra* at New Jaipur, but it was a commodious station belonging to Henry Corp. and, along with its sister installation *Adamcak*, it handled busy traffic while over twenty colony ships were being readied for loading. Nick saw them in their docks as the *Gloriana* approached the station, and the Hotel Amaterasu, which he was approaching on the station's internal transport, provided another view over the main docking arm. The hotel was located on the very edge of the station structure.

Before disembarking, Nick had read the information Henry had sent him.

Henry Corp. had three candidates interested in providing the colony expedition's cyber-security.

Bohemur Inc. was a company focused on finding weaknesses using tailor-made cyber-attacks. At least, that is how Nick understood it. He wondered if it was something like the old military wisdom stating that attack is the best form of defense. Their representative on the station was a man called Oliver Forman.

The other two hackers were both women. The first of them, Carol Laut, worked for Tambor Security, a company mainly engaged in protection against enemy hackers. Given the needs of the colony expedition, this made more sense to Nick.

The third company was Pisces Interstellar, represented by Amira Angami. This firm's focus—at least according to Henry's information—was "intel"—quiet undercover work to obtain information whose owners mostly thought it would never see the light of day.

Just from the company descriptions, Nick felt that the most sensible choice would be the protection company, but Henry probably saw the whole matter in rather more complex terms.

All this was still chasing through Nick's head as he stood at the reception desk of the Hotel Amaterasu.

"Hello. I am Nick Gramo. I work for Horizon News. A room has been reserved for me on behalf of Henry Corp., and I also have an appointment here."

The receptionist was a robot, one of the retro metallic ones with a humanoid figure but no human features, of the sort that had recently come back into fashion. "Aaahh, certainly, Mr. Gramo. Welcome to the Hotel Amaterasu. Do you want to go to your room first, or would you rather go straight to your appointment?"

"Well… maybe the appointment."

"Your guests are waiting for you in the Silverstone Lounge. That's on the first mezzanine."

"Thank you."

Φ

The view from the Silverstone Lounge over the station's docking arm and open space was as beautiful as Nick had imagined. But now he concentrated instead on the trio of people sitting in the attractive easy chairs. They all had tablets in their hands and were communicating with them intensively. Two of them were obviously trying to do something. Were they playing a game against each other?

The first to notice Nick was a woman of around forty. Nick guessed that she was either from New Jaipur or from the Indian subcontinent on Earth, judging by her complexion.

"My name is Nick Gramo, journalist from Horizon…"

"Yeah, we've heard of you," said the woman. "I am Amira Angami, Pisces Interstellar. And those two… well, I suppose they're my competitors, if you want to look at it that way. Oli from Bohemur and Carol from Tambor."

The pair of hackers raised their heads from their tablets. Oliver Forman was tall and maybe a few years younger than Amira. He was hollering at his colleague in a deep voice that was strained through his teeth.

Carol Laut was significantly younger than her two competitors. She was the sort that Nick could imagine in a basement somewhere, breaking through enemy firewalls or building her own. She did not come over as an entirely representative sample of the firm. Her Tambor Security was the protection company that Nick suspected would be the first in line for the fleet protection contract.

"I am Nick Gramo from Horizon News," he introduced himself again, to all three of them.

"Will there be a camera?" asked Carol. "Just because I'll need to switch off my scripts since they'll start to beep. They always do when there's an active camera near me."

"I don't think we need a camera just yet," Nick reassured her, and switched on the audio-recorder via his comlink. "I can record the sound."

"Okay, I'll still need to switch them off then."

"And maybe we can just talk."

Oliver Forman laughed and nodded Nick to one of the couches. "You look wiped out."

"A long journey."

"One of those drinks we have there will get you back on your feet."

Nick looked at the table. Along with various sorts of tea and soda, there were two bottles of different energy drinks, Dulles and StellarShock. He allowed himself to doubt their efficacy, but poured some StellarShock into a glass. This one at least tasted better.

"What was that on your tablets? Were you playing something?"

Carol sat down opposite him. "I was showing Oli a new security protocol. He was trying to break through it."

Amira smiled. "Yeah, that's how we spend our time. There isn't much else to do here. Mr. Henry isn't going to arrive until tomorrow."

"But aren't you actually competitors?"

"Well, yes, but we always are, and there's enough work in the Imperium for all of us," said Oliver, and indicated Nick's glass. "We're kind of like the competition between Dulles and StellarShock. Just pour yourself the one you like best."

"That's true," Nick admitted, "but if those two companies had to compete for who was going to supply an entire colonization fleet with an energy drink—and a new colony, at that—they would be fighting like cats in a sack. And I think that the cyber-security for this expedition will be a huge contract for your three companies."

Oliver burst out laughing. "Yeah, that's true, but I've never looked at it like that. The entire Imperium now needs us hackers. There will always be other contracts."

"Unless the war devastates us so much that civilization falls," Amira added, grimacing. "What is it that the Emperor says, again? 'Civilization must continue.' Cyber-security is a bit hard to do in wooden huts in the middle of a baking desert."

Carol raised her head from her tablet. "I would just like to travel with the colonization party. I have a ton of ideas about how to ditch perimeter protection and set up completely new security concepts for the entire expedition. The FTL receivers will always be the weak link. A ship needs to communicate, and I can't very well stuff a network probe into Gertz space, but I have an idea for what to do instead."

"If they let you," said Oliver.

Carol shrugged. "I'll invent it anyway. If not for Henry Corp., then for someone else." She looked back at her tablet and frowned. "Hmm…"

Nick listened to them for a while longer and noted that, of these three hackers, Amira's feet were most firmly on the ground. She was a woman who thought in connections. Carol came over as a child excited by new toys. And Oliver… he was probably somewhere between them. He was mature, but he saw everything through the lens of his work.

"Maybe we could start with the question of how you came to do this job," he said, by way of introduction. None of them showed any interest in answering immediately. Nick understood. Very few people *really* know why they chose their profession. He too had no idea why he had decided to become a journalist.

It was Oliver who took the plunge and answered first. "Well, I always enjoyed playing with computer systems and then some guy on New Sydney offered me a scholarship."

"You're from New Sydney?"

"Yeah, not from the poorest parts, I was…"

"That's funny," said Carol, still staring at her tablet.

Nick swallowed the comment that it is rude to interrupt an interview like that, especially when none of them were politicians. These interjections would have to be edited out of the interview later.

"As I was saying," Oliver continued, a little irritated now. "I lived in Kieran, one of the better developed cities and there…"

"Something's just crossed the station's security tiering!" gasped Carol.

This time, Nick wanted to say something to her, but then her meaning hit him. He didn't know exactly what it meant, but her two competitors did and immediately reached for their own tablets.

"It's penetrated right through to the life-support system!" Carol continued. "This…"

The lights in the room suddenly went out.

Amira screamed. Nick suddenly felt light, crazily light, he wanted to move, but his feet were no longer touching the ground.

"The gravity is off!"

"Absolutely everything is off! All the life-support systems!" shrieked Carol. "I'm trying to do something about it."

"Leave it to me," said Oliver, his fingers furiously dancing across his tablet. Their devices were the only source of light.

Although they weren't; the stars were still glowing through the observation port, but the light was weaker than Nick had expected, and it took him a while to understand why.

The lights had gone out across the station and in the ships docked at it. Absolutely everything had gone dark.

"Not even the ships outside are lit up," he said.

Carol, Oliver and Amira flew across the room, still tapping at their tablets.

"Yeah," said Amira. "The attack must have gotten through the station to all the docked ships."

The light went on again. A pale, yellowish light.

"The backup generator has kicked in," said Oliver, his fingers still pecking. "Now let's see what we can do about the grav."

"The bastard has created active protection around it. It cut me off just like that," said Carol.

"Let's try a different way."

Nick watched the drops of his StellarShock energy drink float through the air.

Oliver suddenly let out a yell of triumph. "And… got it… brace yourselves…"

Nick started to ask what he needed to brace himself for, then unexpectedly fell onto the ground.

He ended up on all fours, the energy drink raining down around him.

"Owwwww!" roared Amira. "My ankle!"

"I assume that the whole station is full of ankles and fractures now," said Oliver, continuing to tap at his tablet. "That was necessary."

Nick pulled himself together and stood up. "We have to get out of here!"

He ran to the door and pressed the button. It wasn't working. Seized by a wave of panic, he pressed it several times more.

"The fucker has blocked the whole system," said Amira. She clambered into an armchair, also still working on her tablet. "All the doors are shut."

"There must be a manual control here," said Nick. He might not be in space much, but he knew that every electronic door must have a manual backup. He'd read the handbooks and even knew where to find it. He wrenched open a panel beside the door and found a small lever there, which he pulled on several times.

Nothing happened.

"Why doesn't it work?!"

"The fucker has burned through the hydraulics too. A short circuit melted the door pistons," said Oliver. "Well, isn't that clever. There's a small energy cell beside the door and it's close enough to blow the door if the circuit shorts."

By now Nick was really beginning to panic. "But there must be some sort of backup here! Some pyro system that will blast through the door."

"On military ships and installations, yes. This is a civilian station, and we're in a *hotel*, they're not going to clown around with something like that here."

Nick thought. This happened directly after Mr. Henry flew past the station. Hmm…

"Could it be a test?" he asked aloud.

Oliver and Amira looked up. Carol went on working.

"What are you talking about?" wondered Amira.

"Well, they want to test you. Which of your companies is the best for Henry Corp. Could this be part of a test?"

"If it's a test, then Henry Corp. will get its ass sued off," said Amira, indicating her foot. "I only got a bad ankle, but there are ten thousand people on the station and artificial gravity normally has several backups. There will be hundreds or thousands of wounded, maybe even a few dead. This really is *not* a test."

"It's not a test," agreed Carol. "It's too elaborate. Henry Corp. doesn't have things like this. They wouldn't need us if they did."

"What do you mean?" asked Oliver.

"It's some polymorph bastard. An AI, in fact. It's spreading across the station's entire system and adapting. It's the most advanced thing I've ever seen."

Oliver worked for a while. "You're right. Damnit, that thing… that thing is sophisticated."

"What do you mean?" asked Nick, interested. "Can you do anything about it?"

"That thing is *intelligent*," Oliver reminded him. "I'm trying to fight it, but it's adapting… Have you ever solved a Rubik's cube?"

"You mean that… thing, yeah. I was never any good at puzzles like that."

"Well, imagine you're trying to solve an intelligent Rubik's cube that's fighting back."

All three hackers worked on in silence. Nick looked around. His almost dreamy gaze fixed itself on the blocked door.

"We're simply going to wait until someone comes to rescue us?" he said.

"We can't. It's up to us to deal with this," said Amira.

"But with all due respect, the station has its own security systems. There are soldiers and security guards here!"

"And they're all trapped. Like us," said Amira. "I've gone through the diagnostics on all systems. That mofo—or virus, or whatever it is—deactivated all the safety fuses in the reactor, which is now slowly overloading."

Nick's education might be in social sciences, but he did not like the term "overloading reactor", not even a little.

"But there's still loads of safeguards, right? And the reactor staff will get it under control?"

Amira's expression gave him no consolation.

"According to this, the entire reactor section is now open to space. On stations of this type, like *Nelson* and *Adamcak*, the reactors are right underneath. They jut out from the station with the control room at the top. Here the control room has lost pressure, and all the human staff are now dead. The AI shit has deactivated the robot staff too."

"Fuck!" exclaimed Carol. She was probably so absorbed in her work that she hadn't realized that.

"What can we do?"

"Give me a moment," said Amira. Nick remembered that her employer focused on intel, or obtaining information. And that the company's name was Pisces. He wondered if they meant the sign of the zodiac, or just any fish.

"Got it!" exclaimed Amira, after a while. "There's an emergency conduit in the corner of this room. For technicians. There are some things they don't show to tourists. And even a polymorph bastard can't take a hole away."

Nick looked around. "Where, exactly?"

"It should be… over there, by that wall. Maybe a meter from the kitchen door."

Nick went over. In the kitchen he could see a heap of scattered crockery, thrown in all directions by the loss of grav. Fortunately, it was made of unbreakable material.

"Roll back the carpet!"

The carpet was fitted to the wall, but as well as his tablet, Oliver had an unusual knife with many different attachments. Together they cut back the carpet and rolled it away to reveal a hatch.

This time, when Nick tried the manual lever, it opened.

"Awesome!" said Oliver. "So, we can go."

"Go? Where, exactly?"

Carol stood up. Amira did too, carefully, with her bad ankle.

"We must get to the reactor and stabilize it."

Her tone was enormously matter-of-fact.

"But… but… I'm only a journalist."

"And we're only crypto-nerds. But unless I am mistaken, we have approximately two hours before the reactor explodes and blows up the entire station and all the docked ships. And of course, kills the at least sixty thousand people aboard. So would you rather stay here?"

Φ

Any space station, any spaceship, is a great deal of empty space divided by bulkheads. The tangle of corridors empty into several larger spaces. , Every station and every ship is interlaced with thousands of kilometers of service corridors for maintenance and technical robots, as well as the classic passageways for staff and visitors. They are the blood vessels in the space station's gigantic body.

And Nick Gramo and his three companions from different hacker firms were now trudging through one of these tunnels.

The corridor's ceilings weren't *that* low. However, they all still had to crouch, particularly Oliver the beanpole. They weren't crawling, it just felt like it to Nick.

The thing that always fascinated me about journalism was the opportunity to meet people from different fields, he thought to himself. *Expand my horizons, discover new information, send it over the airwaves. I never had the investigative journalist's urge to go undercover in gangs or obscure religious groups, roll around in the mud with militias or run naked through the forest with some cult.*

So how did I end up crawling through this duct here?

The hackers didn't complain. Maybe because they were climbing a narrow shaft and at the same time were still constantly typing away on their tablets.

Sometimes they found a closed hatch, which Oliver quickly hacked into and opened. The manual backup didn't always work, but Oliver always successfully broke into the system another way.

But then things began to get complicated.

"The fucker has thoroughly blocked the emergency hatch to the reactor!" said Amira, who was limping slightly on her ankle. She had taken some painkillers before they set off. "It burned everything," she continued. "It knows we're going to the reactor!"

"Could the bastard, virus, AI, whatever you want to call it, could it also release the oxygen from here and kill us?" asked Nick, not sure that he wanted to hear the answer.

Carol leant on a piece of pipeline and tapped at her display. "It could, and it wants to. I'm preventing it from doing so rather effectively, however. My Imat scripts have confused it a little."

Nick really hadn't wanted this answer, but the word Carol used at least diverted his thoughts.

"Imat? That's the Ralgars' symbiotic race?"

"Yeah. Neither they nor the Imats are any freaking good at programming, but my obfuscation is precisely what's confusing the virus. It's like someone going for you with a super-modern computer and you're fighting them off with a program that runs under T-602."

Nick had no idea what T-602 was, but before he could ask, Amira took over.

"That next hatch ahead of us has a vacuum on the other side. It's let out the air from the rest of the way."

"Yeah, I thought as much," said Oliver. He wasn't as calm as he seemed, but all of them were obviously kept rational by their work and the consciousness that they could somehow influence the situation.

Unlike Nick.

"I suggest we go back thirty meters and through that hatch to the left. It goes further from the reactor. We'll see if it expects that."

"There's a hatch there. I'm already working on it," said Oliver. "What's on the other side?"

"We won't get to the reactor, but there are other options which the AI maybe hasn't thought of."

"So, what is there?" wondered Nick.

"A locker room."

Φ

By "locker room", Amira meant a changing room for spacesuits, in front of the airlock. A room that led *out* of the station.

Only they couldn't go any further.

"All the compartments around us have depressurized," said Carol. "I tried to stop it, but it didn't work. I'm attempting to put together a program that would stop the fucker and sandbox it in the entire system, but it's taking a while. And for the time being I'm entirely sure that it won't reduce the pressure here. And it won't open the airlock's internal or external doors either, in case you were worrying."

Nick had been worrying about that very much indeed.

"How long will the reactor still hold out for?" asked Oliver.

"Maybe an hour," said Amira.

Nick looked around. "Is there anything we can do? Anything at all? Maybe the station's security units have managed to do something already."

Amira shook her head. "No, they're even deeper in the shit than we are."

"There's something that might work," said Carol. She was sitting on the floor, her back against the wall beside the spacesuit cupboard. Her tablet pressed against her knees.

"What?"

"I think I know how to stabilize the reactor. I'll set up a bypass of the reactor's main control routines and throw them into a special sandbox. I'll put it on a chip to get it there. If it works, I'll be able to manually simulate the input parameters from the sensor and the reactor will think that everything is going back to normal. But I'll need help with the manual, Amira. I've never controlled a reactor. And meanwhile I still need to distract the bastard before it overturns all the security systems again. The bypass won't destroy the mofo, but at least it will no longer be able to get to the reactor, and we'll need to find a solution for getting it out of the system until then."

"Awesome. Do you want me to create a DDoS distraction for two AIs? Finally, something decent. I will turn every thermometer and sensor in this station against the fucker. And combined with my hand-held conductor, we'll be able to attack it in a thousand places at once," said Oliver. "Even the most advanced AI must get overloaded with time."

It sounded good. "And how will we get the chip to the reactor?" asked Nick.

"That will actually be quite simple," said Amira. "I did my homework before coming onto the station and I have the complete system documentation. That's where I learned that the main part of this reactor is beneath the station. It's possible to get to it from outside. Then all you must do is locate the access port, stick the data chip with Carol's bypass into it and we are in business."

"While I put pressure on the fucker," added Oliver.

Nick felt his insides cramping.

"So, someone has to put on a spacesuit, crawl through the airlock and go—or rather fly—to the reactor to stick the data chip into a slot?"

They all nodded.

"It'll be like putting the chem into a golem," said Amira. "Do you know the legend of the golem?"

"No. But otherwise it sounds fine. If you all think that we can save the station this way, then I believe you. And who's going?"

They all looked at him.

"No!"

Oliver burst out laughing. "I know that you've been writing a news report all this time, but the rest of us have important work. I can't fly through space and type on my tablet at the same time."

"But I'm not right for this! I've never been in EVA!"

"None of us has," said Amira. "But a spacesuit has buffer thrusters, a safety cable with ascenders and there are rails all around the station's external perimeter. You'll just need to go hand over hand to the reactor and stick in the chip. It's quite simple. You can do it!"

Φ

Oliver helped Nick into a spacesuit. He put Carol's data chip into one of the suit's breast pockets. Into the other went his comlink, which he connected to the suit's transmitter, so the hackers could hear him.

Then the airlock's inner door closed behind him.

"Don't be afraid," said Oliver, in his earphones. "I once got a spacesuit flight in space as a present. You know those experience voucher things?"

"Yeah, and how did it go?"

"I upchucked before the training even started. They didn't let me go into space."

Nick wanted to say something caustic, but the outer door was already opening.

Into his head popped the memory of his journey on the *Gloriana,* and how he had thought about not being in space for a long time.

However, he really did not want to go outside like this.

The only sound he could hear was the echo of his own breath in his helmet. He slowly made his way to the edge and left the station's gravitational field.

He weighed nothing again.

He looked around at the infinite horizon and tried not to think that, if the thrusters failed or if he made a mistake when attaching the safety cable's ascender, he would fly off into open space and nobody would ever find him.

He wasn't surprised that EVAs induced agoraphobia in many people.

Fine, Nick, just keep calm, he repeated to himself, as he listened to his own breathing. *Keep calm. It's like the low-grav gym that we had in school. Nothing unusual.*

He had hated low-grav gym class. He tried to ignore this fact.

He maneuvered around the ascender that was designed to secure the cable even if he himself let go. Hand over hand he went, on and on.

Although he theoretically weighed nothing, he was still perspiring so heavily that the spacesuit must contain a puddle of sweat.

The advantage of moving like this was that he was looking at the station, not into open space.

"You're nearly there already," said Amira, in his ear.

"And that means how long?"

"Maybe another ten minutes."

Nick's impression was that he had been here for several infinities, and that several more awaited him.

"Talk to me!" he begged the hackers. They were all engrossed in their work, and nobody was bothering to make conversation.

"The fucker has infected all the station's systems. It's trying to deactivate all the backup life-support too," said Amira.

"My scripts are preventing that," said Carol. "It's already managed to knock some stuff out, but fortunately it will be hours, probably days, before the air on the station becomes unbreathable, even if the air purifier fails."

"I'm following its expansion and trying to find out how far it's penetrated," said Oliver. "And I'm providing the systems it controls with their own cyber-attacks."

This time, Nick was glad even of their catastrophic reports. He didn't have to think about where he was.

"I'm really not right for this!" he complained.

"You're the only one in the group we could do without," said Amira.

"Yeah, not to mention that not many people with your education are employed in the field," added Oliver, and Nick could even see his sneer. "You're lucky that you're not serving fries!"

Nick's breathing in his helmet was replaced by the sound of grinding teeth. Those comments about his education were embarrassing.

Then, suddenly, he was where he was meant to be. He saw the gigantic dome of the reactor located below the station hull. What is "up" in space, and what is "down" is, of course, arbitrary, even though "above" him Nick could see the unending universe, then closer, Phoebe, one of Saturn's moons, above which the stations *Gar K. Nelson* and *Adamcak* were positioned, so from the perspective of Phoebe, at least, he was "below" the station.

"Well, here I am," he said with relief, dragging himself over the reactor. "Do you have any idea where that access port is?"

"Two seconds…" Amira searched on her tablet. Nick kept on hauling himself round, hand over hand. "Yes, there are two. One on each side of service shield V-18."

"Where's that?"

"There's a sort of yellow board there, maybe a meter wide, on either side."

Nick visualized a yellow board, then hauled himself back to the other side. He found exactly what he was looking for. The port looked like any other port.

"I'm here, and I can see it."

"Insert the chip. and take care that the little thing doesn't fly off."

"Thanks. I hadn't realized I should be afraid of that as well."

The vision of letting go the data chip and seeing it fly off into infinity danced before his eyes.

He unfastened his pocket, and with his hand encased in the skin-tight glove, pulled out the chip and inserted it into the slot.

During that time, nothing reverberated in his suit helmet, because he wasn't breathing.

"It's in. Do I need to press anything?"

"No, that's enough," said Oliver, and chuckled. "Excellent. You pulled it off! A lot of us computer nerds never manage that!"

"It's starting up," Carol interrupted him. "Yes… yes… yeah! We did it!" The young woman burst out laughing. "Yeah, the reactor is stabilizing. And my firewalls will stop the AI bastard from crawling in again."

Nick heaved a sigh of relief.

"What about the rest of the station?"

"We're working on it," said Amira, for all of them. "We've already isolated the bastard. Hold on for a moment."

Nick was suddenly flooded with euphoria.

The fear of the infinite universe and everything was gone. They had saved the station. He'd done it. He was a hero.

Another of the things he'd never reckoned on at the faculty. That he would be a hero.

"Nick, are you there?" asked Amira.

"Yes, I'm here. I'm giving myself a moment of rest."

"Nick, we have a problem!"

"A fucking huge problem!" added Oliver.

Nick did not like their tones.

"What is it? Is it the reactor?"

"No… that is… not this one."

"But this station has only one reactor."

"Yeah, true, but that fucking *fucker* has sent a signal to the reactor on *Adamcak* station."

"What? How?"

"I blocked all the bastard's attempts at outgoing communication, both via the FTL receiver and via the normal channels," said Carol. For the first time, there was something like real horror in her voice. "Only the reactor itself has a transmitter, for sending data to other reactors. I don't know why they built it into this model, maybe as an emergency backup in case there were two reactors on one station, so that one of them could immediately cover if the other one outed. It's not normally used, I couldn't have known it was there…!"

"In practice, it means that *Adamcak*'s reactor now has the same problem that ours had!" exclaimed Amira. Carol probably needed to compose herself a little. Nick had no idea whether she was more horrified by her own failure or the vision of the second station exploding.

"What about the rest of *Adamcak*?"

"I sent the procedures for eliminating the shit to their user interface," said Carol again, a little calmer now. "It won't go anywhere, but their reactor is out of operation again and I don't know if the team who take care of the reactor is alive! And if anyone is, then I don't know if they can do anything with it, depending on what we can see from here—Amira's hacked into the station sensors—so their reactor will go to hell."

"What can we do?" asked Nick. Another station, as big as *Nelson*. Also full of people…

"We have one solution," said Amira. "Actually, a simple one."

"Yes?"

"Take out the data chip. It doesn't need to stay in this reactor."

Nick did so. Again, he placed it in his suit's breast pocket. "Fine. Now what?"

"We'll give you a trajectory. Disconnect the ascender, push off from the station using the thrusters and then fly to *Adamcak* and do the same thing on their reactor."

"*What?!*"

"Disconnect the ascender and safety cable, use the thrusters to push off…"

"I fucking understood that, but it's madness. I can't do that!"

"You must, Nick! Otherwise *Adamcak* will explode in two hours' time!"

"But… but… how far away is it?"

"If you push off and burn the thrusters at maximum for at least fifteen minutes, you can fly on inertia to *Adamcak* in an hour and a half."

"And then your suit's computer will slow you down again. The same length of time that you accelerated," Oliver reminded him. "Otherwise, you'll smash into the station!"

"But you must set the trajectory exactly," said Amira. "Or else you'll just miss the station and nobody will ever find you. Your spacesuit wasn't made for this, but, unfortunately, we don't have any other sort!"

Nick no longer had the strength even to curse.

Φ

According to both Amira and Oliver, Nick pushed off correctly. This changed nothing about the fact that he was terrified half to death as he flew through the vast emptiness. The stations were on opposite sides of Phoebe, barely 500 km apart in stationary orbit of the small moon, but he had to approach *Adamcak* on an orbital trajectory.

For the first few minutes of flight, Nick simply screamed in terror until he ran out of breath. Then Oliver warned him that the more he roared, the faster his oxygen would run out.

He was also glad that the suit had connections and tubing everywhere, because he had lost control of his bladder.

Then he simply flew and flew. The hackers sometimes called him with new information. Carol and Oliver already had ready a system for removing the whole virus from *Nelson*. After an hour they reported that *Nelson* was practically clean, and Carol was extending her antivirus network and firewalls.

By then Nick was already quite close to *Adamcak*. The suit computer automatically turned him around and began to slow him down using the reaction thrusters.

According to the hackers, he should have enough fuel left to maneuver around the station and get to the reactor.

"Nick, are you there?" said Amira's voice in his earphones.

"Yes, I haven't gone anywhere. I'm still decelerating and…"

"Where is your PDA comlink?"

"What? In the other breast pocket of my suit. The one that doesn't have your chip in it. I'm talking to you through it!"

"Destroy it. Immediately."

"What?"

"Don't argue! The bastard came from your comlink! It activated as soon as you switched it to audio in the lounge with us! We only just figured that out now!"

"But… but… how… one second!"

Nick remembered. Mr. Henry had uploaded data about the three cyber-security firms and instructions on where he was to meet their representatives. He'd uploaded it from his comlink onto Nick's.

"That came from Henry!"

"Henry really won't be a saboteur," said Oliver.

"I know he isn't, but somebody must have hacked his comlink and then it infected mine. Nobody even knew that I was flying. Where is Henry now?"

"Still aboard the *Gloriana* on the way to Iapetus."

"Send him a message! Tell him that he must destroy his comlink as well! Now!"

"Yeah, fine, we will, the station's communication systems are starting up," said Amira. "But you destroy yours right now too."

"But then you won't be able to talk to me. If the communications are only starting up now, the spacesuit is normally connected to them…"

"So, you'll cope on your own. Just do the same thing you did on *Nelson*! But you must destroy that comlink. If you get too close to the station with it, it could hack its entire system."

"And how will they find me afterwards?"

"The spacesuit's transmitter and emergency beacon will work and maybe they'll notice someone flying round their reactor!"

The helmet filled with Nick's sigh. "Well, only if they're observant enough there!"

He pulled his PDA comlink from his pocket. It was a new Arcane 9.1 and he had bought it only three months ago. It was tough and sturdy.

Fortunately, the standard equipment in the spacesuit's pockets included enough tools to make destroying the comlink quite easy.

Φ

He decelerated successfully, but this did not stop him from slamming into the hull. Without, however, killing himself, or breaking anything.

He grunted, and with accelerated breath desperately felt around him before managing to grasp hold of a rail. He pulled out the safety cable and ascender and rapidly began to haul himself, hand over hand, over *Adamcak*'s hull.

Only now did he realize how horribly exhausted he was.

And just this morning he had thought that a long flight on a luxury yacht would be tiring!

His muscles ached. What was worse, they were starting to give out on him. Pain can sometimes be ignored, but total exhaustion cannot.

On several occasions, he only grasped the rail on the second attempt. In at least half a dozen instances, he would have floated off into space if he hadn't had the cable and ascender.

In time, he finally reached the reactor dome. The yellow panel on it was the same.

He no longer had the strength to be afraid of letting go of the chip. He was at the port when he realized that his fatigued muscles could cause a tragedy.

Then the chip was in place.

Suddenly it was all over. Maybe it was all over.

He tried the spacesuit's internal transmitter.

"Calling *Adamcak* station, do you hear me? *Adamcak*, Nick Gramo here, journalist… well, no matter. I'm in spacesuit number NKM-4518"—he read the number from his helmet's HUD. "I'm circling round *Adamcak*, but I flew over from *Nelson*."

"*Adamcak* space traffic control here," said a voice after a while. A male voice sounding like someone who had just woken up at their own funeral. "Mate, you have no idea what just happened to us on the station! We just started a mass evacuation, the reactor was in the shit, communications too…"

"Yeah, I know, believe me."

There was a short silence. "Our sensors are picking you up at the reactor. Did you fire it up?"

"Well…. no. Three hackers on *Nelson* helped me remotely."

"Stay where you are. We're sending someone for you."

"Thanks. I don't think I have the energy to go anywhere now."

It is common knowledge that the muscles hurt most on the second day after great exertion. Nick Gramo was able to confirm this. When they'd rescued him on *Adamcak*, massive commotion was reigning everywhere. The stations were jointly coordinating the solution for this unprecedented cyber-attack. The *Gloriana* had gotten involved too. Henry was still sailing on her and had destroyed his comlink, following Amira Angami's instructions.

Carol and Oliver had eliminated the last traces of the hostile AI virus from *Nelson* and, to be on the safe side, they had sent the same antivirus systems to *Adamcak* too. Now they were reviewing everything.

Twenty-two people had died aboard *Adamcak*, most of them reactor staff and a few people who had broken their necks when the gravity was restored. More than one hundred twenty were wounded, mostly fractures, dislocations and the like.

Nick was lucky that only his muscles ached. But for all that, they ached terribly, and he was immensely grateful when Mr. Henry invited him to sit down, again in the *Gloriana*'s observation lounge, after the *Gloriana* had finally docked at *Gar K. Nelson*.

"My comlink was responsible for everything!" said Henry baldly, a combination of rage and chagrin in his voice. "It must have gotten into it when I was in an unsecured network… yes. Every Tuesday I go to the same restaurant for lunch and of course I check my messages and the datanet when I'm there. And last time, when the waiter brought my food, I remember he spilled the drink. He apologized over and over, but I realize now that he also touched my comlink while all that was going on. He must have hacked it with something. Goddamn it!"

"I think you have bigger problems with cyber-security than you thought," Nick couldn't refrain from saying.

"Trust me, I'm taking this very seriously indeed."

Nick was more than willing to believe him. He knew that Mr. Henry hadn't wanted this. But he also knew that this wouldn't help the dead. Not to mention the fact that, because of Henry, he had had to fly through space like some difficult-to-control lump of rock.

"Do we know who did it?" he asked instead. "Who was responsible for the cyber-attack?"

"There are a bunch of possibilities," said Henry. "What's left of our enemies from the New Protectorate, some internal cabal in the Imperium that does not want those colonies, even a competitor. Bunch of possibilities."

"Something tells me that we're going to need extremely good cyber-security for this entire expedition."

"Yes, Mr. Gramo. And that is the reason why I invited you here. The representatives of the three companies on the shortlist. How did they seem to you? Amira Angami, Oliver Forman and Carol Laut?"

"Without any one of them both stations would have been destroyed and your colony expedition would be in ruins," said Nick baldly. "I'm planning to state this in my report too. My editor-in-chief has promised me the main slot on this evening's broadcast."

"That's good, and yes, all three of them acted commendably. I hear that they will all receive the highest civilian honor, maybe even from Emperor Daniel himself. But that does not solve my problem. I would still like to hear your recommendation. Which company should I hire? What is your opinion, Mr. Gramo? Will it be Tambor Security, Bohemur

Inc. or Pisces Interstellar?"

"Do you really want to hear my honest opinion?"

"Yes. And not just because I promised to get you onto the colony expedition. I want your opinion because you and those three representatives saved not just one but two space stations. What do you recommend?"

"My recommendation is simple. Hire them all."

"All three companies?"

"Yes. Those three hackers complemented each other excellently and their firms will certainly do the same."

Doug Henry smiled. "And don't you think that will be very expensive?"

"I think that Henry Corp.'s travel budget will barely notice it. And it will be cheaper than a new colony fleet!"

"You're absolutely right, there, Mr. Gramo. Absolutely right."

VI

"So that was the work of the New Protectorate's agents and allies in the Bornholm Sector?" Varviso asked, to be sure.

"Yes, that's now been confirmed by our intelligence services," said Daniel. "And it wasn't an isolated case. There are many problems across the Imperium. Not just in the Bornholm Sector."

"And similar incidents resulted in Empress Hila's journey to that sector?"

Hila nodded. She still didn't want to talk about it, but she knew that, today, she'd have to. "Yes, yes. That was a kind of tour. To boost morale."

"I understand. You are in fact more popular than the Emperor. Forgive me, sire."

"Don't worry about it," Daniel said.

"You've simply become an icon, ma'am."

"I know, even though the events of the Bornholm Sector may have strained that somewhat."

"You think so?"

Hila frowned. "Well, it's why you're here. If the situation in Bornholm had been… less controversial, you wouldn't have been sent to us. And our protocol expert emphatically did not recommend that we receive you."

"I am honored that you did, but I'm only the ordinary chief editor of a local rag," said Varviso, with false modesty, probably for form.

Hila forced herself to smile. Varviso was strange, but he got what he was after. And he was not a tabloid sensation- or controversy-hunter.

Maybe he liked to rake things over and annoyed a lot of people in doing so, but in his trade, this was practically a matter of course.

I annoyed loads of people during my career. And I dug up loads of shit that they'd have wanted to remain hidden.

"Fine. I think that I should finally talk about the main reason you're here, don't you think?" she asked rhetorically.

Varviso took a mouthful of the coffee that Sean had brought him while they talked.

"If you would be so kind, ma'am."

His electronic recorder was running.

Hila nodded.

THE TRIBUNAL
PART 1

One might think that even a proud mother would, in time, get bored of watching a video of her child on repeat, but Hila couldn't help herself.

The display in her cabin was again showing ten-month-old Elda in motion, crawling across the carpet and finally, with the resolve of an Omega Commando, attempting to climb up onto the couch, with her little hands tenaciously grasping the upholstery.

The attempt was unsuccessful, and little Elda ultimately plopped down onto her bottom. She didn't burst into tears. The sounds she was making indicated that she was hugely enjoying the whole process. She tried it a few more times. The third time she dropped down onto her behind, Jazz the rabbit hopped up to her, assessed the situation with a suspicious eye and then hurriedly hopped away as Elda began to reach out for him.

The little crown princess found a new target and set out in a new direction, toward the play mat, where she had a set of blocks that changed color when she tapped on them. She had a lot of more sophisticated toys that she had received from excited wellwishers when she was born, but the blocks were currently her favorite. Elda threw herself at them, ignoring her daddy's voice, which was off-camera and telling her to wave at mommy.

Hila was interrupted by the buzzer. She paused the video.

"Come in!"

"Hila, are you watching that video of Elda again?"

In came Devika Pradhan, officially a member of the Imperial Guard and commander of Hila's personal bodyguard contingent. However, any stickler for Imperial protocol would probably be driven crazy by how informally these two women spoke to each other.

But Hila had always been closer to ordinary soldiers than to sticklers for protocol.

"It would be more accurate to say that I'm still watching that video. You liked it too, remember?!"

Pradhan grinned. "I know, it's cute. I don't know whether you forced me to watch it four times, or five, but so what, the main thing is that the oxytocin is flowing. And Elda's such a clever little girl! Are you looking forward to having more?"

Hila waved her hand. She hadn't thought much about it so far, but she and Daniel knew that they wanted more than one child, and not just because of their dynastic responsibilities. Over the last few millennia, many books had been written about the ideal gap between children, and none of them agreed on anything. At a time when people could live to be one hundred fifty, and they could have children at an advanced age using an artificial uterus, they frequently weren't in any hurry. There was an age gap of fifteen years between Daniel and his sister Radana.

Hila and Daniel didn't want to wait that long, particularly not in this uncertain age, and they had agreed to discuss it when Hila returned home from her current journey.

Pradhan smiled when Hila didn't answer. "Well, in any case, I came to tell you that we're approaching our destination. We'll arrive in the Enugu System in half an hour."

"Good," said Hila, laughing. "So, I'll have time to watch this again, right?"

Φ

Hila had already been traveling for over three weeks now. She had set out from Hub, the Central Imperium's main planet, through the FTL gate into the Bornholm Sector, where she had first visited the eponymous planet. Her "tour" continued to Arnhem, New Canaan and Kanchanpur, and she was now heading for Enugu, where there would be more handshaking, bows and speeches. One of the things she had to do there was ceremonially open a new school and some accommodation for war orphans. Then her Imperial yacht would continue to Ridiger, the last stop on her journey.

She still couldn't entirely get used to the fact that she—*she*, Hila Eban—could fill a town square. That people would fly in from all over the planet to see her. She could try to delude herself that they were interested in her title, in seeing the Empress—or rather the Empress Consort—but no, they were interested in her. The war was still all too vivid in their memories, and Hila's deeds had become legendary, as had her relationship with Emperor Daniel.

That was partly the reason for her journey today. The Imperial couple had traveled frequently since the war ended. But traveling together wasn't always possible, so on this occasion Hila was heading for the Bornholm Sector on her own, while Daniel—and ten-month-old Elda—remained at home in the Imperial palace on Hub.

If Hila disregarded little girl waving goodbye—which was never entirely possible—she knew that she would rather be on this journey than at home in the palace in the new capital city of Belfeld. Daniel was constantly dealing with a thousand and one tiny problems, along with his prime minister and members of both chambers of the Imperial Parliament. Hila understood this, and had eventually accepted her role as Empress, just as in the past she had accepted the role of commando or journalist. Years ago, she had dealt with what was expected of her, but there was a world of difference between *deal with* and *be enthusiastic about*. She still felt that high politics was not for her, and however much she had once hated politicians who only gave speeches and cut ribbons, she'd enjoyed the contact with people. And however much it surprised her, the people loved their Hila. They might consider her husband a hero and the savior of the Imperium, but they considered her *one of them*. Members of the armed forces saw it in the same way. One of them. Hila had won the hearts of ordinary astronauts, marines and soldiers simply by refusing an officer rank.

Traditionally, when someone who had previously served in the armed forces married into the Imperial family, they automatically received the title of either High Admiral or Field Marshal. Hila had refused it, saying that she had left the Omega Commandos as a sergeant, and a sergeant she would remain. An enlisted soldier.

The head of protocol had protested, but even he hadn't argued much. Finally, he came up with a compromise.

And Hila had become a Sergeant Major of the Imperium. If she insisted on remaining a member of the enlisted, she would at least hold the highest non-commissioned rank.

It seemed like ridiculous theatricals to her, but Daniel had explained that even ridiculous theatricals need to be played. He hadn't failed to add that the people who filled the town squares would take it seriously, and she should too.

It didn't bother Hila. She felt close to soldiers. She was already looking forward to visiting the astronauts, marines and soldiers in the Fifth Fleet at the end of her journey.

She banished her thoughts and looked around the cockpit.

At the helm sat Hila's personal pilot, Martin Mureau. Hila could still pilot the ship herself, in case of emergency—she'd learned as an Omega—but this wasn't something she would insist on.

"Dropping to the second Gertz level in five, four, three, two, one," Mureau said, and the Imperial yacht *Hawk* switched its reactionless drive to a speed slower than light.

They continued across the star system toward the planet Enugu, one of the most densely populated worlds in the Central Imperium.

Hila was sitting in the co-pilot's seat, with Pradhan at the navigator station behind her. Maybe it wasn't the most appropriate place for the Empress, but that was another thing the head of protocol could tear his hair out about; Hila certainly wasn't going to. What's more, the *Hawk* wasn't a typical Imperial yacht. It was a combat transporter of the same class that the Omega Commandos had used. Hila had received this ship as a gift from an ally and had decided to use her as a yacht too. Nobody could object that the *Hawk* was insufficiently armed. These toys were built to be unobtrusive, but they were armed like a small frigate.

"Arriving in Enugu's orbit in eight minutes," said Mureau. "And… ma'am… there are warships in orbit."

"Imperial IFF," Pradhan added.

Hila rapidly pressed a few buttons at her own station and soon saw what she needed to on the display.

It was true: several of the Fifth Fleet's warships were right there in orbit.

Since the end of the war, there had been a lot of unrest in the Bornholm Sector. A lot of saboteurs were still operating here, after breaking away from the New Protectorate's fleet as it withdrew. Piracy was also flourishing. The Fifth Fleet was positioned at Ridiger, where it was practically at the center of the threatened area. Ridiger itself was barely habitable and had only a small population, but the presence of the fleet had suddenly put it on the map.

And there was something else that Hila knew. The Fifth Fleet would need to double its number of ships to guard its area of operations. Admiral Alender had already informed the Admiralty—and the Emperor, personally—of this, several times, and his most recent reports had been frustrated and barely courteous. Alender was proud of the fact that he had started as a rank-and-file astronaut, and he had sharp, peppery expressions at his fingertips.

A month ago, the Admiralty had decided to send Alender two brand-new *Nagaland*-class battleships, the first two models in the entire Imperium, which had increased the number of battleships in the fleet to twenty. But everyone knew that this was an empty gesture. The Fifth Fleet didn't need two new battleships; it needed at least sixteen new cruisers and other light vessels to defend the sector.

And therein lay the problem. The Central Imperium currently *did not have* many light vessels, just as it didn't have many battleships. The shipyards were running at full speed, but the post-war economy still prevailed, industry was only beginning to get going properly again, and those warships that the Imperium still had were needed across the entire Imperium, to put out hundreds of other small fires.

Alender understood this, but he didn't have to like it, and he couldn't stop his frustration from showing.

A personal visit from Empress Hila would at least boost morale. Everyone in the Fifth Fleet, from Alender to the lowest astronaut, knew that Hila was no dolled-up fine lady who would rattle off a few phrases, then fly back home. She would be interested in what they told her. They all knew about her military background, her career in journalism, and primarily her reputation as the Emperor's right hand, who had fought— physically—at his side, when the survival of civilization was literally at stake. They were looking forward to meeting her.

And now it seemed that they would meet her sooner than expected. Four battleships and ten cruisers were currently orbiting Enugu, according to their IFFs. That was a quarter of the Fifth Fleet.

"Signal them," said Hila, although she knew that Mureau had already done this some time ago. Meanwhile, she watched the display and saw the IFF transponders.

She saw that the three battleships were the modern *Hubei*-class and one, which was ten percent larger, was the most modern, most powerful *Nagaland*-class.

The transponder said it was the *Quezon*.

Mureau was sending a verbal signal too. "To the forces of the Imperial Navy in the Enugu System, this is Imperial Two, I repeat, Imperial Two. Designation INAV *Hawk*, LAV-1816. We are flying into the star system on arrival vector seven six at two four six."

In the Central Imperium's radio communications, Imperial Two was the designation for any ship on which the monarch's spouse was traveling.

"Incoming transmission," said Mureau. He turned on the speaker.

"This is INS *Quezon* for Imperial Two. Please clear the flight area as soon as possible and land on the planet in accordance with your flight plan."

Hila bent toward the microphone.

"Hila Eban here. What's going on in the star system?"

"The *Quezon* here. We cannot talk to civilians about… uh…Your Majesty?"

Yes, she should probably have announced herself as the Empress. She could imagine the expression on the wretched dispatcher's face as he worked out who she was.

"I think that my security clearance is higher than yours, astronaut," said Hila, a small smile playing around the corners of her mouth.

The dispatcher was silent for a moment, then replaced by a different voice. She imagined that he'd called his officer for assistance.

"Your Majesty, welcome to the star system. Unfortunately, we really must ask you to land in accordance with your flight plan."

"Is there a threat?" asked Pradhan, behind Hila. She was responsible for Hila's safety.

"No threat. Task Force 52 will soon set out and civilian traffic is being re-routed."

This was probably normal procedure. The orbit was not busy, so nobody needed to get out of anyone's way.

Hila understood that needing to explain something to the Empress was the last thing they wanted. If this task force was setting off for combat action, they probably all had enough work already.

But if something was brewing here, she should know about it.

And what was more: she *wanted* to know about it.

She looked at the display. The transponders and signals from the entire task force betrayed not just the names of the individual ships but also told her that the *Quezon* was the task force's flagship and that it had the Fifth Fleet's deputy commander, Vice Admiral Vu, on board. This new battleship and her sister ship had joined the Fifth Fleet as planned, barely a week ago, so Vu had had to move to her immediately and come straight here.

"Please connect me to Admiral Vu."

"Who is Vu?" asked Pradhan.

"The deputy commander of the Fifth Fleet."

The other end was briefly quiet, then someone said: "Just a moment."

It took almost a minute. Finally, the face of an approximately sixty-year-old officer with Asian features appeared on the screen. He looked like he was dealing with several things at once.

"This is Vice Admiral Tom Vu. Your Majesty, I heard that you were arriving on Enugu, but I didn't know exactly when. I apologize, but we're preparing for a combat mission."

"I already figured that out. Are you leaving immediately?"

"Within a few hours. Two battleships are on their way to join us."

"Excellent. That gives you enough time to brief me on the situation."

Vu hesitated. "Your Majesty?"

"I'll come aboard."

"Hila," said Pradhan, behind her, but her charge just shrugged.

"The speeches can wait."

Φ

The *Hawk* landed aboard the *Quezon*. She was the *Nagaland*'s sister ship, one of only two currently in the Navy. Construction work on these battleships had been scheduled to start just before the war against the New Protectorate broke out. As soon as it was over, Daniel and the Admiralty had accelerated production and the first two ships, the *Nagaland* and the *Quezon*, had been sent here. The battleships had the most advanced equipment for combat management and the greatest amounts of space for an admiral and their staff, so it was no wonder that Admiral Alender and Vice Admiral Vu had each taken one of these ships as their flagship.

A guard of honor was waiting in the hangar, lines of astronauts and marines, and the speaker announced her:

"Her Imperial Majesty Hila Eban, Empress Consort of the Central Imperium, Sergeant Major of the Imperium."

The description was bizarre, but accurate.

At the head of the crowd beside the *Hawk*'s ramp, Vice Admiral Vu was waiting.

"Welcome aboard, Your Majesty."

"Thank you, Admiral. I understand that you weren't expecting me, but as you are setting out on a mission, I felt that I should make an appearance on board."

Vu undoubtedly had his own opinion here, but to his credit, he didn't argue. For Hila, it was enough to look at the faces of the astronauts in their lines—she could see they were delighted that she was here with them.

Like a kind of golden goose.

The Admiral had undoubtedly realized this too. He was experienced and knew that morale was worth millions in such situations.

"Please, come with me, Your Majesty."

They walked through the bowels of the *Quezon*. The ship still had the new-car smell. The space tests had been completed only a few weeks ago. Vu must have brought his flag aboard only a few days before being forced to head here from Ridiger.

They reached the *Quezon*'s conference room, where the admiral nodded to indicate she should sit down. Devika Pradhan stood behind Hila, assessing the other officers with the careful eye of an experienced bodyguard. It was nothing against them, just auto-pilot.

In addition to the admiral, members of his staff also joined them. Hila was surprised that this included the senior warrant officer designated head of on-board security.

"We received a report about the movements of one of the New Protectorate's super-battleships," said Vu. "I don't know how familiar you are with the New Protectorate's tactics here in the sector…"

"I know that the New Protectorate left a lot of saboteurs as it was withdrawing through the Bornholm Sector, and a few heavy ships to sow chaos here. To attack our convoys, colonies and so on. I guess they left a few of their super-battleships, the ones they call dreadnoughts."

"Correct, Your Majesty. Those ships are three times bigger and stronger than our battleships, including the newest *Nagaland*-classes. The New Protectorate's fleet left three—the *Subjugator*, the *Siege*

Breaker and the *Harrowing*. They each fly paired with a light battleship, or monitor, as they call them. They can get the better of any Imperial ship and by the time the Fifth Fleet can get enough battleships together to destroy one, it's too late. And as you probably also know, we can't monitor them closely enough here."

Hila nodded. Normally it was possible to monitor a ship moving through space using the FTL sensors that worked on a similar principle to the FTL Gertz drive, but while it was withdrawing, the New Protectorate had destroyed many sensor platforms across the sector, making continuous monitoring impossible.

The admiral went on: "Six months ago, we managed to destroy one, but not before it had destroyed two of our battleships and sent the third to the docks, where she still is. What's more, we found them and drove them into a corner largely due to chance and luck. That was the *Harrowing*. The remaining two kept on getting away from us. Until now."

"You somehow found the location of one of the ships?" Hila asked.

Vu smiled. "Something much better. We know where she'll be in four days' time. The Imperial Investigator in Arnhem has uncovered a network of traitors supporting the New Protectorate. From them, she learned that those two ships will arrive in the Kaffer System in four days' time, where they will re-fuel and take on supplies on the *Kaffer Minor* station."

This time, Hila couldn't look on the ship's computer, but she searched her memory instead.

"The refueling stations in the Kaffer System are owned by a firm of Enners, right?"

"Exactly. There are eight gas giants in the Kaffer System. Most of the hydrogen for fusion reactors is extracted in inhabited star systems, but here someone spotted the financial potential and put in a claim. By Imperial standards, it's a relatively small company, and it belongs to an Enhans called Francis Ebell. And according to the Imperial Investigator, precisely this individual is in it up to his ears. During the war he was associated with various groups declaring the natural superiority of Enhans."

Hila nodded inadvertently. Back when the Protectors had ruled humanity, they had created their own caste of superhumans, the Enhans. The Enhans had a stronger metabolism, a higher average intelligence, greater resistance, stronger bones and muscles… They were originally intended to rule all subsidiary colonies. In time, their status had changed, and they had lost their privileged position. When, over a century ago, the Protectors had practically died out and Emperor Olaf had transformed the Commercial Empire into the Central Imperium, he consolidated the government and significantly limited Enhans powers.

Enhans still had their own chamber of parliament, named the House of Families. At the same time, a lower chamber was created, and the constitution was amended to state that the prime minister could not be an Enhans. Enhans powers varied from world to world. On some, they had fallen victim to public lynching, but on others, such as Haveloc, their rule was still almost absolute.

Despite this, many of them felt that they were losing the privileges they were entitled to. Some of them had thrown in their lot with the New Protectorate, in the hope their original power would be restored.

Hila felt the anger bubble up inside her as she remembered the millions—billions—of dead on the consciences of Enhans such as Arian Lardon, or his brother Conan, Maya Kutevska and even Daniel's own uncle, Haskel Hankerson. She had seen atrocities while in the Omega Commandos secretly committed by other Enhans families, such as House Hartveit or House Maina.

Daniel Hankerson, Hila's husband, was an Enhans. And because the Enhans gene was dominant, Hila and Daniel's daughter Elda was also an Enhans. Many Enhans were highly promiscuous, deliberately spreading their genes wherever they went. Maya Kutevska, who had caused such huge damage on Earth at the end of the war, was one of these illegitimate Enhans. Many great Houses used their illegitimate children as reliable agents or assassins. Before the war, Enhans had even had their own military unit.

Francis Ebell was another such illegitimate child, connected with powerful Houses, and wanting to exploit that.

And when the House he was related to fell in the war, he started to help the New Protectorate directly, not just via his patrons.

He wasn't just an opportunist. He was one of the maniacs who believed in the natural superiority of his own genes.

Some of them even called themselves *homo superiori.*

Vu monitored his Empress's expression. "Yes, I can see from your body language that we are of the same opinion. If you'll forgive the presumption, Your Majesty."

"That's fine. You are correct. I assume that this information has been verified?"

"As well as we possibly can," said Vu. "I don't know if you know who the Imperial Investigator Annika Sparbo is?"

This time Hila brightened up. "Of course I do!"

Sparbo was legendary. She was a woman with almost four decades of experience in the role of Investigator. Hila had first met her, indirectly, when she was still with the Omegas and Sparbo was working for Imperial Interpol. After the war with the New Protectorate, she had been entrusted with working in an entirely new organization.

It wasn't an organization. Elias Rosenthal, the new Minister of the Interior in Prime Minister Gilbert's government, came up with the idea of selecting special investigators who would be responsible only to the government and the supreme court, and even that in a very indirect manner.

The New Protectorate had very nearly destroyed the Central Imperium in many ways, one of them being that their sympathizers— mostly various Enhans—had crawled into all corners of state administration, large corporations and the armed forces. Many of those traitors were still in office and many of them were also in control of police bodies too. Therefore, Minister Rosenthal set up the special investigators, who functioned outside well-established structures, spoke with the authority of the whole Imperium—or rather, as Rosenthal wrote in his memorandum—with the authority of *civilization*. The Central Imperium's motto was, in fact, civilization must continue.

The government selected these investigators with the greatest of care, and there were only sixteen across the entire Imperium.

Annika Sparbo was the most successful. The seasoned Investigator had uncovered and smoked out an entire network of New Protectorate supporters belonging to the Enhans House Lardon on Haveloc in the first few months after the war. She had then become something of a legend. She didn't live anywhere, she had no home, she traveled from planet to planet and exposed traitors to the Imperium. Her hitherto greatest catches had been two senior managers in big corporations, three generals, two admirals, the rulers of three planets, and even one member of Prime Minister Laura Gilbert's cabinet.

Hila was reassured by her involvement in all this and was immediately inclined to grant credence to the information available to the Fifth Fleet.

"Sparbo was on Arnhem," Vu went on. "While she was there investigating the financing of some anti-imperial politician, she came across an entire network of conspirators. And gradually she established a connection to Francis Ebell and the New Protectorate. She sent the information directly to the Fifth Fleet and Admiral Alender ordered us here immediately." He threw up his hands. "I flew from Ridiger straight away, with four ships. Two more are flying in from Nuuk. Two days' flying will take us to near Kaffer."

Hila nodded. "And what is the plan? I assume that six battleships and ten cruisers are enough against a dreadnought and a monitor." She didn't add that she knew there would be losses, that there are always losses. "But I would be more afraid of the enemy attempting to avoid battle."

"There is always that risk, and we will try to pursue the enemy, if we can," said Vu. "In the meantime, we plan on waiting until the super-battleship—dreadnought—docks at the station. We're counting on their operational approach being that the monitor will drop anchor first, and the dreadnought will patrol. Then they'll switch."

"And what if they don't dock?" asked Hila, attempting to play devil's advocate. Maybe she was automatically and subconsciously closer to the enlisted than the officers, but Vu was not stupid and had had a lot more time to think everything through.

"They'll dock there. At least, Investigator Sparbo's information says they will. It's interesting. They seem to be doing something else with that hydrogen. Or with the other substances mined there. Sparbo says they've already moored there several times. It's strange when we consider that the New Protectorate's fleet spent several years flying here and they have lots of supplies aboard their super-battleships. Not to mention the fact that the ship can fill up with hydrogen from anywhere in deep space. But evidently the station is worth them mooring at."

"Won't they see us arrive? The sensor network in the sector may be damaged, but each ship has some FTL sensors."

Hila didn't realize that she had said *us* and not *you*. Behind her, Pradhan uttered a disapproving sound in the way only a professional bodyguard can.

Vu, however, paid no attention to Pradhan, but answered Hila's question: "We're doing the same thing that the New Protectorate did to us during the war. We attach ourselves to freighters flying into the star system to mask our Gertz signature. And we have several freighters for this purpose. The second step will be boarding the station at the time an enemy ship is docking there. We'll use one of the freight ships that shuttles between the main station *Keffer Major* and the smaller station *Keffer Minor*. The classic Trojan horse tactic." He shrugged. "Honestly, we didn't want to do that, but Admiral Alender insisted that we must obtain as much information from the station's computers as we can and also secure some prisoners."

Hila was not happy about this. She understood the need for

intelligence, but the marines they would send there would be incredibly vulnerable. The New Protectorate could simply decide to destroy the station.

Admiral Alender was right. But he saw the situation like pieces on a chessboard.

His pawns would not be delighted.

"How many marines will you send there?"

A moment of silence. Someone cleared their throat.

Vu hesitated but finally answered. "Well, that's the problem. We have very few marines in the fleet. There's only a handful of them aboard the *Quezon*. The *Provence* and the *Baluchistan* don't have any aboard at all. Undoubtedly you know that the Fifth Fleet needs supplies, staff and new ships. Half a dozen of our cruisers are overdue for an overhaul. And they should have been sent to the docks for repairs long ago, but weren't, because we don't have anything to replace them with. And when we were sent here, there weren't many soldiers or marines in the whole Imperium, and those we did have had to be sent to secure some key stations and bases. So, for this mission, our marine assault team will be reinforced by the ship's police. They'll be led by Senior Warrant Officer Tarsen here, the *Quezon*'s head of security."

A tall blond man nodded at Hila. So that's why the warrant officer was here. The ship's security officer was an important role but was more like a cop than a soldier.

That's why Vu did not look thrilled.

"So that's our plan, Your Majesty. I think we have a good chance of intercepting the enemy. As I'm sure you can imagine. You were in a lot of battles during the war."

"I can, and I can imagine all the variables that your boarders will have to face," she said, smiling at Tarsen. Her head was full of too many botched Omega operations. "Only too well."

"So, you understand us."

"I do."

Vu observed her for a moment. There was a question in his eyes. Or maybe a suspicion. Maybe he had noticed that Hila had said *us* and not *you*. He wanted to ask, but he was searching for the words.

Hila felt Devika Pradhan's eyes burning holes in the back of her neck. Her bodyguard knew her well. Maybe too well. Vu didn't know her, but he did know her reputation.

He suspected.

"I hope you still have some room on your flagship, Admiral," she said, finally, and Pradhan didn't even attempt to suppress her sigh. "I'm coming with you. I think it will only help the morale of your people. Not to mention the fact that I'm a former commando. I'm sure I can advise your people somehow."

Tarsen grinned. Vu sighed, much less obviously than Pradhan.

"Fine, Your Majesty. But I am in charge of this mission. Even if I must go to the Emperor about it."

"Don't worry. I'm not going to argue. I'm more of an observer."

"Yes. And the second thing: you will stay here on the ship. You're already in danger as it is, but you will *not* join the boarders."

Hila opened her mouth, but despite all protocol, it was her bodyguard who spoke.

"Don't worry, Admiral. Her Majesty is *very aware* that she won't be joining the landing force for the station."

There were some battles that even Hila couldn't win.

PART 2

Sooner or later, wars always stop being called wars and terms such as *cleansing actions* are used instead.

This was also true of the war in the Central Imperium. Even though nobody had formally declared war, or declared peace, the conflict officially started when the New Protectorate's fleet attacked the planet Paskin and ended at the Battle of Hub not quite two years later.

Everything that came afterwards was merely a cleansing action.

Although it makes absolutely no difference whether the enemy fire tearing you to pieces is part of a cleansing action or a war; Hila had found this out long ago.

She could easily imagine what the landing force was currently going through on the station *Kaffer Minor*, while she herself sat safely in the *Quezon*'s auxiliary tactical center, listening to the unfiltered, uncensored voices of the marines and security officers in the front line.

During the journey of several days on the *Quezon*, Hila had spent a lot of time with Warrant Officer Tarsen and his security team. She was attempting to train them, to hand on her knowledge. Most of them had never seen combat action, which was why they had marines on board. Even though the fleet didn't have enough of them right now.

Fortunately, Hila had training experience herself. As an Omega, she had trained guerrillas on several occasions, on worlds dominated by Enhans that the Emperor wished to dispose of.

So maybe the members of the ship's police had learned something.

Fortunately, the landing force was led by marine units from the battleships *Burgundy* and *Haryana*, which had full complements. The *Quezon*'s unit, with units from other ships, formed the backup.

Now Hila was watching them advance on a large screen, on which she could see a diagram of the station and icons indicating the advancing marines and security officers.

The astronauts around her were, as usual, thrilled that the Empress was sitting there with them, instead of on the bridge with Admiral Vu, so they were being highly forthcoming.

Hell, I wish I could just be here with them! As a commando or even a war correspondent. What's the point of being Empress?

"Dagger Alpha here, the main linking corridor is secured."

"Dagger Gamma, advance toward the central control room."

"Striker Alpha in position." That was Tarsen's voice. The *Quezon*'s boarders had the call sign Striker.

"Dagger Alpha for Striker Alpha, keep yourself in reserve."

"Camper Alpha, we have secured a group of mechanics, two were armed. No resistance."

They found everything exactly as described in the information supplied by Imperial Investigator Annika Sparbo. Francis Ebell, the man who owned all the mining stations in the star system, had been scheming here with the New Protectorate for quite a long time and practically all his staff on the station *Kaffer Minor* must have known this, just like the crews of the freight ships shuttling between the stations.

Last year's war had convinced Hila that she could not be surprised that there were so many traitors in the Imperium.

Fortunately, everything had gone according to plan, so far. When the marines and security officers seized the transporter, the crew hadn't managed to warn anyone. Tarsen was personally leading this first part. During the journey, Hila had discussed possible tactics for securing the ships with him. Tarsen and his team had gotten on board under the pretext of a visit from another freighter—the same freighter behind whose Gertz signature Vu's task force was hiding.

It was challenging and complicated, and because they didn't know in advance which freighters were going to be moving around the star system, Tarsen had had to improvise. However, he had dealt with the problem excellently and his people immediately got the better of the small crew. Nobody was killed, and nobody managed to call for help or warn the enemy.

Here his police experience had paid off. And, as Hila was willing to admit, so had her advice about infiltration.

So, the transporter *Vanessa* moved across the star system toward *Kaffer Minor*.

Where they found what they were looking for. In the upper layers of the atmosphere of a gas giant, near the station, one of the New Protectorate's super-battleships was anchored. A smaller light battleship—called a monitor—was holding position nearby and keeping watch.

The New Protectorate had been founded by the Protectors when they lost power over the Central Imperium. They had created a new caste of warriors and rulers whom they called the Chosen, something even better than Enhans. The Chosen maybe regarded Enhans as some sort of evolutionary dead end in the best-case scenario, or worse, with contempt. Clearly this did not bother Enner bastards like Ebell.

She was interested in what sort of future the New Protectorate would have had for Enners over the long term, if…

"Contact! Contact!" came over the speakers. "Dagger Gamma here, encounter with New Protectorate troops! I repeat: There are Protectorate janissaries on the station!"

Φ

"Striker Alpha, control here, move forward to cover Dagger Gamma."

"Striker Alpha. Understood!" said Senior Warrant Officer Tobias Tarsen and turned to his people.

The police from three ships together had very provisionally formed something that marines might be willing to call a company. Command had fallen to him, and the security chiefs from the three other ships were responsible for individual platoons.

They were only here as backup. Tarsen realized that despite all their training with Her Majesty during the journey here, despite all the plans and briefings, nobody had *really* believed that they would be used as a military unit in a pitched battle. Securing the freight ship *Vanessa* was something else, that was police work, the work of strike teams, a third of his people had experience. But this…

He pushed all doubts out of his head. His work was investigating, not fighting, but so what? Her Majesty had also imagined her career somewhat differently. Not to mention her husband.

"Jenkins!" he shouted at his deputy. "Double time, triangle formation! Let's go!"

Thirty security officers began to run.

Ahead of them they could already hear shooting.

"What's happening?"

Baroness Yurrela Barn was sitting on the bridge of the dreadnought *Subjugator,* and she almost whispered this question. She practically never lost her temper. She didn't raise her voice. She didn't give in to her emotions.

That was why the New Protectorate had chosen her to lead this mission. Many of her fellow Chosen tended to constantly demonstrate their superiority; they thought the fact that they had survived the ritual, in which they had consumed a piece of Protector tissue, gave them natural intelligence or superiority.

Barn was calm and contemplative. By the time she had asked the question, she already knew what must have happened.

"An Imperial landing force!" said the *Subjugator*'s captain, looking at the display. "It's encountered some of our janissaries aboard… and now Ebell's calling us for help!"

The station head. An Enhans, useful, but just like some Chosen, Enhans tended to be arrogant.

But this was a known variable, and Barn had immediately allowed for it.

"Send all the janissaries we have to the station."

"My lady," exclaimed the astronaut at the sensors. "We have enemy contacts on the sensors! Imperial ships, at least… six battleships and ten cruisers!"

So, this was not just an enemy landing force on the station that had probably got there on that freight ship. No, this was an organized trap.

The *Subjugator* was still docked at the station. A short distance from the station, the monitor *Cepheus* had been patrolling. It had already set off to meet the enemy ships.

"Emergency disconnection from the station," she ordered.

Her calm, quiet voice made some people nervous.

The captain did not ask, but sent the order on, and then looked at his superior. "Even an emergency disconnection will take at least two minutes."

"I understand. The *Cepheus* may attack at will."

She knew that she this order was condemning the ship to death, but death threatened all of them. Now they must inflict the greatest possible losses on the enemy. They wouldn't be able to withdraw in time anyway.

"The janissaries are still embarking on the station, my lady," someone notified her.

"Let them continue until we disconnect the tunnel. Right until the last moment."

That meant that any janissaries with the bad luck to be in the tunnel at the moment the ship disconnected would fly into space. Barn was not in any way troubled by this. More collateral damage.

Nevertheless, a dreadnought was at least able to face six battleships with honor.

The captain transmitted the orders and, as the ship began to move and he had a little time, he turned to his superior.

"My lady, we haven't yet brought all the panasin aboard."

"I know," said Barn. "But our allies on Arnhem already have enough in any case to implement our plans on Ridiger. That was only the last of the supply."

With these words, the *Subjugator* disconnected the last refueling pipe and the connecting tunnel.

The pipe spurted gas into space. Janissaries flew out of the tunnel. Nobody heard the screams of the artificially tank-grown soldiers.

Φ

The entire Imperial task force began to move. As the moment of surprise subsided, Admiral Vu gave the order for his ships to set sail immediately.

The Gertz drive was reactionless, so Hila didn't feel the acceleration or any g. But she knew that the ships were moving at a speed that would correspond to 0.02 c in relativity space. The second level then accelerated them to 0.15.

They would arrive at *Kaffer Minor* in a few minutes.

The astronauts around Hila said nothing. They were breathlessly watching the marines and security team advance, but only from a distance; they were expecting a battle now. And although their numbers were superior, they knew that they wouldn't escape from a monitor and a dreadnought unscathed. A good half of those present were young, around eighteen years old. They were too young to have experienced the recent war. The other half were old hands. They had experienced the war and maybe had a better idea of what was about to happen. Both groups were silent.

Maybe this really was only a cleansing action, but you can still die in one of those.

Beside Hila, Devika Pradhan looked rather resigned. She was worried about her charge but knew that she couldn't be anywhere else.

That is, she could, and wanted, to be with the landing force, where a genetically modified Omega could be of some use to them. But she would have to do that over Pradhan's dead body. Literally.

"Contact! Striker Alpha reporting contact! Fire from grenade launchers!"

Φ

Tarsen had never much understood the strange divisions of all those genetically modified people. The Central Imperium had had Enhans for centuries. Their power was diminishing more and more, which the head of this station, among others, found very hard to bear. The previous Emperor had created genetically modified Omega Commandos, like Hila Eban, as a counterweight. Meanwhile the Protectors, in their new territory, had created their own nobility, whom they called the Chosen, and then they had grown many cloned warriors in tanks. Or slaves, whatever you wanted to call it. They were known as janissaries.

There were a great many of these modified humans, it confused people, and Tarsen didn't trust any of them, except possibly the Empress.

Right now, it was important to know that the Protectorate's janissaries apparently obeyed every order and willingly went to their deaths.

Which most of them were now doing, as they met Tarsen's unit.

There were a great many janissaries, they had grenade launchers and were blasting down both corridors leading to the control room. The marines and security team had to advance slowly, themselves clearing the corridors with grenades and flak cannons.

"Pressure loss, pressure loss!" Jenkins cried.

They might not be marines, but they had served in space and didn't wait when they heard that shout. They reacted automatically and sealed their helmets. The corridor was deep within the station, so the loss of pressure was probably not caused by the firefight. The station commander had let the air out.

Then the grav went off. But all the landing force members were equipped with magnetic boots.

So were the janissaries.

Tarsen personally fired another projectile from his flak as a group of janissaries surged toward them. The charge dispersed into hundreds of tiny, destructive needles and tore apart the attackers' bodies. The room was filled with red bubbles and flying chunks of viscera.

But there were more behind them, and still more.

Φ

The light battleship was flying directly at Task Force 52. Hila had to admit that the ship's crew was brave. It was headed for them like David against six Goliaths.

Just as she hadn't felt the ship start to move, she also didn't feel it shooting. But on the display, she watched the task force open fire. The ships maneuvered rapidly, the computers attempted to predict the ray trajectories or their opponent's courses.

Now everything was happening quite fast.

The Imperial battleships wiped the light battleships from their paths.

Not one of her beams found a target. She only delayed them a little, but to Hila's delight, all of Task Force 52's ships got away undamaged.

However, their luck would soon start to run out.

They were continuing to aim at the super-battleship that had just disconnected from the station.

Admiral Vu had wanted to catch her unawares, but the ship's commander must have had nerves of steel and disconnected from the station almost immediately.

Now it was six Davids against one Goliath.

The beam guns of all possible calibers now opened fire. The ships maneuvered. Hila watched it as closely as her human senses allowed. Her brain couldn't process everything.

However, she knew that the first shots had found a target.

The gigantic colossus was convulsing under the stress of fire. The super-battleships or dreadnoughts were the biggest things to have any power in their arsenals. Six battleships with a cruiser escort should be able to make short work of her, and nobody expected any other outcome.

But nor did they expect to come out of this without any losses of their own. The ship was too powerful, too well armed, for that, and even when damaged, she was dangerous, like a wounded animal.

Several rays hit the hull of the battleship *Burgundy*. They pierced the hull's armor, burned holes in the bulkheads and destroyed everything in their path. But the battleship remained whole and continued flying. The cruiser *Adeye* was worse off. She had caught a full salvo intended for another battleship and Hila closed her eyes as the cruiser, with four hundred people aboard, vanished in one large explosion.

Φ

"Continue firing!" Yurrela Barn's voice was no longer quiet, not because she was panicking, but she had to shout over the screams of the wounded and dying, as the *Subjugator*'s bridge had taken a hit. The captain was dead. So was the first officer. But she was standing there, an oasis of calm in the middle of all that chaos.

They had successfully accomplished their mission. It was fortunate that they had been isolated here, at their last stop. The Fifth Fleet would still be destroyed…

Another enemy ray found the bridge and Barn died with this thought.

A minute later, all that was left of the *Subjugator* was a warped, charred wreck.

PART 3

"Your Majesty?"

It took Hila a moment to realize that the voice coming from the speaker was calling her, and that it belonged to Admiral Vu.

"Yes, Admiral?" she said, her eyes still fixed on the consequences of the battle outside.

"Station manager Francis Ebell on the line. He wants to negotiate. I would like you to be present."

Hila's face twisted. The station commander had it coming. His patrons had been destroyed, and he now wanted to weasel his way out.

She wasn't sure if there was any way she could help, but the admiral probably wanted to have the Empress to hand.

It didn't take her long to reach the flag operations center, the faithful Pradhan at her heels.

To her great irritation, the marine at the entrance announced her officially, but everyone was looking at their work. She walked up to the admiral.

"How is the situation on the station?"

"The landing force is holding position. There aren't many janissaries left, but they won't surrender, of course. Unlike Ebell, who has locked himself in the control center and wants to talk to us."

"I assume that our people will be able to get into the control center even so?"

"Yes, but they first need to eliminate the final pocket of janissary resistance and then cut their way through four hermetically sealed doors. It will take time. And Ebell wants to negotiate."

Hila nodded. "I'm here as an observer only, Admiral. If you want my opinion, I'll be happy to tell you, but you're in command. Meanwhile

I'd like to hear what Ebell wants to tell us."

"I agree," said Vu, nodding to the officer at the communications section. A moment later, the face of a black-haired, dark-skinned man appeared on the screen on the admiral's panel, with fear, guardedness in his eyes.

"This is Francis Ebell. I am responsible for mining on all gas giants in the star system. And… well, doesn't matter. I want to negotiate."

"This is Vice Admiral Tom Vu, deputy commander of the Fifth Fleet of the Central Imperium. You want to talk? So talk. Undoubtedly you realize you have been caught aiding and abetting the enemy. And whatever happens, our marines will soon be in your control center."

Ebell was briefly silent. "I'm not going to defend myself with unnecessary speechifying, Admiral. It wouldn't interest you anyway. But I can make you an offer."

"What offer?"

"In the control room I have computers with a complete database. This ship was not the only New Protectorate vessel to stop here. I know what they loaded here, what they wanted. And I also got onto their computers. Without them knowing. I have part of the encoded database. I could format everything forever by pressing one button. But I want to give it to you."

Vu raised his eyebrows. "You want to?"

"Yes. Hell. I'll express myself more clearly. I know I can't wriggle out of this, but I can make a few calculations. I'll give you the entire database, in exchange for not being sentenced to death. I want to strike a deal. That's fair, isn't it? Isn't it?"

"The Imperial Court will decide on your punishment."

"Really, Admiral, you can do better than that. I helped the New Protectorate, I even believe in it, but I don't want to die for it. If I know that a bullet or a vacuum awaits me anyway, I'll just delete that database."

Vu started to answer, but then he stopped, and turned to Hila. He silenced the broadcast with a hand gesture.

"What do you think, Your Majesty? This is diplomacy. I can't promise him that he won't face the death penalty. But you can."

"Me?"

"Yes, you, or your husband Emperor Daniel."

"We are not above the law!"

"Maybe not, but you can grant an Imperial pardon. Both the Emperor, and yourself, as his spouse, have the right to release someone from prison, stop court proceedings or reduce a punishment. That's what Imperial pardon means. You can promise him that." He stopped short. "Of course, it's your decision, but I think that the potential gain is probably worth it. My intelligence officer will certainly agree."

Hila had never considered Imperial pardons. Yes, she knew that she could do something of the sort. These rights were guaranteed to the Emperor or Empress's spouse by the Central Imperium's constitution, as a counterweight to the power of the ruling Houses. The Imperium's inhabitants thought that anyone marrying into the dynasty having the same powers was a good balance.

Personally, she had a problem with it. About five years ago, Daniel's great-uncle, Emperor Adrian, had caused controversy by pardoning the son of a friend who had been convicted for embezzling a great deal of money. Hila had always seen this responsibility as something powerful people could easily abuse.

But now it was dawning on her that Vu was right.

She could play her role of Empress.

"Okay, fine," she said, and stood so that Ebell could see her on camera. "Turn on the sound."

The Enhans station chief's mouth dropped open when he saw Hila.

"Do you know who I am?"

"Yes. Everybody knows you. I didn't know you were on board, you…" he looked as if he wanted to say something else but thought better of it. Undoubtedly, he would have liked to regale Hila with any number of other expressions, but this was not appropriate when negotiating and pleading for his life. Instead, he simply said: "You heard my offer."

"Yes. And you undoubtedly know that *I* can guarantee you won't be executed."

"Well, yes, but I also know that you're a vindictive bitch."

"I can only promise it. And I'll happily record it in the ship's log—everything I say here will be recorded. It's up to you whether the guarantee is enough. Your friends have just caused the death of hundreds more Imperial astronauts and marines. So, if you decide that my word isn't good enough and you want to get yourself killed straight away, I'm *not* going to try and talk you out of it."

Ebell hesitated, but not for too long. He must have considered that he really wasn't going to get a better offer and that he *literally* had nothing to lose.

"Fine. I accept. I hereby officially surrender on behalf of the entire star system. My people will not put up any resistance."

"And what about the janissaries?"

A small smile appeared on Ebell's face. "I sent away the few who were with me in the control center. They're programmed to be loyal to the New Protectorate and probably wouldn't have responded well to my… negotiation. And your people have already taken care of most of those outside. You'll have to attend to those remaining yourselves. Again, that's the most I can do."

Ebell obviously wasn't going to cry his eyes out if any of the remaining janissaries killed an Imperial marine or security officer.

The bastard, thought Hila. She would keep her promise that he would not be executed, but…

What a bastard.

Φ

"We've found out that one of the things they were getting from that gas giant was panasin," said Senior Warrant Officer Tarsen. He had a healing bandage on his head, a souvenir of the janissary who had struck him there in the last phases of the battle. If Jenkins, his deputy, hadn't saved him, Tarsen wouldn't be here. Jenkins himself had died shortly afterwards in a suicide attack by another janissary.

This was one of the reasons why Tarsen wanted to help the fleet's intelligence officer analyze the information they had obtained. He wanted to do something. He wanted to be useful. He wanted to convince at least himself that his people hadn't died for nothing.

Hila got it only too well.

"And what exactly is panasin?" Admiral Vu wanted to know.

More than twelve hours had passed since the battle in the star system. In addition to Hila, Vu and his staff, the hologram of Admiral Alender, commander of the Fifth Fleet, was also present in the *Quezon*'s conference room. They had used one of the FTL retranslation stations to connect with him.

"It's a rare gas, sir. In the Imperium it's only extracted in five or six places." Tarsen shrugged. "From the shreds we've obtained from that captured database so far, it seems that the New Protectorate wanted to use it to damage the Fifth Fleet. But that's about all we know for the time being."

"And how would they want to damage it?" Alender asked, as his hologram flickered slightly.

"I don't know, sir. I discussed it with our forensic specialist. Yes, panasin is toxic, but there are many more effective toxins that are also easier to get hold of. It can also be volatile in the right combination, but again, we have lots of better explosives. I don't know, sir."

"And do we have any information about those other marauding New Protectorate ships?" wondered the admiral.

Tarsen exchanged a rapid glance with Vu's intelligence officer. Under normal circumstances, the intelligence officer would command an entire team of specialists, intelligence officers like Daniel had been before he became Emperor. But even here the Imperium was short of personnel, so the ship's police helped with this too. The intelligence officer nodded and Tarsen went on.

"We don't know anything yet, Admiral. That is, yes, from interrogating Ebell and the station crew, we established that those two super-battleships also loaded up on supplies at the station—the *Siege Breaker* and the *Harrowing*, before we destroyed them six months ago. We'll see if we get anything more from the database. It could take weeks."

"Nevertheless, if the New Protectorate thought that they could somehow disable or destroy the Fifth Fleet, we have to take it seriously," said Alender. "Admiral Vu, return to Ridiger as soon as possible."

"Aye aye, sir."

The fleet commander's hologram now turned to Hila. "Your Majesty, I understand you will now continue your tour. Would you honor the Fifth Fleet with a visit under more better circumstances?"

"Yes, Admiral, of course. I'll look forward to it. I've changed my plans a little by joining this mission, but my… assistants," she glanced at Pradhan, "are telling me I'm still expected on Enugu."

"I understand. In any event, I am glad you joined Admiral Vu and helped to train our people." Admiral Alender's feet were firmly planted on the ground, and he held it as a badge of honor that he had worked his way up from being a rank-and-file astronaut. A roguish smile flickered at the corners of his mouth. "I think that the legend of the great Hila Eban has grown a little more, Your Majesty."

"Thank you, Admiral."

"I will look forward to meeting you in person again."

PART 4

The better circumstances never arose.

"Incoming message…" called Martin Mureau in the *Hawk*'s pilot's chair, and Hila felt him stiffen beside her. "Code Citadel! Code Citadel!"

He didn't say anything more but immediately pressed a few buttons and the ship activated all her active sensors and weapons.

Behind Hila, Pradhan breathed in sharply.

In the Imperial Navy, Code Citadel meant only one thing: Area under attack.

They all still vividly remembered the battle against the Protectorate ships in the Kaffer System, but two weeks had already passed. On Enugu, Hila had given her speech as planned, she had cut ribbons, and ceremonially opened a new school and a home for war orphans. She'd had lunch with the children, as she had with various other dignitaries, including soldiers, volunteer firefighters, and many others. "Empress Hila's" tour, then, was going according to plan. Her protocol experts would probably be delighted that her image had again been boosted by her personal involvement with the mission to the Kaffer System. "Empress Hila is back in action," read the headlines across the entire Central Imperium. Sometimes, Hila told herself, she played the role of Empress in the same way she had played the roles of servant, lover, manager or journalist when infiltrating something for the Omega Commandos.

Journalist was at least a role that came close to what she wanted to do, which was why she had studied journalism when her career with the Omegas was over.

Of course, she was very good at meeting her obligations as Empress, and she had thought that the remainder of her tour across the

Bornholm Sector would be quiet.

Evidently, she was wrong.

"What do you see on the sensors?" she asked, while Mureau silenced the beeping alarm signals.

Behind Hila, Pradhan was already watching the sensor display. "The Fifth Fleet is orbiting the station *Varsity*, in Ridiger's orbit… there are a few other ships in the area, but it looks like normal traffic. It certainly doesn't look like an invasion."

In the co-pilot's seat, Hila turned to her bodyguard. "And that fleet is definitely ours, right?"

"Yes. We're picking up their IFF responders."

"Martin, send our signal."

"I already did," said Mureau.

"So do it again! And add verbal confirmation."

Mureau ran his fingers through his short beard and pressed a few buttons. "To the Imperial Navy forces in the Ridiger System, this is Imperial Two, I repeat, Imperial Two. Designation INAV *Hawk*, LAV-1816. We are flying into the system on arrival vector zero eight two to one four eight."

Imperial Two was the designation for any ship on which the monarch's spouse was traveling in the Central Imperium's radio communications.

The *Hawk* continued another six minutes into the star system, but nobody responded. Even without FTL communications, that was enough time for the signal to get there and back again twice.

"We'll try one more time," Hila decided. But this was already suspect. "Devika, find the *Nagaland*'s transponder. I'll connect directly with Admiral Alender."

Pradhan briefly flicked through the list of ships whose transponders she was picking up, then shook her head. "I can't find it. There's no incoming signal from the *Nagaland*."

"That's strange."

"Incoming message!" exclaimed Mureau. "Audio and video from the battleship *Quezon*. That's Vice Admiral Tom Vu."

An unpleasant feeling settled into Hila's stomach.

The admiral's familiar face appeared on the screen. He looked like he'd aged several years in those few weeks since they last saw each other.

"The *Quezon* here for Imperial Two, ah, it is you, Your Majesty. I'm sorry that nobody reported earlier, but we fell victim to sabotage."

"What happened?" Hila asked.

"This morning, we arrested a saboteur aboard the supply ship *Platypus*. He was attempting to poison the cleaning filter set for the entire fleet and..." He shook his head. "Come aboard the *Quezon*, my dispatchers will connect with you and guide you."

"We were supposed to go aboard the *Nagaland*," Hila objected, but from Vu's expression, she could already guess what he was about to tell her.

"The *Nagaland* exploded. Probably the work of the same bastard from the *Platypus*. We lost the entire crew. There were no survivors."

Φ

The *Nagaland* and the *Quezon* were practically identical. On her way through the *Quezon*, which she already knew, Hila experienced an even greater awareness that the *Nagaland* had been destroyed. With her entire crew. More than eight hundred people. People like those she was meeting here in the corridors.

Hila had lived through much larger massacres, both at Daniel's side aboard the *Hermes*, and before, with the Omega Commandos. Maybe it was the suddenness of everything here that had caught her off guard. As if the cold ruthlessness of the universe intended to snatch her from the calm and peace that had reigned within her since Elda was born. She realized that not even the battle in the Kaffer System aboard this very ship had aroused such feelings in her. She'd expected it there. That was a combat operation....

But this...

The fleet was still in chaos, but Vice Admiral Vu had already satisfied himself that no immediate danger threatened, so he met Hila and his staff in the *Quezon*'s conference room.

"What exactly happened, then? What do we know?" Hila asked, as Vu led her to the head of the table and himself sat down beside her. Pradhan took up her position at the door.

"This morning a technician on the supplies ship *Platypus* reported a fault in the air cleanser filters," said Admiral Vu. "The filters had come from the *Platypus*'s rapid printers and two different computers had certified them. The duty officer also personally confirmed this. With thorough confirmation, it turned out that the filters were saturated with some substance containing panasin, the same muck that the New Protectorate were extracting on Kaffer. And there were also plenty of other substances, the New Protectorate's bio-tech." Vu shrugged. "I don't understand it. The ship's doctor explained it to me in lay terms. All told, it's some biological muck and ordinary instruments wouldn't detect it. We were lucky that we had tweaked the sensors to pick up panasin. If those filters had been installed into the air cleansers on one of our ships—exactly what they were intended for—they'd have killed the entire crew within a few weeks."

"A few weeks?" asked one of the other officers sitting at the table, Captain Stephen Palmer, whom Vu had introduced as the fleet's deputy chief engineer.

The chief engineer had been aboard the *Nagaland*.

"That doesn't sound like an effective weapon to me," Palmer continued. "It would be discovered quickly enough."

"That's the problem," said Vu. "It depends on what you want it to do, Stephen. This acts slowly but can't be cured and it's a long time before any symptoms appear. By the time the first people fell ill, it would be too late."

Hila could imagine this only too vividly. More Protectorate nasties. She remembered how New Protectorate agents had cold-bloodedly killed the Imats, the Ralgar's symbiotic race, so they could blackmail them with the threat of killing more. Or how they had used a biological weapon to eliminate the third sex of the alien race Silmani. Their civilization still hadn't recovered.

Mainly she could imagine the hundreds, thousands of crew members who died slowly, in corridors, in the mess, at their stations, because nobody knew what would help.

"How many ships were the filters intended for?" she asked.

Vu's answer indicated that imagining thousands of astronauts was rather too optimistic.

"The entire fleet. The *Platypus* is currently our only supply ship with large industrial rapid printers, and it produced the filters for all the other ships. This delivery was the first to be infected, but within a few days the entire Fifth Fleet would have received these filters."

"And do we know for sure that this was the first?" Palmer asked. "What if there are already some on a few ships? Here, even?"

Vu shook his head. "No, Admiral Alender was able to tackle that with me. He gave an order to all ships for the engineer and medical teams to immediately inspect everything for the presence of panasin. Maybe a standard scanner wouldn't have caught that gunk in the airlocks leading onto the ship, but the medical scanners will reliably find it, particularly if they know what they're looking for. The fleet is clear."

"And while I'm thinking about it," Palmer went on, "Why didn't they find it aboard the *Platypus* sooner? Admiral Alender ordered immediate panasin scans as soon as we flew in from Kaffer."

"And what's more, there were random inspections with manual scanners," said Vu. "It seems that someone hacked the computer so it wouldn't consider this a threat."

Hila nodded. Enemy hackers had recently attacked an entire colonization expedition.

"What does all this have to do with the *Nagaland* exploding?" she asked.

Vu frowned. "The *Nagaland* exploded shortly after Admiral Alender gave the order to check the entire fleet's filters. I think that that son of a bitch who planned… forgive me, Your Majesty…"

"I've already heard the word a few times. Not to mention the fact that

I spent a few weeks on a Ralgar planet once. Go on."

"Okay. So, the bastard probably planned to have our flagship explode while those filters were being distributed. He probably thought that nobody on any ship would inspect a routine filter delivery during the mayhem after the flagship was destroyed."

"To be on the safe side, our engineers are inspecting the other ships too, but they haven't found any bombs or charges planted there," Palmer added.

"And do you know what caused the explosion?" Hila asked.

Palmer shrugged. "Admiral Vu entrusted that task to me before you arrived. We still don't know the exact cause, but we do know that there was an explosion on or near the Gertz generator."

Hila nodded. The Gertz generator was the basis of the ship's reactionless drive that enabled the vessel to travel between stars. It was also a device that could destroy an entire ship if it critically malfunctioned or exploded.

However, for that reason, Gertz generators were secured with a great many safeties and backups.

"My people will study the records from the black box aboard the *Nagaland*," Palmer continued. "It was continuously backed up in the database on the station *Varsity*, so we have a complete record up to the moment of the explosion."

"Don't you have a guesstimate?" Hila asked.

"I don't want to speculate…"

"We're not in court, damn it. Speculate all you like."

"Very well, ma'am. In that case I would guess that somebody put some chemical or biological corrosive material on the generator cover. It would only need a drop, and again, could have been some muck that our scanners wouldn't have detected. Could be panasin again, or something similar, whatever that bastard had access to."

"From what you're telling me," said Hila, her eyes flickering over the officers, "I assume that you have a suspect."

Vu nodded. "Yes, ma'am, we do."

Φ

His name was Henry Kotulan. He worked as the chief supplies officer aboard the *Platypus*, he certified everything personally, and was personally responsible for the panasin scan. His eyes looked as if they were a size too big for his head and otherwise uninteresting face, which was dominated by a small brown goatee.

Hila watched the first interrogation on a monitor connected to the camera in the interrogation room. The suspect was brought aboard the *Quezon* directly from the *Platypus* and Senior Warrant Officer Tobias Tarsen personally took charge of him.

The Imperial Navy didn't have a non-military investigation organization, but Hila had already seen Senior Warrant Officer Tobias Tarsen in action, and she knew that the ship's security officer and his deputies would discharge their duty well enough. It was much more Tarsen's routine work than the recent combat landing force. One glance was enough to assure Hila that the landing force was still fresh in Tarsen's memory, along with the deaths of many of his friends. He took charge of the investigation with the enthusiasm of a varahasaurus chasing its prey.

"The system has your personal signature that you used to certify those filters," Tarsen was just saying to Kotulan.

"I always do that," snapped the suspect. He seemed more irritated than terrified. And he also seemed like someone who would repeat the same statement again and again.

"But this time you certified the contaminated filters," said the interrogator.

"Both scanners evaluated them as safe."

"Somebody hacked the scanners."

"Yes, and? That could have been anyone! We have two dozen people in the entire section who could have done it."

"But you were the only person who had the opportunity to check the filters the whole way until they were loaded onto the supplies shuttle."

"That doesn't mean anything," Kotulan's irritation reached new heights. "You only suspect me because I'm an Enhans!"

Behind Hila, Pradhan sucked her breath in sharply. "I was waiting for the bastard to spring that on us."

All these Enhans fuckers had one thing in common. As soon as the situation went against them, they started to howl about discrimination.

Tarsen responded to this accusation with relative calm. "No, nobody suspects you for that reason. But in addition to the fact that your personal code and electronic signal approved everything, there's another thing here. Petty Officer Divar—she was responsible for checking the filters manually—confirmed that you offered to take over that delivery yourself and check them personally."

"I don't mind getting my hands dirty."

"You, a lieutenant-commander, will do the manual work of a second-class petty officer?"

"Is it forbidden?"

"No, but it's strange that you did it for the first time after serving on the *Platypus* for eight months."

"I wanted to give that girl some time off!"

"And two weeks previously, you personally delivered some supplies to the *Nagaland*."

"The fleet's chief supply officer invited me to a meeting. Along with other officers!"

"And the *Nagaland* exploded entirely by chance on the same day that the filters you approved were supposed to be distributed?"

"That's nothing to do with me!" said Kotulan, more defensively than before. He folded his arms. "I'm not going to tell you anything more. You're biased against me. All of you."

Hila looked behind her at Pradhan. "Well, it's not going to be that simple."

Φ

When, that evening, the FTL communications center on the main planet of Hub established its regular contact with the Fifth Fleet, Hila personally initiated her husband, Emperor Daniel Hankerson, into the situation.

At first, Daniel appeared on the display with little Elda on his lap—and sent her several more videos—but the situation was too serious for them to be able to deal with family matters, so Daniel rapidly handed Elda over to his robot, Sean, when Hila started to talk about what had happened. Daniel already knew that the *Nagaland* had been destroyed, and about the other sabotage, from the first rapid report sent by Admiral Vu. Hila now told him her observations.

"Do you think that Kotulan did it?"

"The other crew members who had the opportunity are also being vetted, but Kotulan comes out worst. Frankly, I don't know. And I think that the ship's security team aren't ideal for investigating a crime of that sort."

Daniel shook his head. "If it is him, then he's one more Enhans who's angry with the current regime."

"They should be glad that we let them keep their house of parliament after the war!" Hila couldn't stop herself from saying.

She was very sore about this persistent injustice. People like Arian Lardon, by exploiting their position in the House of Families, had almost destroyed the Imperium. The House of Families was, overall, a group of privileged people who had come to power automatically just by being Enhans, and who belonged to one of approximately eighty remaining families.

Hila would have preferred to abolish the House. And she would also have preferred to abolish the whole monarchy and, instead of being Empress, just be Daniel Hankerson's wife.

But she understood that the Imperium was already fragile and vulnerable enough, and that the ruling House Hankerson functioned as a unifying element, whether it wanted to or not. Daniel and Prime Minister Laura Gilbert had retained the House of Families for the same reason but had permanently excluded from it any families directly involved in the conspiracy.

Or rather, realized Hila, bitterly, *those families whose guilt had been proven. The others could bend over backward to point at the Lardons and a few others and shout "Not us, them! Don't judge the whole barrel by a few bad apples!"*

Hila had no doubt that there were still plenty of traitors in the House of Families that they hadn't caught, but she understood the pragmatism that Daniel and Ms. Gilbert had to act with, and she didn't argue with them about it. Daniel bore the weight of the entire Imperium on his shoulders; he had to make difficult decisions, and he didn't need his wife kicking up a fuss at home.

That's why Daniel didn't even react to her frustrated comment.

"Do you want to come home?"

"Vu asked me the same question. I guess he's afraid of more sabotage and doesn't want to have the Empress on his conscience on top of everything else. But the crews of those ships are terrified, and I'm not surprised. They haven't just lost their commander and newest ship; those contaminated filters were prevented from spreading through the whole fleet by a hair's breadth. I think I can raise their morale just by being here with them for a bit."

"I know that the astronauts and soldiers love you. Quite a lot more than they love me."

"Your Majesty! Are you *jealous*?"

Daniel laughed. "No, I'm really not, not about that. But Vu is right. What if there is more sabotage?"

"To be on the safe side, the Admiral has ordered a shutdown of all Gertz generators, except those in the cruiser squadron going out on patrol. If the fleet needs to move to another star system unexpectedly, it will take the ships a little longer to set sail. Vu thinks it's worth it."

"I guess so."

"Exactly. And, as I say, it'll help with morale. I'm still their Empress— and you and Ms. Gilbert are always reminding me that I have plenty of powers of my own. I think I can help."

"But don't forget that we can't interfere with process. That's up to the investigatory bodies."

"I know, I know. The Emperor or his spouse can at most grant a pardon, but they can't investigate anything. I'm more worried by the thought that the fleet is still actually front-line, Daniel. Maybe they destroyed one raider dreadnought, but there's at least one more here. You remember the great pomp with which we sent them those two gigantic battleships? And one of them exploded. Just like that. For them, it's very different from losing a ship in battle. And to be honest, if you had seen Kotulan's arrogant expression…"

Daniel made a face. "Yes, but please, don't cut off anything."

"Don't worry, I know it's not appropriate for an Empress."

"But here's some good news for you. The Interior Ministry has already reacted. Annika Sparbo, who gave the fleet that tip about the Kaffer System, has received an order to go to Ridiger."

"Sparbo?" Hila suddenly felt a burden drop from her shoulders. Any Imperial Investigator would be great, but Sparbo had been legendary even before Hila had recently seen the results of her work in person. "That is good news—the first I've had today. I've heard so much about Sparbo!"

"I thought you'd be pleased. But I don't think it's the only good news. Maybe Elda would like to wave to mommy again…"

PART 5

Annika Sparbo resembled a sweet old granny from a fairy-tale, but there was something more to her. Hila might be the Empress—or the Empress Consort, depending—but she would never be able to carry herself as regally as Sparbo did. But it wasn't just a matter of how she moved, or any superficial sense of superiority. No. Sparbo was, purely and simply, a lady.

"Welcome aboard, Ms. Sparbo," Vu greeted her, as the older woman disembarked from her shuttle in the *Quezon*'s hangar. "I am Vice Admiral Tom Vu. And I assume I don't need to introduce Empress Hila?"

Sparbo smiled radiantly. "No, definitely not! I am glad to see you again, Your Majesty." Instead of shaking hands, she dropped an elegant curtsey which, in her old-fashioned, long crimson dress, also looked like it came from a fairy-tale.

"The pleasure's all mine," said Hila. "We're very happy to see you here."

Sparbo turned to Vu. "And congratulations are undoubtedly in order for your victory in the Kaffer System, Admiral."

"It wouldn't have been a victory without you, Ms. Sparbo. And unfortunately, that victory has a bitter aftertaste, given what happened next."

"Unfortunately, yes. But the tragedy that happened here does not diminish your victory in any way. Nor does my tiny contribution to obtaining the information that led to it. And if I understand correctly, there's something else I should congratulate you on? This morning the Admiralty confirmed you as the new commander of the Fifth Fleet."

"Yes… thank you, Ms. Sparbo. But I must say again that I could wish for it under other circumstances."

The Investigator's smile vanished. "I understand. Believe me."

"May I show you to your cabin?"

Sparbo looked almost shocked. "But Admiral, if Hub thinks that I am needed here so much that they recalled me from the other side of the sector, I think I should start work immediately. What do you say?"

"As you wish."

"I studied the details on my journey here. The suspect isn't saying anything?"

"No. And unfortunately he covered his traces well."

"Only those he knew about," said Sparbo.

Φ

Vu summoned Palmer, Tarsen and Aukrust, the ship's doctor, to the flag conference room. Security chief Tarsen was the first to initiate Sparbo into the situation. He also had the smallest number of new things to tell her. Kotulan was continuing to insist on his innocence, and that they had no further evidence against him. There were other suspects among the *Platypus*'s crew. Kotulan might be the only one to have access to everything and to certify the filters, but it was still possible that several people had worked together.

Next was Palmer, the fleet's newly appointed chief engineer, promoted under the same unpleasant circumstances as Vu.

"I've been viewing the records from the *Nagaland*'s black box. In the machine room, we're constantly comparing them with the *Quezon*'s records. The ships are identical, so the *Quezon* can act as a model for what happened on the destroyed ship."

Sparbo smiled. "I hope you don't plan to copy the *Nagaland*'s fate too closely, Captain."

It wasn't that funny. Palmer just nodded. "No, ma'am. We haven't found anything yet. The *Nagaland*'s Gertz generator was behaving entirely normally until twelve microseconds before the explosion. When we slow down the recording, we can see that part of the generator's casing burst. It was a microscopic fissure. But it was enough to destroy the whole ship."

"And do you yet know what caused it?"

"Unfortunately not, ma'am. Kotulan, or someone else, could have placed something on the generator. We're trying various spectral analyses on the camera records too."

Sparbo shrugged. "I'm afraid that isn't my field, Captain Palmer. What are you talking about?"

"If the casing was damaged by some corrosive material—and provided it was essentially of organic origin, as we assume—we could capture it on the camera and holographic record. And work out from the spectrum type whether it was panasin or something else."

"And then who put it there. I don't envy you your work, Captain Palmer, but I know that this part of the investigation is in good hands."

Hila saw Palmer's eyes glow in his tired face and suppressed a smile. Sparbo could say ordinary phrases in a way that made you believe them.

The ship's doctor Aukrust was the next to speak.

"The substance that Kotu… that someone used to contaminate those filters contained panasin, but it was also a blend of many other things. I already sent you the full analysis. However, the scanners were specially tuned to panasin, and the *Platypus*'s scanners should have picked it up."

"But they didn't," said Sparbo. "Could anyone have bypassed the scanners to smuggle it aboard?"

"With great difficulty," said Vu. "It occurs to me that some co-conspirator could have put it through the airlock, if Kotulan hacked the system so the airlock opening wasn't recorded. But that co-conspirator must have come from somewhere. Flown in from a ship, emerged from a space suit from another vessel. And if it was one of the fleet's ships, they'd have had to deal with the scanners *there*. So realistically, I don't see it."

Sparbo thought briefly. "Doctor, what was in Kotulan's medical history? Was he taking any meds or anything?"

The doctor checked his records. "My colleague on the *Platypus* sent me his medical records, but there isn't anything material there. He'd been complaining of allergies for the last few months. He bought himself some meds on the station *Varsity*. Diexil."

"Why did he buy it on the station? Why didn't the *Platypus*'s doctor prescribe it for him?"

"The Imperial Navy uses Klienol for these things. Diexil is more expensive and a slightly gentler substance, but it works just as well. Apparently Kotulan preferred to spend his own money." The doctor made a face. "A matter of status. He buys the most expensive to show he can afford it."

"Doctor, please could I ask you to send me the exact composition of both substances and any known side effects?"

"Certainly, ma'am, but it may not have anything to do with this."

"I know. I just want to check everything." She looked at Vu. "Admiral, I need to check something else as well. Please could I send a request to the Central Imperium's navigation control computer?"

Vu nodded. "You have access, but we won't have our regular connection to Hub via FTL communications for another three hours."

"That's fine." Sparbo looked at the computer terminal and her half-closed eyes flickered for a moment. Hila realized that the Investigator was sending an order via the chip in her brain. She had a similar one, as did all members of the Imperial family. Imperial Investigators had automatic access to all the databases held by the armed forces, the civil security agencies and other institutions. These computers were called navigational, because historically, that had been their function, but now they were the backup for all the Imperium's security systems and databases.

After a moment Sparbo opened her eyes and smiled at those present. "I think I know how Mr. Kotulan smuggled that substance aboard. I need to verify something. As soon as the answer arrives, I'd like to question him myself."

The security chief nodded. "That won't be a problem, ma'am."

"I must confess that I'm very glad of the opportunity to get to know you better, Your Majesty," said Sparbo. She'd invited Hila into her cabin while waiting for the results from the computer. "We never managed to have a proper chat during our previous meetings. I've always admired you."

"I admired you. But for god's sake, please drop the crazy form of address," said Hila. "I'm Hila."

"I'm rather old school, but I can call you ma'am."

"Isn't that what I should call you?!"

"We can both be ma'am. There are no laws against it." Sparbo smiled and took a bottle and two glasses out of a small cupboard in the corner of her cabin. "Admiral Vu supplied me with this. Or maybe he saves it for all his visitors. It's Mohawk cognac, Calliar, it's a relatively good brand. I hope you won't refuse."

"No, I definitely won't," Hila said. She found it a bit strange that a woman more than twice her age was serving her, but she recognized that the Investigator *wanted* to.

Cognac wasn't something Hila would have chosen, but it was still better than the peaty Scotch whiskies that Daniel loved so much.

"I'm glad you're here," said Hila, when they had drunk. "Really. The crew might be hiding it, but the air has been crackling with tension for the few days before you arrived. Someone destroyed the flagship. Someone tried to kill them all. Then there was nothing they could do except wait and see whether by any chance the saboteur tried something else. One ship exploded, so why not more? But someone like the Imperial Investigator immediately raises their morale."

"Well, I think that the raised morale is largely down to you. You still identify with rank-and-file astronauts, even as Empress, and you've spent most of your time in the enlisted mess, am I right?"

"Yes, you are."

"And they must ask you about your experiences." Sparbo sipped her cognac. "I confess that I entirely get where they're coming from. I have followed your career enthusiastically. Tell me, did you really do… that… to the Lardon on Folna? Cut off his…?"

"Yes, that's true. And no, I'm not exactly proud of it."

Sparbo chuckled. "None of us can be proud of such things, but the entire Imperium is talking about it gleefully. And what can I say? That Enhans bastard deserved it."

"Well, yes. But the Enhans aren't the Imperium's only problem. The New Protectorate wouldn't have almost destroyed us if an entire section of society hadn't helped them. The Enhans alone aren't enough for that."

"You're right. I have my own experience."

"Yes, I read that you smoked out all of Lardon's henchmen on Haveloc. That's when you became a legend."

Sparbo waved her hand. "Well, let's say that I have personal reasons for fighting people like the Lardons. I'm sure you know where I'm from."

"The same place as me. Colbran."

"Exactly. I'm a child of the slums too."

"I know. You were born in Port Hansen on Colbran, is that right?"

"Yes. Practically the whole city belonged to one corporation. Barani Corp. Ninety-five percent of the population worked in their factories. Today we call pirate states like Kalinga barbaric, because they have slavery. Well, Port Hansen also had what was called 'work opportunities.' Barani Corp. controlled the money, but everyone had enough to support their families, if they were lucky. But they couldn't travel, and they couldn't go to the competition—there wasn't any, not there. That's how Barani sucked the life out of several generations. And they're still in Port Hansen. They've made several superficial changes, but the situation is only slowly improving."

"I should try and do something about that as Empress," said Hila.

"Maybe it's necessary, but I understand that there are dumpster fires all over the Imperium that need putting out. Like this one here. It's hard. I worked in a Port Hansen factory from the age of twelve. They had younger children there too—nobody was bothered that child labor is forbidden under Imperial law. They found some legal loophole to get around it. Many of the Enhans shareholders evaporated after the war. The management changed, but not a lot else did. They all spout bullshit about changes needing to be introduced gradually because of the economy." She finished her cognac.

Hila studied this remarkable woman, and her journalistic instincts woke up.

"So how did you finally get out of the slums?"

"Not as elegantly as you. I wasn't invited to join the Omegas, nor was I terminally ill. At twenty I joined a gang. I'm not proud of it, but I had to survive somehow. But my gang-mates weren't much better than the Enhans bastards ruling us. We were all arrested during a scuffle. The local police inspector was fair, given he worked for the private police agency belonging to Barani Corp. He made me an offer. I turned state's evidence against my gang-mates and helped to uncover the whole gang. Then I found out that I had two possibilities: either become a criminal and ultimately end up face-down in a puddle somewhere in the slums, or join the other side and try to change things from within. I got probation and the local inspector gave me a reference for the Police Academy. I spent the next eight years on Colbran, keeping order, but I was also moderating the greatest excesses of our rulers." She smiled. "I dug up enough dirt on them too. And when, after eight years, I had saved enough funds to get off the planet and apply to join Imperial Interpol, I had enough ammunition to be able to rap some of those bastards over the knuckles, hard." She waved her hands. "And then I spent my entire life slapping the wrists of people like Kotulan here. In the end I became the Imperial Investigator."

Hila drained her glass. "You're awesome."

"Oh, please. I'm not fishing for compliments. But let's say that my experience gives me a unique perspective. I agree with what Emperor Olaf said: civilization must continue. But not the civilization that the Enhans jerks want, people like the Lardons, the Hartveits, the Mainas or even the Hankersons, not your husband of course, but rather his traitor of an uncle. And let's face it, even Emperor Adrian was no saint."

Hila wished she could disagree, but she couldn't. Emperor Adrian might not have trusted other Enhans, but the way in which he created the Omega Commandos—including Hila—could not be considered ethical.

The terminal beeped. Sparbo pulled out her personal tablet and tapped on something on the screen several times.

"Aha, the information from the central computer has arrived." She became engrossed in reading the data on the display.

"What did you actually want to know?"

"Everything about Kotulan. I know his service records, but I've been able to establish, with my Investigator powers, as much as possible about whom he met over the last three years, where he bought what, where he paid for what. And I have his medical records. They're necessary for the investigation."

Hila whistled. "For that you'd normally need several days and a ton of authorizations."

"Precisely. I cannot abuse these things, of course, but I probably don't have to tell you that it's sometimes necessary for the good of the Imperium."

"Or rather for the good of the people in it, but yes."

Sparbo continued going through the records in silence for a little while longer. Hila watched her and could see the other woman's brain working.

Finally, the Investigator smiled. "Gotcha, you bastard." She looked at Hila. "Instead of waiting for permission, we can tighten the screws on him right now."

"What have you found out?"

"I'll happily show you when I throw it into his face." She looked at Hila. "I admit that I don't entirely know what to do with you, ma'am. You're a member of the executive, so you shouldn't be part of a criminal investigation, but this isn't a court, only an informal hearing."

"I don't have to take part…"

"Nonsense. I'd be happy to see you there; I'd be very glad of your insights. You have a unique perspective, just as I do."

"Thanks. I'll try not to disappoint you. I can watch the interrogation on a screen again."

"I think that's a good idea."

Hila and Pradhan were again sitting at the monitor. A pair of marines brought Kotulan into the interrogation room, accompanied by Warrant Officer Tarsen, who also stayed in the room, looking fixedly at Kotulan, while Sparbo studied something on her tablet, for effect.

"Lieutenant-Commander Kotulan, I am Annika Sparbo, the Imperial Investigator."

This made an impression on Kotulan; at least, as far as Hila could read him. For a moment he didn't move, then he seemed to relax. "And what's supposed to happen?"

"She's making him nervous but he's trying not to show it," said Pradhan.

"I'd be nervous too!" Hila agreed.

Sparbo went on. She asked the same questions that the head of security had asked. She repeated herself. Kotulan's self-confidence increased a little. He folded his arms.

This pretense went on for around ten minutes, then Sparbo looked at him with an expression that reminded Hila of Daniel when he played poker.

"I have discovered that, two weeks ago, on the station *Varsity*, you bought a drug called Diexil."

"I have allergies. I've never denied that."

"But didn't you always take Klienol for your allergies? It was regularly prescribed to you by the *Platypus*'s doctor and the doctors on your previous postings."

Kotulan gave nothing away. "What business is that of yours?"

"Just that it's very interesting. And I've also discovered that, a month ago, while you were on leave on Arnhem, you bought various interesting substances in a different pharmacy. And then you visited a bar where various sympathizers of the New Protectorate regularly meet. You picked up the tab. And someone on Arnhem also smuggled synthesized panasin onto New Protectorate ships. You used it to contaminate the air filters. I've managed to map its journey from New Canaan, which was once attacked by that same marauding ship from the New Protectorate that mined the filthy stuff on Kaffer."

"That proves nothing! Two full liners from the Fifth Fleet were flying to Arnhem. Several hundred astronauts."

"You are correct. But only you could have received the substance and smuggled it through the ship's scanners. Using various ordinary substances that you bought on Arnhem, you hid that bioweapon in your own body. It became part of your organism and then you carried it through the scanners. When you were sure that you had aroused no suspicion, you bought Diexil on the station. One of Diexil's side effects is flushing the kidneys. The substance with which you mixed the bioweapon inside you was released on contact with Diexil and you simply urinated the bioweapon out."

"That's ridiculous!" snapped Kotulan.

"Not at all."

"If it's so deadly, why didn't it kill me?!"

"You also had the antidote. Your Protectorate friends gave it to you."

The corners of Kotulan's mouth quivered, but he controlled himself. "Nonsense. That's just guesswork. How're you gonna prove it?"

"You made sure you could do everything in the peace of your cabin. I know that. But something always remains in the body that you need to get rid of gradually, by natural means, so to speak. We found traces of panasin in your toilet on the *Platypus*. And there's no other way they could have got there. Not aboard the ship or into your cabin!"

Behind Hila, Pradhan whistled.

All emotions swirled across Kotulan's face, then finally it contorted with anger.

He exploded.

The mask dropped.

"The damned Central Imperium is sending all of civilization to hell! Enhans are becoming second-class citizens! The Emperor himself is an Enhans and he's hypocritically cutting our rights one after the other! Look at me! I was well on the way to being captain of a ship, but after the war it wasn't proper for people like me to be in command, so they sent me to a supply ship!"

"So, you decided to kill everyone in the fleet?"

"Yes! Yes, that's exactly what I wanted to do! Destroy the entire fleet! This is war. A war for civilization. The New Protectorate is ruled by the strongest! It provides stability and prosperity! That is what civilization needs!"

Kotulan breathed out loudly. The anger and frustration inside him must have been seething for a long time. Hila recognized the expression of the confessing criminal. He suddenly relaxed. He'd wanted to shout everything out to the world.

Sparbo didn't show any signs of triumph or victory; she remained aloof and factual. She knew that it would be easy now. Kotulan would tell them everything.

"How did you sabotage the *Nagaland*'s generator?"

"I had nothing to do with that."

The Investigator was taken aback, for the first time. "We know that someone sabotaged the *Nagaland*."

"Not me."

"Come, now, Mr. Kotulan. You've already confessed to one crime. Why are you lying now?"

"I'm not. I had nothing to do with destroying the *Nagaland*!"

Sparbo said nothing but observed the offender. Hila and Pradhan were doing the same, via the monitor.

"What do you think?" asked the bodyguard.

Hila studied Kotulan's face. He was behaving exactly as she had assumed. His anger and frustration were no longer bottled up inside; he now wanted them to know how much he despised their laws and the lives of the people he'd endangered.

But he didn't tell them what they'd expected to hear.

"He isn't lying," said Hila, surprised herself by how sure she was. Maybe she had learned more about reading people from Daniel. "He had nothing to do with the *Nagaland*. He doesn't know who did it."

"But that means there are other saboteurs in the fleet," said Pradhan.

Hila did not like that thought one bit.

PART 6

"Are you sure he's telling the truth?" asked Admiral Vu, as Sparbo and Hila sat at the table in the flag conference room. Head of security Tarsen, engineer Captain Palmer and several other officers were already waiting for them. Pradhan assumed her traditional position by the door.

"I'm afraid he is," said Sparbo. "And not just because he no longer has any reason to lie. Even if he had any accomplices, taking it all on himself would benefit their schemes rather than not. Yes, he's arrogant, but I'm sure that he really is not behind the destruction of the *Nagaland.*"

"That means we have other saboteurs in the fleet," said Vu. "An entire conspiracy."

"I'm afraid that's how it is, Admiral."

Vu looked at Palmer. "Any new indications of what could have destroyed the *Nagaland*?"

"We're still working on it, sir, but nothing yet."

Vu rubbed his eyes. "I admit that I'm finding it hard to believe that we have one traitor in the fleet. But two? Or a whole group?"

Hila nodded. "Just like a few years ago we couldn't believe that so many politicians, officers and corporation bosses would try to destroy the Imperium from the inside."

Sparbo raised her hand. "I know it looks horrifying, ladies and gentlemen, but the list of suspects probably isn't that long."

Palmer twitched. "But we have thirty-six thousand people in the fleet."

"That is true. But how many of them could access the Gertz generator in the flagship? And I think we can narrow it down still further. Only the ship's technicians can access the generator, that goes without saying. Did any of them survive the destruction of the ship?"

Tarsen consulted his terminal, then shook his head. "No. Eighteen crew members survived the destruction of the *Nagaland*. People who were either working on other ships or on leave on the station. But none of them worked anywhere near the engine room."

"I would like to question them anyway, if only for the sake of completeness. What about visitors from other ships?"

"There's one possibility here," said Palmer, checking something beside him. "Yeah, here it is."

"The *Carina*?" asked Tarsen.

"Yes, the *Carina*." To Hila and Sparbo, he added: "That's the repair ship in the Fifth Fleet. She sent a repair team to the *Nagaland*… two weeks ago," he said, reading from his information. "They helped change the coils in the Gertz generator."

"Where the explosion was?" Hila asked.

"No, but if the saboteur was one of that team, there'd be no great difficulty in placing something on or near the generator cover where it did explode."

"How many people were in that team?"

"Twenty-two. Fifteen of them came aboard the *Nagaland* that time. Plus, eight service robots."

"Please check the robots in case someone hacked them. And invite the members of the repair team for questioning."

Tarsen looked questioningly at the Admiral, who nodded. "As Madam Investigator suggests. By the way, the way you discovered that Kotulan's toilet still contained traces of pasanin was amazing. How did you even think of looking there?"

Sparbo smiled. "Send the forensics team to his cabin. Maybe they actually *will* find something in his toilet."

Hila burst out laughing. She couldn't stop herself.

Φ

They decided to question the repair team in the somewhat less formal environment of one of the briefing rooms on the ship.

A sturdily built woman with olive skin and a set of blue tattoos on her temples was the first person led into the room by Warrant Officer Tarsen. The woman looked guarded and was a little taken aback to see Hila sitting there with the Imperial Investigator.

"Your Majesty…"

"At ease. I'm only here as an observer," Hila twinkled. "And as someone to assure you that you really do have nothing to be afraid of."

But the woman looked confident enough as she sat down at Sparbo's invitation.

"As Her Majesty has already said, there's nothing to be afraid of. I will only add that this is not a court. I merely need to verify a few facts."

"Understood, ma'am," said the woman.

"Please state your name, rank and number for the records."

"Chief Petty Officer Joanna Lors, service number 07-41029-1."

"What is your posting?"

"Head of repair team 14 on the INS *Carina.*"

"And where do you come from?"

"I was born on Davenport."

"On the tenth of this month you and your team visited the ship *Nagaland*, is that right?"

"Yes, ma'am. We changed defective coils in the Gertz generator."

"Was the defect anything unusual?"

"What do you mean, ma'am?"

"Was the defect a routine type?"

"Yes, lots of coils wear out quickly. The new ones need to be fine-tuned."

"Could the coils damage the ship in any way?"

Lors slowly shook her head. "Do you mean, could the faulty coil destroy the ship? No, ma'am. If the coil broke down, the generator would stop working but not explode. Only the central chamber of the generator can explode, and only if the casing is damaged."

Sparbo frowned. "Chief Lors, while you were conducting repairs on the *Nagaland*, did you notice anything that may at that moment have seemed innocent, but in retrospect could have been a sabotage attempt?"

"Do you mean by one of my people?"

"Yes."

"No, that isn't possible."

"Really? You could always see all of them, the whole time? You know very well that not even a security camera will pick up everything."

"I couldn't see them all the whole time, the Gertz generator room is big and my people, like the *Nagaland*'s technicians, were working all around it. But I know my team and none of them would be capable…"

"Chief, I understand your loyalty and none of your people is accused of anything. But hypothetically, if one of your people wanted, for example, to rapidly put some corrosive material on the generator casing, so it ate through it unobtrusively, would they have the opportunity?"

Lors looked at Hila, who smiled encouragingly. She understood what the Chief—as Chief Petty Officers were addressed—was going through. She didn't want to betray her people, but Sparbo was right. This was about whether someone was hypothetically able.

After all, Daniel also had no idea that his own uncle would try to kill him, but it happened.

"Yes, ma'am, I think it would be possible."

"Thank you. Last question: Was anyone from your team aboard the supplies ship *Platypus* in, let's say, the last two months?"

Lors may have been taken aback by the change of subject. She stared frowningly into the distance. "I think… yes. A month ago. All our team helped the supplies guys from the *Platypus* to patch up a defective reactor intended for a cruiser."

"Thank you, Chief. Thank you very much. You may go for now."

"Thank you, ma'am." Lors stood up and Tarsen motioned her out.

"Bring the next one in, please, Mr. Tarsen."

The fourth person to be questioned was a young man who might have been nineteen or twenty. Gangly, dark-haired, eyes high up on his face, he looked like a puppy on its first visit to the vet.

The sight of Hila didn't reassure him much, but Hila and Sparbo again assured him that he had nothing to be afraid of and that this was not a court.

"Please state your name, rank and number for the record," Sparbo ordered as he sat down.

"Specialist second-class Ingar Feigins, service number 17-51108-1."

"And your posting?"

"I'm a member of repair team 14 on the INS *Carina*."

"And where do you come from, Mr. Feigins?"

The terrified expression became even more terrified. "I was born on… on Ferrel Kast."

Sparbo narrowed her eyes. "Fine. On the tenth of this month, you and the rest of team 14 were involved in repairs on the ship *Nagaland*. What exactly was your responsibility?"

"I—we—did a lot of stuff. Chief Lors entrusted me with changing coil eight and then I analyzed the generator casing."

"On your own?"

"No, Specialist Evans and Specialist Gotano helped me."

Sparbo fixed her eyes on him. "You know that you really do have nothing to be afraid of, Mr. Feigins?"

The youth nodded jerkily. "I know, ma'am."

Sparbo smiled. "Are you too warm? You look flushed to me. Should I turn down the heating?"

"No-o, ma'am. It's fine. I'm not too warm."

"Aha, my mistake. I apologize. Tell me. While you were repairing the generator, did you notice anything…"

Sparbo continued to ask questions, as she had of all the others before him. This time, Hila watched the Investigator more than the young man. What was she driving at when she asked if he was too hot?

When she focused on Feigins, she didn't notice anything strange about him. He was afraid, maybe even actually terrified. That was obvious, but probably because he was being questioned by the Imperial

Investigator and, in addition, Hila's presence did not give a calming impression. She didn't know what was meant by the comment about being warm. Feigins wasn't sweating, he was well built but still looked like a child.

"That's everything I wanted to know, Mr. Feigins," said Sparbo, ending the interrogation, and smiling at him in a grandmotherly sort of way. "I hope I haven't kept you for too long. I know that this investigation isn't pleasant for any of you. Please accept my apologies." She stood up and held out her hand to the young man.

Feigins stared at her in surprise, then took her hand. Sparbo pressed his between both of hers, as if they knew each other well.

"Once again, my apologies. I hope the rest of your shift today goes well."

"Th-thank you, ma'am."

The youth left. As the door closed behind him, Tarsen, who was probably as confused as Hila, turned to Sparbo. "Should I bring in the next one?"

"No, hang on a moment," said Sparbo, and reached for the terminal. "I need to find Specialist Feigins' medical records."

"What for?" Hila wondered.

"I recognized it from a distance. He wasn't too warm, but he was warm. And when I shook his hand, I confirmed it."

"You confirmed what?"

"Feigins is an Enhans."

Φ

"You're going to have to explain that," said Admiral Vu, when they met again in the flag conference room. "I admit that I don't know that much about Enhans. I get that they're more resistant and more intelligent, and that the Protectors created them way back as a sort of ruling class, but I don't know much about their physiology. Why do you think that Specialist Feigins is an Enhans?"

"Among other things, Enhans have a significantly faster metabolism," said Sparbo. "Because of their greater stamina and similar things, but they also have a higher body temperature because they burn calories faster. Normals have a body temperature of around thirty-seven degrees, but for Enhans, it can be as high as forty. Their bodies are adapted to it, but for us normals, it feels like they have a fever when we touch them."

"That is true," Hila confirmed. "Sleeping with the Emperor under one blanket is like sleeping next to a small reactor."

Something in Vu's expression indicated that he did not wish to imagine everything. "Fine. But how come we didn't know this about Feigins?"

"And I would also like to ask if it's absolutely certain that he's an Enhans?" added Vu's chief of staff, Captain Tidemand. "He could have a raised body temperature for any number of reasons."

"I'll answer the second question first," said Sparbo. "I am convinced that Feigins is an Enhans, but I will verify it. I thought that I would send Warrant Officer Tarsen here, or his opposite number on the *Carina*, to search Feigins' cabin, to obtain DNA samples from his hair and so on. But if security offices pried into his cabin, there'd be no way of keeping it secret on a repair ship, and I don't want to scare Feigins off. So, I sent a query to the Imperial Navy's central register and requested access to a sample of Feigins' DNA."

"But that database can only be used to identify remains. Using it for a criminal investigation isn't allowed!"

"No, not under normal circumstances, certainly not, but I have that special jurisdiction as Imperial Investigator. What's more, I won't use the DNA as evidence, only to establish the facts." She turned back to Vu: "And regarding your first question, Admiral: I don't know why we didn't know about Feigins. An individual's genetic status is a required field on the Imperial Navy's application form. In addition to Enhans, we can also identify members with various defects or people from worlds where their bodies have mutated in some way. For Enhans it was always a matter of prestige. They wanted everyone to know they were superior."

Hila remembered thinking this about Daniel, when she met him for the first time. It was no longer her opinion of him.

On the other hand, families like the Lardons or the Hartveits still thought like that today.

"And how could they get round it?" Vu wondered.

"I've already sent the query to Hub. He came in via the recruitment office on Ferrel Kast. They did his entrance medical there. He could simply have bribed the doctor who examined him to lie in his records. And then, his training school would have just accepted those records. The *Carina* is his first placement in space, and he must have had to report to the chief doctor there. I'll check out how that went."

Hila remembered her own genetic modifications that had made her an Omega agent. And which she had kept secret with the help of the ship's doctor. He was forbidden to say anything.

"I think that the doctor could maintain medical confidentiality," she said aloud. "Particularly when it didn't endanger the fleet."

"I'm not sure about that danger right now," said Sparbo. "Why would Feigins conceal it?"

"And do you know it for sure now?" said Vu, going back to his original question.

"Not yet, but I will in two hours, when our center on Hub connects with the *Quezon*." She turned to Tarsen. "In the meantime, I would limit Feigins' movements, and at the very least keep him away from the critical parts of any ship."

"That won't be easy," Tarsen said. "Particularly not if you want to be unobtrusive."

"We can keep all of repair team 14 aboard. We'll think of a pretext."

"Just a moment!" exclaimed Vu. "Do you have any evidence that Feigins has committed anything at all? All we know—or rather suspect—for now is that he's an Enhans. That doesn't make him a saboteur."

"Maybe not," said Sparbo, looking briefly at Hila too. Hila didn't know what to think. "But Feigins lied about being an Enhans. Why?

Practically no other Enhans hides the fact. He joined the Navy only after the war, he could have been planted there from the very beginning, waiting for exactly such a situation. He had access to the generator on the *Nagaland* and just like that, his team also visited the *Platypus*."

"None of that is direct evidence," said Vu. Hila understood his attitude. She was opening her mouth to add something, but then Tarsen spoke up.

"No, Admiral, it's not direct evidence, but nobody is accusing Feigins of anything yet either. We only want to continue the investigation. At the end of the day, we don't even know how many other ships someone may try to sabotage. We must get to the root of the problem."

"Mr. Tarsen is right," said Sparbo. "We should…"

She was interrupted by a beeping comlink. Vu reached for his transmitter and pressed a button. "Admiral here."

"Captain Palmer here, sir," said a familiar voice. "Is Imperial Investigator Sparbo with you?"

"Yes. And the Empress too."

"Please could you all come into the engine room? We've discovered something."

Φ

Palmer was waiting for them in the *Quezon*'s engine room with the ship's chief engineer, captain, and a group of technicians. When Vu, Sparbo, Hila and their group arrived, the room by the window overlooking the Gertz generator became rather too full.

"Your Majesty, Admiral, Madam Investigator, we've discovered something very interesting. When I compared the status of the *Nagaland*'s generator with the records from the ship's black box, I used the *Quezon* for comparison purposes, because the ships are identical. The vessels sailed away from the docks only two days apart. Their eight sister ships are now completing space tests on Hub."

"And what have you found out, Captain?" Sparbo asked.

"The explosion really was caused by a crack in the generator's casing. We have discovered that the casing was weakened in several places, under the influence of some sort of radiation that was active for some time. And when we checked the generator cover on the *Quezon*, for comparison purposes, we found the same weakened cover. Exactly the same."

"So, the saboteur was here too and tried to destroy this ship as well?" asked Sparbo. This was pointing increasingly at someone who had access to all vessels in the fleet, like a member of a repair team.

"No, ma'am," said Palmer. "A radiation weakness couldn't be caused by one saboteur. The casing must have been subjected to it regularly for months on end. Not even the ship's engineers could do that."

"Did you say months?" Vu asked. "But the *Nagaland* and the *Quezon* only arrived a month ago."

"Exactly, Admiral. I sent a request for information the last time we had contact with Hub. The casings were supplied by a firm from Palawan. One of our new military contractors. It seems that they supplied cases for the first ten generators intended for *Nagaland*-class ships, but a radiation leak was reported in their factory six months ago now. But nobody realized that it had caused defects in some generator cases."

Sparbo threw up her hands. "I'm afraid I'm lost, Captain. What are you trying to tell us?"

Palmer took a deep breath. "I mean, ma'am, that the sabotage of the *Nagaland* was not sabotage. It was an accident. A tragic accident caused by a manufacturing error."

PART 7

Hila realized she was in high spirits as they returned to the conference room. An accident caused by a manufacturing defect—a defect that would undoubtedly be thoroughly investigated by the Imperial inspectors—was tragic and had taken eight hundred lives. But that was still better than deliberate sabotage.

Palmer had confirmed everything, and documented it, and the Admiralty on Hub confirmed that the other *Nagaland*-class ships also had the defect. The faulty cases were currently being uninstalled from all ships and the *Quezon*'s technicians were currently working on the one aboard.

But Annika Sparbo did not look so confident. Nor did Warrant Officer Tarsen.

"I find it very hard to believe that it was an accident."

Vu frowned. "If Captain Palmer and his entire team of engineers confirm that it was an accident, then it was an accident."

"Could it have been sabotage in the factory, sir?" suggested Tarsen.

"Possibly, but I doubt it. If I wanted to speculate about such matters, there are many other ways of sabotaging a fleet. And many more effective ways." He looked at Hila, who nodded. The admiral was right.

"It looks as if the explosion of the *Nagaland* really was a tragic accident and has nothing to do with the sabotage attempt," she said. "No wonder Kotulan knew nothing about it. Maybe it was a crazy coincidence that it happened at the same time, but I've experienced similar things both with the Omegas and as a journalist."

Sparbo raised her hand. "Before we start congratulating ourselves and patting each other on the back, let's take a step back and look at it dispassionately. The mere fact that the *Nagaland* was not sabotaged does not yet mean that we don't have a conspiracy here. It is possible that other sabotage attempts are in preparation in the Fifth Fleet."

"We don't know for sure that there is a conspiracy here. Kotulan insisted that he had no collaborators, and you believed him."

"Well, indeed, Admiral. Kotulan didn't need to know his accomplices. That way he couldn't betray them if he was caught. Do you really think that he would have almost managed to kill all people in the fleet if he had no accomplices?"

Vu snorted. "It would be difficult, but definitely not impossible!"

Hila watched them. Most of her instincts were telling her that Kotulan could have acted alone. During the war, one saboteur had killed the entire crew of the station *Coral Star* with radiation.

"We should interrogate Feigins again," said Sparbo. "He still lied to us about being an Enhans. Why would he do that if he didn't want to hide it?!"

"I agree, Admiral," Tarsen added. "Whatever Feigins may have done, he withheld information on his application form, and that's illegal. They could give him a dishonorable discharge for that."

"That doesn't make him a saboteur, though," said Hila.

Sparbo nodded. "That's true, ma'am, but even so, we should continue to interrogate him. If only to prove his innocence."

Hila's stomach cramped. "Ms. Sparbo, he is innocent. He is innocent until proven guilty."

Sparbo looked at her with her gracious, grandmotherly expression. "Of course he is, ma'am. That's what I meant. I meant that further interrogations would confirm his innocence definitively. For his sake. Whether he was mixed up in the conspiracy or not, people will gossip about him. We need to smack down any suspicion against him."

Hila bit her tongue. She didn't like this. She didn't like this one little bit.

Vu was frowning, but he nodded. "Okay, fine. You're the Imperial Investigator; it's up to you. But I intend to assign the JAG officer as Mr. Feigins's representative."

"That won't be necessary, Admiral. This isn't a court of law."

"So, nobody will mind if a JAG officer is present."

Sparbo smiled. "Of course not, Admiral."

Hila didn't know what to think. She observed Sparbo's sweet, grandmotherly smile. The woman was an experienced Investigator. Maybe she should trust her.

Φ

Hila, accompanied by Pradhan, entered the lecture theater in which Sparbo conducted her interrogations and stopped short.

The hall was packed.

Mainly by *Quezon* crew members, but Hila recognized several people from the crews of other ships by their shoulder patches, and plenty of civilians, probably from the station.

Feigins sat on a small podium and looked as if he were in the stocks on the main square.

That parallel seemed only too apt to Hila.

Tarsen came up to her. "Your Majesty, a seat has been reserved for you at the back there, there's space due to your security and…"

"Why is this inquiry public?" hissed Hila.

Tarsen shrugged. "Ms. Sparbo wanted it, Your Majesty."

The Investigator was just preparing to sit down at a long table opposite the person under interrogation. Two assistants were preparing documents for her.

In a few long steps, Hila was beside her. She lowered her voice.

"What does this mean? Why are you putting on a spectacle for the public?"

This time Sparbo wasn't smiling. She was serious. "Members of the armed forces and a few civilians from the station aren't exactly the *public*, ma'am. In my experience, a long, secret investigation benefits nothing and no one, least of all the person under investigation. It leads to speculation, and then the public gets the impression that we're not telling them everything."

"You just used the word *public* too."

"Let's not quibble, ma'am. The other thing is that spies and conspirators cannot stand being the center of attention. They prefer to hide in the shadows. This is an effective method."

Hila looked at the unfortunate Feigins. The pressure was working.

But that did not mean that he was guilty of anything.

However, Sparbo did not intend to argue with her further, and not even the Empress should sit around and pretend she was interfering in the investigation. She found Admiral Vu among the spectators. He looked even more unhappy than she was. The JAG officer assigned to Feigins wore a strictly neutral expression.

Hila sat down and Pradhan took up position behind her.

"I don't like this, Devika."

"Before we start," thundered Sparbo's voice. "Allow me to remind you again, Mr. Feigins, that this isn't a court, and that you are not accused of anything. Do you understand?"

Her reassurance was as convincing as a doctor's "don't worry, this won't hurt".

"Ye…yes, ma'am."

"Mr. Feigins, is it true that, as a member of the repair team aboard the *Carina*, you have access not only to spare parts, but to various industrial chemicals and rapid printers?"

"Yes, ma'am. But an officer must approve use of the rapid printers."

"I understand. I also believe that your team recently visited the ship *Platypus*."

"Our team travels around the entire fleet, ma'am."

"When you were aboard the *Platypus*, did you meet any of the ship's logistics department?"

"Yes, probably. I met a lot of enlisted members."

"Did you take any chemicals aboard the *Platypus*?"

"No, ma'am."

"Did you meet Lieutenant-Commander Henry Kotulan?"

"No, ma'am!"

"Really? One of the chemicals that Kotulan used with panasin to mix the toxin he wanted to poison the entire fleet with is found in the *Carina*'s stores, to which you have access."

Hila was taken aback. She knew nothing about this…

"I didn't have anything to do with that!" yelled Feigins.

"And what about the Gertz generator on the *Nagaland*? The generator that you worked on a few days before the *Nagaland* and her entire crew exploded. What if I told you that its casing was weakened by a corrosive chemical made from a mix of panasin and the substance to which you also have access?"

Hila looked up sharply. She saw that Admiral Vu had almost jumped up.

That wasn't true, that wasn't true…

"I had nothing to do with that either!" Feigins looked like he wanted to cry. Suddenly he looked exactly his age. Like a lost puppy.

Sparbo got tougher.

"How can we believe you, Mr. Feigins, when we already know—I repeat, we *know*—that you are a liar. You lied when you completed the application form for the Imperial Navy!"

An expression of pure horror appeared on Feigins' face.

"Isn't it true that you didn't mention that you are an Enhans on the form, Mr. Feigins? That you bribed the doctor in the recruitment office to not mention this in your records. And I must ask why you needed to conceal the fact that you are an Enhans? And why, on your first posting, the entire fleet was endangered with the help of another Enhans?"

A hum began to fill the hall.

"Is it true, or not, Mr. Feigins? We're all waiting! Answer!"

The JAG officer rushed over to Feigins and rapidly whispered something to him. The youth was really trembling now. Tears ran down his face.

"Based on the advice of my representative, I in-invoke Article Ten of the Constitution of the Central Imperium… a-and I refuse to answer these questions."

Φ

They met again in the flag conference room.

Once again, the mood was completely different from before.

"You lied," said Hila, as she sat down. "You lied about what caused the destruction of the *Nagaland!*"

Sparbo looked at her with an astonished expression. "And when I lied to Kotulan about finding traces of the chemicals he used for the sabotage in his bathroom, you didn't mind?"

"That was…" Hila stopped short. She'd been about to say that that was different, but it wasn't. Only then it had seemed okay to her, because…

Because why? Because then, she had lied to the arrogant Enhans Kotulan? And now she's lying to the terrified puppy Feigins? Who is also an Enhans… but so is my little Elda.

"You're right. I didn't mind then, and maybe I was wrong not to."

Sparbo shook her head. "Nonsense. It's a tried-and-tested technique for turning up the pressure. And it works."

"It didn't work on Mr. Feigins. He confessed to nothing," said Vu. The admiral was angry.

"That doesn't mean that it didn't work. He backed himself into a corner until finally he refused to testify, by which he gave away everything possible. That he's afraid to tell us his real reasons, among other things."

"But you can't take it like that!" exclaimed Hila. "Article Ten of the Constitution guarantees his right not to testify, and that his silence cannot be considered proof of guilt."

"Your Majesty," said Sparbo, switching to the more formal title, as her tone slid into condescension. "Of course. I realize that. However, as I have continually repeated, this is not a court of law. I am an Investigator. I have very broad jurisdiction from the government, and I intend to find the truth and uncover the conspiracy that has appeared in this fleet. And clearly, we do have a conspiracy here. Kotulan confessed."

"Yes, Kotulan confessed, he will stand trial and pay for his crimes," said Hila. "But that has nothing to do with Feigins. We have no direct evidence against him."

"He is an Enhans and hid this fact. He joined the Navy shortly after the war, when a great many Enhans and their sympathizers and agents of the New Protectorate went underground. Can none of you really make that connection?"

"It's not about connections," said Vu. "It's about a member of my fleet, *my* fleet, being accused, despite the fact that you have no evidence against him."

"We will have evidence. Clear evidence. As soon as we interrogate other witnesses, as soon as we search through Feigins' history, we will find evidence." She looked at Hila. "Compared to what you did during the war and before, to that bastard on Folna, for example, this is absolutely nothing. Just as you and I both work for the Imperium. For civilization!"

"That was war," Hila objected automatically, but stopped short. She suddenly remembered what she herself said when she and Vu's task force had been flying to Kaffer.

Every war develops into a cleansing action. But you can still die in one of those.

Was Sparbo not doing anything different from what she had done in the war?

And what did that say about Hila?

"We're at war now too!" said Sparbo, with another smile. The grandmotherly expression had, however, now been permanently replaced by condescension. "The war was never over for our enemies. They only changed the way they fight. What if, next time, we don't succeed in stopping someone like Kotulan or Feigins? What if tens of thousands of people die and it knocks out an entire fleet? Someone like Kotulan or Feigins could destroy the whole Central Imperium. That's why there are Imperial Investigators like me. We're foot soldiers in this war, and when at war, we must fight with all means possible! *Inter arma enim silent leges*, as they say."

Hila knew that Vu had obtained a classical education before joining the Navy—they had come back into fashion in recent decades—so the Admiral didn't even blink when the Investigator switched into Latin. "'In times of war, the law falls silent.' Cicero. So, you see us as a twenty-eighth century Rome?"

Sparbo shook her head. "No, Admiral, Your Majesty. We are not Rome. We are a civilization. A civilization that must continue, and I will do anything to ensure it does. And that isn't all. I have jurisdiction to do so." She stood up. "And now, if you will excuse me, I have further interrogations ahead."

She left the conference room.

Hila waited until the door closed behind her, then looked at the admiral.

They had the same opinion of the situation.

"Can you stop it in any way, Your Majesty?" asked the admiral baldly.

Hila shook her head. "I… can't. As Empress I have very limited jurisdiction in criminal investigations. Even my presence at a hearing depends on the Investigator's permission."

Vu thought briefly. "The Imperial Investigator does not fall under my command, so I can't restrict her in any way. But I can contact the Admiralty. I'll tell High Admiral Toscano what's happening."

Hila nodded. "Actually, I can do something."

"What?"

"I can make use of my experience as an Omega, and particularly as an investigative journalist. I'm going to do an interview."

"Who with?"

Hila nodded at Pradhan. "With Specialist Feigins."

PART 8

When Pradhan led Feigins into the cabin, Hila tried to soothe the boy, but without much success.

"Sit down, Mr. Feigins. You can leave us, Devika."

Pradhan took up her position outside the cabin door as it closed.

Feigins sat down, looking like an animal seeking an escape route.

Hila knew that she could be sweet and kind, but so was Sparbo, until she started to tear into him. She probably shouldn't beat around the bush.

She sat down opposite him.

"Believe it or not, I really have not come to interrogate you. As the Empress I don't even have the power to do so. Maybe my title will soon be Empress Consort; the protocol experts have been arguing recently about whether to rename the position, because it's a bit different to being the Emperor in the way my husband Daniel is. Have you heard of Daniel?"

Feigins nodded. "Of course, ma'am… Your Majesty. And of you too. About everything you did during the war. I know about your missions to Lundin, Barrondo, Folna, Valakor, about the battles on Earth and then on Hub. How you fought your way through the station *Hub Central* together. It was like something out of a legend."

Hila would have liked to say that it wasn't advisable to believe everything you hear, but most of her war experiences were so bizarre that they really couldn't be embellished much.

"Tell me something about yourself, Mr. Feigins. I believe you're a mechanic. Do you want to obtain an education in the Navy, then find a job in the private sector?"

"No, ma'am … Your Majesty."

"'Ma'am' is fine."

"Ma'am, I… admit that I wanted to join the Navy after the war. I always knew that I was good at mending stuff and my stepfather always helped me. But then the war started. It wasn't terrible on Ferrel Kast, not like other places, but there was fighting at the local military base too, against sympathizers of the Emperor's uncle. Some local Enhans were also on the side of our… well, the enemy side."

"And you decided to join the Navy after the war, right?"

"Yes, ma'am. I… the recruitment officer on Ferrel Kast told me that the Navy always needs good mechanics and that the technical training the Navy provides is at least as good as any university, and he was right. I was able to be part of something bigger than me. To help somehow. I guess I was a patriot. I remember how thrilled I was when they posted me to the *Carina*. My first deployment."

He looked at the top of the coffee-table between them. "And now it's all over. They'll throw me out of the Navy. I'll go to prison."

"If you're innocent, nobody will hurt you," said Hila. "I guarantee you that."

"But I am not innocent! I didn't sabotage the ship, I didn't collaborate with any enemy agents, but, hell, I really did rig my application form and bribe the doctor! I'm an Enhans!" He was staring at the tabletop again. A tear appeared on his face.

Hila pushed the box of tissues toward him, with a glass of very sweet juice. She suppressed the urge to stroke his head. "It's okay. It's okay."

"It isn't, ma'am. You don't know what the atmosphere immediately after the war was like. The recruitment officer warned me. Everyone saw the Emperor as a hero, but other Enhans… no one trusted them. My mother was Sebastian Calvador's lover. An Enhans who lived on Ferrel Kast. One of the promiscuous ones who deliberately spread their genes. And my mother probably wanted an Enhans child. Then, after what happened on Tarlin, if you remember? Where they killed the Enhans? She didn't boast about it so much after that. And I decided that I'd keep it a secret in the Navy."

He wiped his eyes and drank some of the sweet juice. "That will probably count against me, won't it, ma'am?"

Hila automatically shook her head. Not all Enhans sat in the House of Families. There were many like Feigins.

Nothing of what Feigins had told her proved his innocence. But Hila didn't need proof—and not just because he was innocent until proven guilty under the law.

"Nobody will hurt you, Ingar," she said, using his first name. "I will do whatever is in my power."

"But you said yourself that you don't have that power," said Feigins. "And Ms. Sparbo emphasizes repeatedly that this isn't a court. What can you do for me?"

Hila knew what she could do. Sparbo was zealous, and maybe couldn't see the wood for the trees, but she was reasonable. It wasn't about power; it was about what was right.

"I will help you," she promised.

Φ

"Tell me, Chief Lors," Sparbo asked the woman she was interrogating. "When you and your repair team visited the ship *Platypus*, did Specialist Feigins or anyone else of your people meet Lieutenant-Commander Kotulan?"

"No, ma'am," said Lors, looking like someone who'd spent the last hour walking round a minefield. "None of us met him."

"And did Specialist Feigins talk to any other of the *Platypus*'s crew members?"

"Yes, when we went to eat in the ship's mess. He sat with some crew members there."

"Can you specify whom, exactly?"

Lors was surrounded by mines now. "It was an innocent social gathering."

Sparbo put on her grandmotherly smile. "If it was so innocent, why are you afraid to tell me their names? After all, Chief, I don't want to hurt anyone. I just need to ask those people a few questions so we can be sure of what happened on the *Platypus*."

Lors sighed. "I know that he was sitting with Specialists Volkov, Abran and two others whose names I don't know. I only knew those two because I met them last time I was aboard."

"You see! That wasn't so difficult, was it?"

Hila crossed the hall and stopped beside Sparbo. "Ma'am, I need to talk to you."

The Investigator raised her head. "Of course. How about this afternoon?"

"No. Now."

Sparbo sighed, like a parent when a child interrupts their work. "Well, fine then, ma'am. I've pretty much finished here. Thank you, Chief Lors, you can go."

The head of the repair team was evidently glad to be released.

Not long afterwards, Hila and Sparbo were alone in Hila's cabin.

"Will you have some more cognac?" asked Hila.

"No thank you, ma'am. I'm on duty. There will be a lot of interrogations today."

Hila was briefly unsure of how to continue. She remembered Daniel and his eloquence, how he had convinced the rebellious crew of a warship to join him.

Hila was not nearly so eloquent.

"Ma'am… these interrogations will have to stop."

Sparbo sat up straighter. "What do you mean, Your Majesty?"

The more formal form of address, again.

"As I said. The interrogation of Specialist Feigins went too far. We have no direct evidence against him, and you lied to him about what caused the explosion of the *Nagaland*."

"As I have already explained, that was a method of turning up the pressure that you approved when I used it on Kotulan." Sparbo stood up and began to walk around the cabin. "I cannot believe that you're saying this to me. You! An Omega who spent her entire adult life fighting Enhans intrigues and various traitors to the Imperium! You, whom the entire Imperium admires and looks up to! Maybe even more so than they do Emperor Daniel. And you're saying this to me?"

"Yes, I am, and I am serious."

"Are you aware that you do not have the power to give me orders on anything? As the Imperial Investigator, I answer to almost nobody, and certainly not to you."

"I know, and I'm not ordering you to do anything," said Hila, in a more conciliatory tone. "I'm asking you. Begging you. Ma'am, I admire you too. I admire your work on Haveloc, and then later on Arnhem. We achieved victory at Kaffer thanks to your information. You are a model of devotion and self-sacrifice, but this time you have gone too far. You are persecuting an innocent man."

Sparbo chuckled. "And how do you know that he is innocent?"

"I talked to him."

This time the Investigator could only roll her eyes in disbelief. "Let me guess. He told you that he's only an unfortunate victim of circumstance. Did he add any tragic story from his childhood?"

"His childhood wasn't so different from yours or mine. His family was only trying to survive. Yes, Feigins made a mistake when he lied about not being an Enhans on his application form, but that does not make him a saboteur or a traitor."

"How can you be so naive?! Enhans tried to destroy the entire Imperium! They allied themselves with the New Protectorate. They intrigued for decades to regain their old powers!"

"Not all of them."

"Oh, please, spare me phrases like *they're not all like that*! Every Enhans whom I've found guilty of something said that to me. Best case scenario, they then add something like *don't judge the barrel by a few bad apples* or *I've been discriminated against because I'm an Enhans*."

She was saying exactly the same phrases that, only a few days ago, Hila herself had detested.

"The Emperor is also an Enhans! And Feigins is the illegitimate son of an Enhans. His mother was the lover of some big shot. There are hundreds, probably thousands of such Enhans love children in the Imperium."

"Yes, and one of them was, ooh, Admiral Maya Kutevska, who used her ship to bomb Earth at the end of the war, because another Enhans ordered her to. An Enhans who was a member of the ruling family and who intended to kill his own daughter in that attack!"

"Yes, and he paid for his crimes, as did Kutevska. But we have no proof that Feigins has committed anything!"

For a long moment, Sparbo observed Hila. Her mouth moved soundlessly as she studied the Empress. As if she were seeing her for the first time. As if, suddenly, she saw her completely differently. In a new way.

Finally, she shook her head.

"I'm an idiot. I've been so naive. I understand what the problem is, Your Majesty. After all, it's absolutely clear!" This time she pronounced the formal title almost as if it were an insult. "You married an Enhans. You have an Enhans child. Of course you're starting to take their side. You've lost perspective. Of course you believe that Feigins is innocent. He's no longer a potential enemy, even if he infiltrated his way in under false pretenses. No, he's *one of you*. That's how you see it, isn't it? You're the Empress now, the mother of the Enhans heir to the throne. It's logical that you would take the Enhans side and you don't care how many lives they endanger."

Hila was speechless. It was like a slap in the face. An enormous slap in the face, from Sparbo. Now, for a change, it was Hila's turn to observe the other woman for a long time. Inside her, an icy anger began to burgeon, like a giant fist clenching.

"My Enhans husband saved the entire Central Imperium," she said hoarsely. "As did some other Enhans."

"Yes. After that same Imperium was betrayed by members of his own family! Do you know how many corpses his uncle had on his conscience? A member of the family *you* married into. Hundreds of millions? Billions?" She sighed. "You know what I've been doing in recent years, while you were living in your ivory tower with your new family, cutting ribbons, being the patron of charity foundations and giving speeches? I traveled from planet to planet. I lived and slept in hotels and shuttles. I don't remember the last time I saw my family. But that's a sacrifice I'm happy to make, because I believe one thing that used to be the motto of the ruling family, before they turned their backs on it: Civilization must continue. And despite all its problems, the Central Imperium is that civilization. And Enhans like Kotulan and Feigins are a danger to that civilization."

Hila slowly stood up. She refused to argue any further. She stared Sparbo right in the eye.

"The investigation of Ingar Feigins is over. Admiral Vu has already contacted the Admiralty, and I will happily go see the prime minister and inform her of what is going on here."

The trump card appeared in Sparbo's eyes. "I have news for you, Your Majesty. I am here on government authorization. Prime Minister Gilbert has a great many problems of her own and Minister Rosenthal has my back. He knows what I'm doing here, and he approves my work. And as for Admiral Vu, he will report for interrogation tomorrow morning. His recent activities have cast suspicion on him."

She smiled. "I think we have now discussed everything you wanted, Your Majesty. Or are you going to run to your husband the Emperor? That would create a wonderful constitutional crisis. Maybe you don't realize this, but you cannot intervene in my investigation. No one can."

She headed for the door, but before she departed, she stopped and turned around for the last time.

"And by the way, Your Majesty. As a member of the executive, you had access to criminal investigations with my permission only. I withdraw that permission. You may not attend any interrogations from now on."

Φ

"Warrant Officer Tarsen!"

The head of the ship's police stopped and, somewhat surprised, raised his eyebrows, when he noticed that Hila, followed by Pradhan, was chasing after him.

"Your Majesty?"

"I need to talk to you."

"Certainly."

They were standing in the corridor in the *Quezon*'s starboard linkway. Other crew members were walking past them, but Hila judged they could still hold the conversation here.

"Warrant Officer, I want this investigation to stop. I know that Sparbo has charged you with searching for other conspirators, but… stop."

"I don't understand, ma'am."

She sighed. "This investigation has gone too far. We must stop it."

"But there are saboteurs in the fleet. Kotulan confessed."

"Yes, he did, yes. But the others…"

"Feigins has also confessed."

"Hell, no. He hasn't. He refused to testify. That's not the same thing."

Tarsen still didn't understand her. "Ma'am, I lost friends on *Kaffer Minor*. Other conspirators killed them."

"That isn't Feigins' fault!"

"Ma'am, with all due respect, the Central Imperium has enemies! We must find them! And if that means Feigins' life is a bit more difficult, even if he's innocent, then so be it. I won't say for the good of the Imperium, but maybe it will mean that I won't have to stuff more kids into body bags!"

Hila opened her mouth, then closed it again. Tarsen was glaring at her, maybe respectfully, but determinedly.

She wanted to order him to stop but couldn't. She didn't have the authority.

Admiral Vu couldn't and didn't have the power either.

She understood where he was coming from. She even understood where Sparbo was coming from. She'd been there once.

And when had she stopped seeing things the way they did?

She said nothing. She let Tarsen go and headed for her cabin.

PART 9

Devika Pradhan had already seen her charge in various situations. She wouldn't have stated that this was the worst, but Hila Eban, just like her husband, Emperor Daniel Hankerson, was proud of always being able to find a solution to the problem. It wasn't always simple, or pleasant, but there always was one. They both hated feeling powerless, as they did when they simply *didn't know* what to do.

This was probably how Hila was now feeling.

The Empress was used to direct methods, but she couldn't use them now. She couldn't go to the prime minister, or her husband the Emperor, and force them to recall the Imperial Investigator. She just couldn't.

Pradhan was trying to suggest that they could simply leave. Return home. They'd already spent more time with the Fifth Fleet than originally planned. Of course, the presence of the Empress was a big boost to morale—they adored Hila.

But they could go home. There wasn't anything more they could do here. This was at least what Pradhan suggested, but Hila wouldn't hear of it. She invited her bodyguard into the cabin. Now they were both in pajamas, sitting on the sofa and watching the video of little Elda.

The ten-month-old girl didn't have to deal with any major life obstacles. When she tried to climb onto the sofa and fell, she didn't say that climbing wasn't for her. She tried again.

It might seem inspirational to Pradhan regarding their current situation, but she knew that Hila was watching it differently. She was in raptures over her amazing daughter. She didn't see a determined child or the heir to the throne of the Central Imperium. She saw her little girl.

A little girl who was going to live in the Central Imperium that was reshaping itself around her.

Her little Enhans girl.

Devika Pradhan knew Hila Eban well enough to know that this thought was currently occupying her, but at the same time, it was obvious that there was more.

"Do you want some more hot chocolate?" she asked quietly, and Hila nodded as she started to replay the video from the beginning again.

Pradhan went into the tiny kitchen and made them both another cup. She opened one cupboard and smiled. "Hey, look at this! A box of chocolates! Royal Isis! They're the best!"

She brought this new find with the two cups of hot chocolate, and Hila helped herself.

Then she took a second, and a third.

"Do you know what terrifies me most of all?" she asked suddenly.

Pradhan took a sip of her hot chocolate. "That Elda will one day live in a world full of women like Sparbo? And that someone will blame her *de facto* just because she's an Enhans?"

"No... well, that too, but..." Hila took another chocolate. "What most terrifies me is that Sparbo and I aren't that different from each other. If I hadn't met Daniel, if I hadn't had to reassess my opinion of Enhans... I'd probably think in the same way as her. That's what terrifies me most of all!"

"I can't imagine that you'd ever be like her."

"Why not? Only a few days ago I admired her as she made nailed those Enner traitors during her investigation. Before then, she obtained information about Kaffer from Arnhem, and God only knows how. And if you'd known me at the time I was still with the Omegas... let's say that I saw the world more black-and-white than I do now."

"That's entirely understandable, given what you went through."

"Maybe it's understandable in Sparbo. But it's not forgivable. Not in me either. This..." she shook her head. "This is a witch-hunt. Now. In today's world! And I can't do anything!"

Pradhan also sampled a chocolate. "Are you sure that you can't do anything?"

"We discussed it. I can't just ask the judiciary to stop the investigation, not to mention that the Imperial Investigator answers to practically no one. Maybe that was a mistake. There's no one to watch the watchers."

"But there is," said Pradhan.

"Who?"

"You. And Daniel Hankerson."

"But I was saying that I can't influence the investigation, put pressure on witnesses, the Investigator or anything of the sort!"

"I didn't mean pressure. You like direct methods. And I think that the constitution still gives you some. It gives great power to the Emperor's wife to balance the hereditary power of the ruling family. Someone who marries in compensates for that. Or that's the theory, at least." Pradhan shrugged. "You understand it better than me, but we both know you can do something."

Hila thought. Something popped into her head. Something she'd done in the Kaffer System. Very unwillingly.

"You're right. I can only do one thing, but it's really poking the hornets' nest."

Pradhan made a face and helped herself to another chocolate. "And when in your life have you ever not poked the hornets' nest?"

Φ

Hila put on her most formal outfit, the one she wore to the official events that Sparbo had pejoratively called ribbon-cutting and speech-giving.

Well, yeah. I'm going to give a speech. Just you wait.

The Investigator had continued her public interrogations, or rather hearings. In addition to the spectators admitted to the interrogations, cameras were broadcasting the proceedings to the whole fleet.

She wasn't bothered by the thought that this would have a bad effect on morale, even though she was questioning the fleet's commander.

Hila walked through the door to the hall. Pradhan marched behind her.

At first nobody noticed her. Admiral Vu was sitting in the raised chair and speaking.

"These interrogations are contrary to all the established practice of the Imperial Navy, and I have already raised a formal protest."

Clearly it was only just beginning.

Annika Sparbo sat calmly, her lips pressed into a thin line, watching the admiral. She let him talk, then continued as if he'd said nothing at all.

"You recently led a Fifth Fleet task force in the battle in the Kaffer System, didn't you, Admiral?"

Vu probably judged that it wasn't worth protesting further. "Yes, that's true. We were fighting against the New Protectorate's super-battleships."

"During that battle you lost one cruiser and one of your battleships was severely damaged. And then you promised the Enhans collaborator an Imperial pardon. You promised to intercede with the Empress, is that also true?

"Yes, that's true. It's stated in my report."

"Is it true that the gases extracted from that station, under the supervision of that collaborator, were key for making the substance with which Henry Kotulan intended to poison the entire fleet?"

Vu hesitated only for an instant. "Yes, that's true."

"And yet you promised a pardon?"

"I was willing to accept an agreement in which he provided us with valuable information in exchange for not receiving the death penalty. But I didn't have the authority for that, so I raised the proposal with the Empress."

A few people started to turn around. They could see that Hila was in the hall. But Sparbo went on, focusing only on Vu.

"Yes, the Empress's involvement in all of this is something we will deal with later. Tell me, Admiral, did you expect to become commander of the fleet so soon?"

Vu narrowed his eyes. "Of course not. But as Admiral Alender's deputy, I was prepared to assume command in the event of his absence or death."

"Yes. And that's what happened. The Admiralty—including Admiral Toscano, the Emperor's great friend—confirmed you as fleet commander. You'll probably soon be promoted from Vice Admiral to Admiral too. Admiral Alender's death was a positive for your career."

"What are you insinuating?"

"I mean that you have actually benefited from the explosion of the *Nagaland.*"

"The explosion of the *Nagaland* was an accident!"

Hila was expecting Sparbo to amplify her lie for the audience in some way, but she again completely ignored Vu's answer and instead, pretended to change the subject again.

"Admiral, tell me, what did you do in the war with the New Protectorate?"

Vu glared at her. "I was captain of the battleship *Sokoto.*"

"And tell me where the *Sokoto* served."

"In the Sol System, near Earth, as part of the Second Fleet."

"But the Second Fleet didn't serve the legitimate government of the Central Imperium, did it?"

Another glare. "The Second Fleet fought on the side of Emperor Daniel against the New Protectorate at Hub. We lost a lot of ships."

"That was at the very end of the war, when the entire Second Fleet rapidly came over to the winning side. Whom did the Second Fleet serve before?"

"Haskel Hankerson ruled on Earth and declared himself the legitimate Emperor. The Second Fleet obeyed orders."

"Obeyed orders?" Sparbo pronounced those words like an insult. "Obeyed orders? And what did you do, Admiral? How did you fight for the Central Imperium?"

"We all did what we could," Vu insisted. "There was lots of confusion, nobody knew what was going on, or even who was in power. A lot of captains were recalled. I had no way of preventing any of this. If I had spoken up or intervened in any way, they would only have relieved me too, and possibly killed me. That happened to dozens of other captains, commodores and admirals."

"Instead, you preferred to keep your mouth shut and fall in line, so to speak, did you? You shut your mouth and watched your step, even though one of the battleships had started to bomb Earth? How many people died then? Twelve thousand? More? I wonder how you can sleep at night, Admiral."

Near the entrance, Warrant Officer Tarsen squirmed uneasily. He looked from Sparbo to Vu and back again, repeatedly. But then he noticed Hila.

Who had just decided to make her entrance and was striding toward the podium. Toward Vu.

Sparbo finally caught sight of her too. "Your Majesty, you do not have access here. I have clearly asked you not to intervene or try to influence the criminal investigation. You cannot abuse your influence or your privileged position! I must ask you to leave immediately."

Hila stopped in front of the chair Vu was sitting on and gave the admiral an encouraging smile. "Don't worry, ma'am, I'm not here to abuse my influence. I came to assert the power the law gives me."

She'd noticed that Feigins was also sitting in the hall. He was staring at Hila, wide-eyed.

"Your Majesty!" exclaimed Sparbo, but Hila stopped her.

"You'll understand soon enough, but I'm glad that we have an audience, and that this recording will be broadcast to the whole fleet and possibly the whole Imperium. That will be an advantage."

She remembered witnessing two similar public confrontations of Daniel's. But today it was up to her.

"But first, I'd like to say something. Article Eighty of the Criminal Code gives anyone the right to say something in defense of an accused. And before you object that this isn't a court of law it *is*. You have made it a court and the terms we use to describe it are irrelevant. Allow me, all of you, to talk about what is going on here. It started when we caught a saboteur in the fleet. A man who confessed his guilt and who will pay for his crimes. But that wasn't the end. Then suspicion fell on another man, Specialist Ingar Feigins. He had nothing to do with the sabotage, but his genetic background automatically made him a suspect in the eyes of the Imperial Investigator. Mr. Feigins is, in fact, an Enhans. His mother was the lover of an important leader and a member of one of the ruling families. There was no evidence against Mr. Feigins. The entire case was based on conjecture and the fact that he is an Enhans.

"The Central Imperium's motto is 'civilization must continue'. Without doubt, we all know this motto, but what is civilization? Is it civilization to destroy an innocent man because he has the same DNA as some traitors? And because Admiral Vu attempted to support him, he is now being interrogated himself, accused of not doing more in a difficult situation several years ago? Have we really fallen so low that we allow this sort of procedure? That we have started to think in this way? This is not a civilization that must continue!"

Sparbo's eyes were still fixed on Hila, but she decided to ignore her speech.

"Your Majesty, you have no authority here and I hereby ask you to leave for the last time, or I will have you removed. I have the authority to do so."

Hila looked at Tarsen, whose expression was unhappy. The security chief also wanted to uncover the saboteurs, and he'd lost a lot of friends at Kaffer. But he did not want to remove the Empress from the hall in front of the entire galaxy.

"I will willingly leave, but I have one more thing to say," said Hila. "Or rather, to do. You are wrong about one thing, ma'am. I have one power. A power granted to me by the constitution and confirmed by the new parliament that met after the war. In my power as Empress, I hereby grant an Imperial pardon to Specialist Feigins and to Admiral Vu, and I halt this investigation."

Sparbo leaped to her feet. "You can't!"

"Oh, I can, and I just did. My official order has already been entered in the Imperial database. The investigation is over. You were right. I cannot influence investigations, but I can stop them. And that is what I have just done. I grant Imperial pardons."

"You can't!" Sparbo repeated, her strict self-control collapsing. "How dare you! You, who cover traitors and consort with Enhans, how dare you prevent me from doing my job? My work for civilization?! You can't! You mustn't! That is an insult to everything I and all the good people of the Imperium have ever achieved! You will regret this! Do you hear me? You will regret this! I have already destroyed much bigger fish than you! You who are in cahoots with the Enhans Emperor, like a whore! You who prostituted yourself to him as soon as you sniffed power! You will not trifle with me!"

Everything she said went to every ship in the fleet. The FTL receiver would then send it to the entire Imperium.

Sparbo pointed at Tarsen. "Warrant Officer, arrest the Empress and take her to her cabin. The investigation will continue, and the Ministry of the Interior will examine these illegal processes on the part of the Imperial family!"

Tarsen gaped at the Investigator, his eyes bulging.

"Now!"

The order in the Investigator's voice forced Tarsen to move. Pradhan started out to meet him, but Hila stopped her with a gesture. She went toward him until they were standing a meter apart.

Tarsen swallowed.

Hila's voice sounded calm. "Warrant Officer, please escort Ms. Sparbo to her cabin. The investigation is over."

Sparbo was now only trembling furiously. Tarsen's eyes flitted from her to the Empress and back again.

Hila half-smiled. "You have to make a decision."

Tarsen reached for his belt and withdrew his weapon from its case. Then he swallowed again and turned to Sparbo.

"Please follow me, ma'am."

Sparbo said nothing now. She was a broken woman.

The hall was silent as the grave as Tarsen led her away.

PART 10

This time the flag conference room was quiet and empty.

Only Vice Admiral Tom Vu was sitting at the head of the table. He raised his head as Hila entered, accompanied by the faithful Devika Pradhan.

Vu immediately got to his feet. "Your Majesty…"

"Admiral."

"I wanted to thank you. You did something that nobody else could have done. I…"

"Believe me, Admiral, it took me a long time to pluck up the courage. An unnecessarily long time." She smiled at Pradhan. "And on occasion, somebody needed to give me a nudge."

The smile was rather automatic. Pradhan had prodded Hila, but Hila had been disgusted. With herself, with Sparbo, with everything…

Vu indicated the table. Where his tablet was lying. He opened a file on it. Hila noticed there were two new reports. "This arrived this morning. When I was still sitting in front of that tribunal. I've been promoted to full admiral. The ship's supply officer has brought my pips. I feel… well, strange."

"How is Feigins?"

"The boy will recover. JAG will investigate his misdemeanor of falsifying documents, but… he may receive an official reprimand. It'll end there. I'll arrange for him to be transferred to another ship in another fleet. It'll be better for him, after all that pillorying that he got here."

It probably really would be the best thing for Feigins. But Hila wouldn't be surprised if he simply wanted to leave the Navy after everything he'd been through.

He probably wouldn't be the only one to think of doing so, either. Suddenly Warrant Officer Tarsen came into the room.

"Admiral… Annika Sparbo has left the ship. It's over." He looked at Hila, then back to the fleet commander. "And I… I should resign."

Vu had no answer, but Hila spoke up.

"Nonsense, Warrant Officer."

"I… I helped her. I wanted her to be right, about everything! What sort of police officer am I, that I wanted everyone to be guilty?"

"If I were to judge myself as harshly—and believe me, I'm inclined to—then I should have retired to some secluded place a long time ago. But I can't entirely resign from the position of Empress."

"But you stopped it!"

"And ultimately, you helped me."

This time Tarsen was silent, and Vu spoke.

"Warrant Officer, don't exaggerate things with that resignation." He tapped on his tablet, which was lying on the table. "Before you arrived, I was just saying to Her Majesty that I have received two messages. One of them promotes me to Admiral. But the second one will interest you more. Imperial Intelligence has cracked the data you obtained from the destroyed Protectorate ship in Kaffer. We have discovered the planned movements of the New Protectorate's remaining super-battleships and confirmed them via other contacts." He smiled. "And we didn't need a witch-hunt to find this out."

Hila's mouth opened. This was news to her.

And to Tarsen, it seemed. The admiral went on.

"I'm sure I also speak for the *Quezon*'s captain when I say that I think you should stay aboard. We're going to need you."

Tarsen hesitated briefly, but finally stood up straight. "Very well, sir. Thank you, sir."

"The Fifth Fleet is going into action again?" Hila asked.

"Yes. I think it will be good for morale too, after the events of the last few days. And now we have the chance to stop the New Protectorate's acts of sabotage in the whole sector once and for all." He looked at Hila.

"I assume that you will want to participate again, ma'am?"

Hila did want to participate. She wanted to set off with the fleet, she wanted to be with these people when they flew into danger.

But she was aware of something else.

She was the Empress. She had other work to do. Important work. Work that could change things. Save other lives.

The witch-hunt hadn't been stopped by Commando Hila or Journalist Hila, but by Empress Hila.

Maybe that wasn't what she had wanted to be. Maybe she felt that the entire concept of a hereditary monarchy was nonsensical and old-fashioned.

But as Daniel would say, these were the cards fate had dealt her. And she should finally learn to play them properly.

"Thank you for the invitation, Admiral, but I must decline. I think it's high time I returned to Hub. I have done everything I could here. It's time for me to go home."

Φ

"I have to tell you that your public stunt caused quite a stir in the Imperium," said Daniel, from the monitor, when the *Quezon* had again connected with the FTL communications signal from Hub.

"I learned from the best," said Hila.

"And now I will probably learn from the best myself. You caused a small earthquake here. Sparbo might have withstood it if she hadn't ripped into you. Whatever ordinary people on the street think about me as Emperor, they adore you. Sparbo cut off the branch she was sitting on when she so publicly denounced you for… well, practically everything."

"So, the investigation is over?"

"That's not all. Sparbo was recalled and the parliament has convened a special commission to assess the suitability of the Imperial Investigators. Minister Rosenthal has already resigned and distanced himself from Sparbo." Daniel heaved a sigh. "I admit that I'd always primarily seen the advantages of an Imperial Investigator. I saw that well enough, but not what it could lead to."

"Sparbo was a fanatic. She couldn't rise above her own life experiences."

"That's not what I mean. That's not the only thing. We would all have admired her if she'd only nailed Kotulan, but when it went further… I feel… unclean. My great-uncle the Emperor founded the Omega Commandos, and I had no idea how he could do such a thing. Now I see that I did something similar myself."

"It wasn't your idea."

"No, it was Rosenthal's, but I could have tried to veto it…"

Hila smiled. "I don't think you made as big a mistake as I did. I trusted her. I admired her. I… I helped her. I didn't realize what was going on quickly enough." She shook her head. "You might say that, as a journalist, I'd understand, but I thought that we'd moved on a bit. That we don't organize witch-hunts; we don't have an inquisition. And then, suddenly…"

Daniel grinned. "Not every villain looks like one. A lot of people think they're doing good, but…" he shrugged. "This time it's over. And I think that we've talked about work for long enough. Elda wants to wave to mommy."

Hila instantly forgot about most problems as their daughter appeared on the screen.

The future belonged to her.

Hila would do everything to ensure it was the best future possible.

ABOUT THE AUTHOR

Jan Kotouč has published over two dozen novels in his native Czech, with many being translated into English. His work includes the futuristic *Central Imperium* series, the *Czech Lands* alternative history series, and the military sci-fi *Hirano Sector* series. He has contributed to numerous anthologies and universes—including stories for the *Honor Harrington* series by David Weber—and the *1632* universe by Eric Flint.

Other work has included creating the atmospheric setting and story background for the *European Cybersecurity Challenge* held in Prague in 2021, and is often the lead in charge of book-related program tracks on many convention committees, including the Comic-Con Prague.

He is also a lecturer at the Prague School of Creative Communication where he teaches writing workshops.